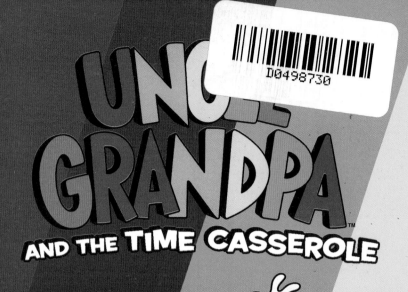

UNCLE GRANDPA
AND THE TIME CASSEROLE

CREATED BY
PETER BROWNGARDT

UNCLE GRANDPA AND THE TIME CASSEROLE, March 2016.
Published by KaBOOM!, a division of Boom Entertainment,
Inc. UNCLE GRANDPA, CARTOON NETWORK, the logos, and
all related characters and elements are trademarks of Cartoon
Network. (S16) All rights reserved. KaBOOM!™ and the
KaBOOM! logo are trademarks of Boom Entertainment, Inc.,
registered in various countries and categories. All characters,
events, and institutions depicted herein are fictional. Any
similarity between any of the names, characters, persons,
events, and/or institutions in this publication to actual names,
characters, and persons, whether living or dead, events, and/
or institutions is unintended and purely coincidental. KaBOOM!
does not read or accept unsolicited submissions of ideas, stories,
or artwork.

For information regarding the CPSIA on this printed material,
call: (203) 595-3636 and provide reference # RICH – 665289.
A catalog record of this book is available from OCLC and from the
KaBOOM! website, www.kaboom.com, on the Librarians Page.

BOOM! Studios, 5670 Wilshire Boulevard, Suite 450, Los
Angeles, CA 90036-5679. Printed in USA. First Printing.

ISBN: 978-1-60886-791-2, eISBN: 978-1-61398-462-8

UNCLE GRANDPA
AND THE TIME CASSEROLE
CREATED BY PETER BROWNGARDT

Story by
**PETER BROWNGARDT
& KELSY ABBOTT**

Written by
PRANAS T. NAUJOKAITIS

PRESENT DAY
Art by **PHILIP MURPHY**
with colors by **CASSIE KELLY**
& MADDI GONZALEZ

MOON CITY
Art by **ALEXIS ZIRITT**
with colors by
KATHARINE EFIRD

THE '90S
Art by **DAVID DEGRAND**

ANCIENT ROME
Art by **CHRISTINE LARSEN**
with colors by
KATHARINE EFIRD

ANCIENT EGYPT
Art by **GEORGE MAGER**

**5TH CENTURY
ENGLAND**
Art by **MATTHEW SMIGIEL**

CAVEMAN TIMES
Art by **PRANAS T. NAUJOKAITIS**
with colors by
WYETH YATES

Letters by
TAYLOR ESPOSITO

Cover by
PETER BROWNGARDT

Designer
KELSEY DIETERICH

Assistant Editor
ALEX GALER

Editor
SHANNON WATTERS

With Special Thanks to Marisa Marionakis, Rick Blanco, Curtis Lelash,
Conrad Montgomery, Meghan Bradley, Rossitza Lazarova and the wonderful
folks at Cartoon Network.

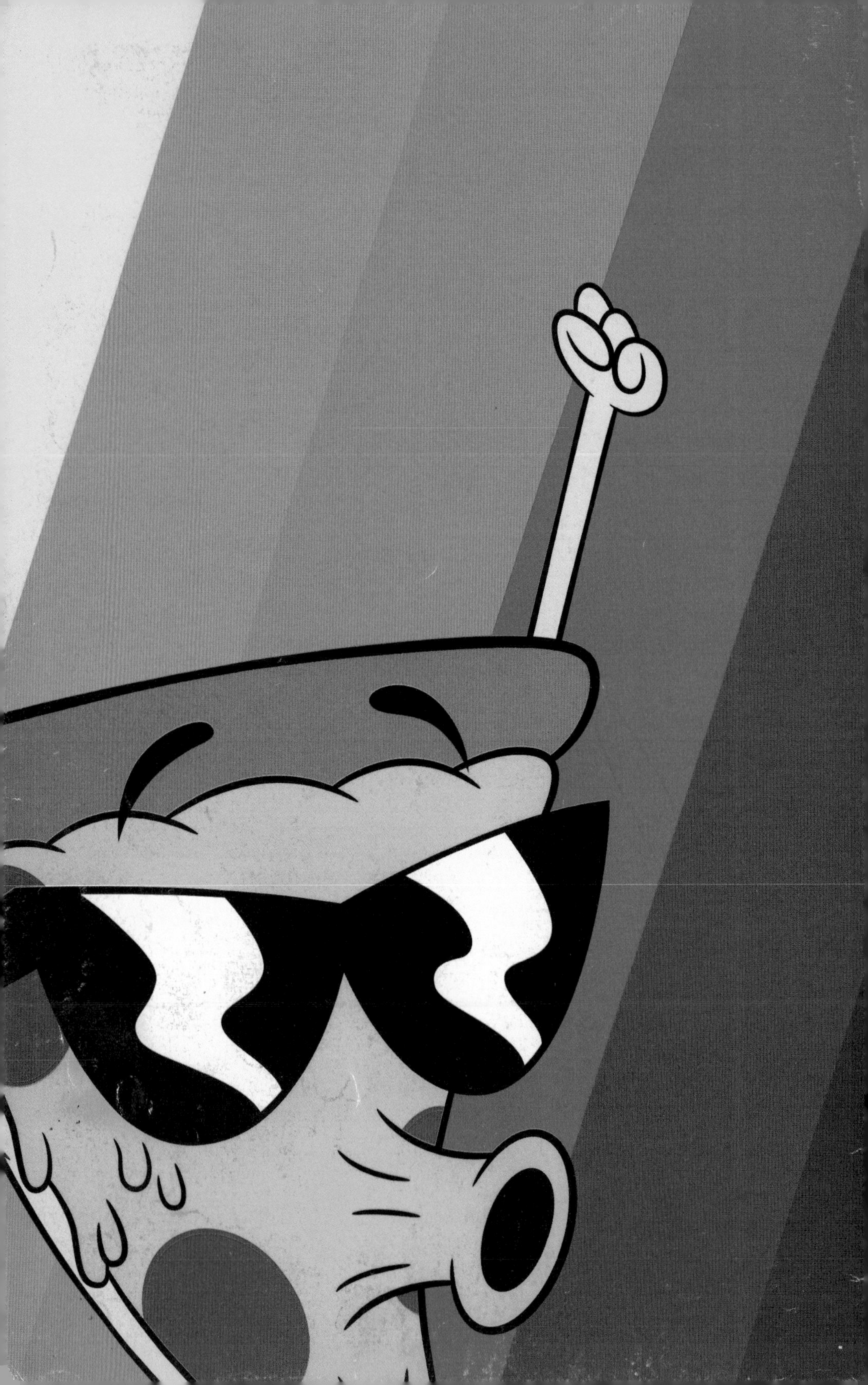

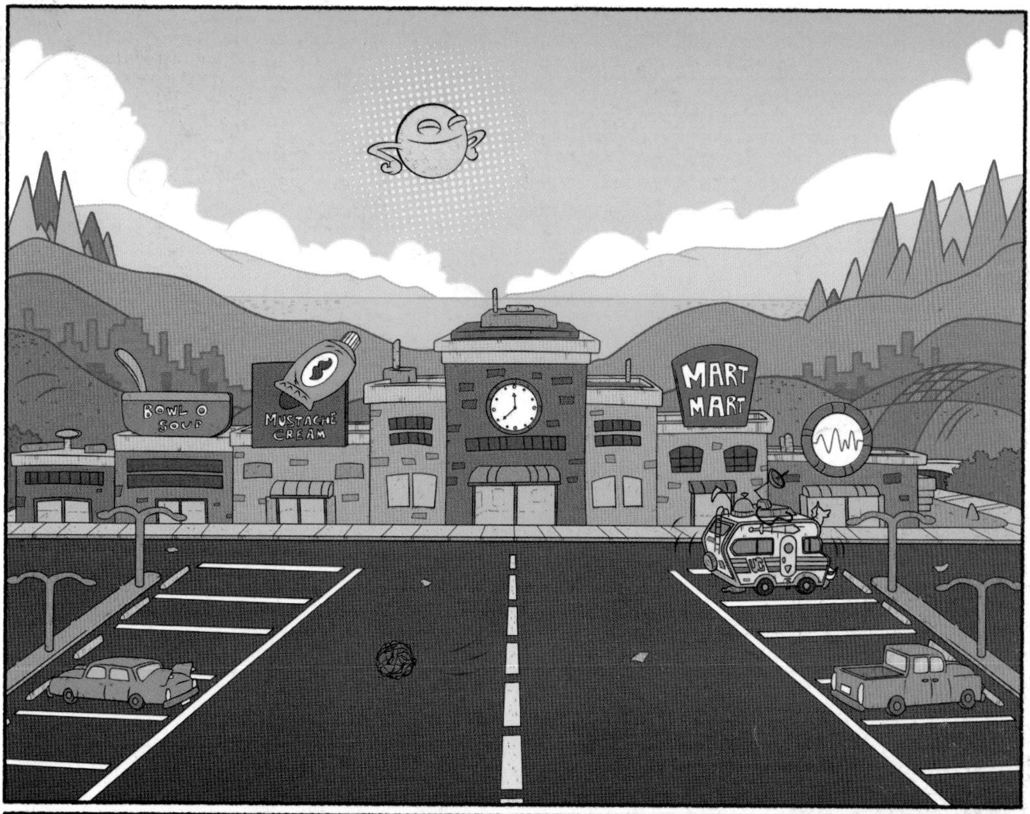
BOWL O SOUP
MUSTACHE CREAM
MART MART

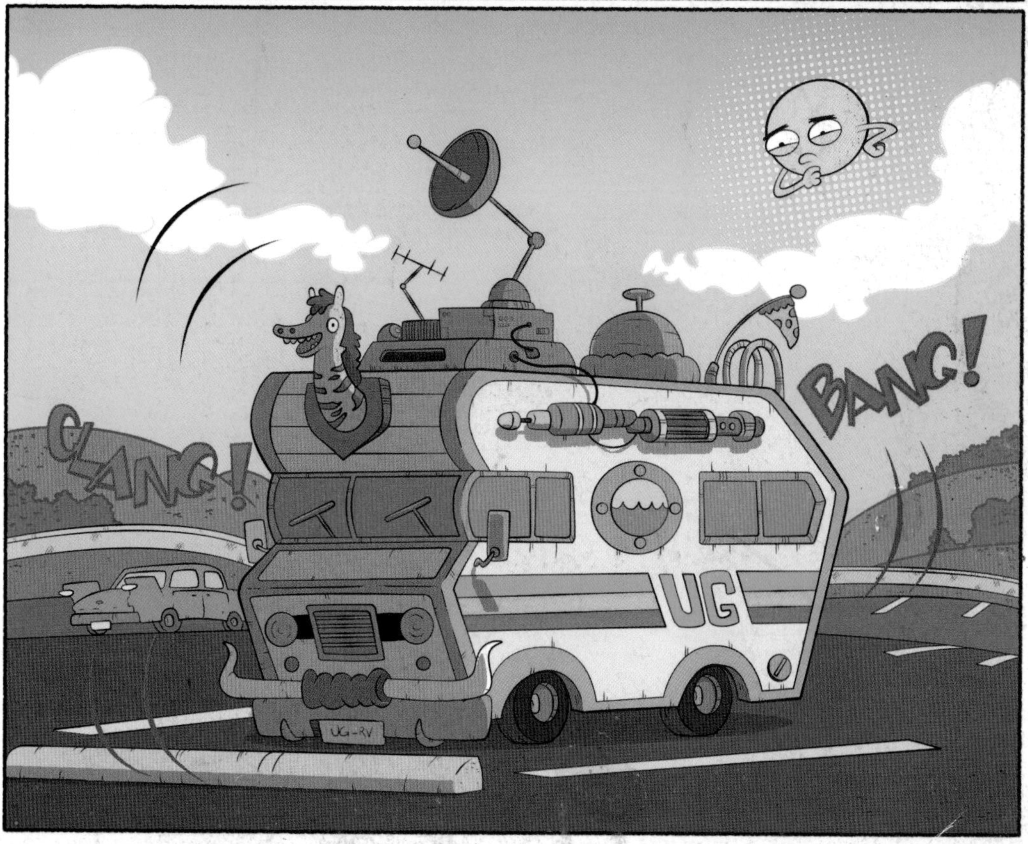
CLANG!
BANG!
UG
UG-RV

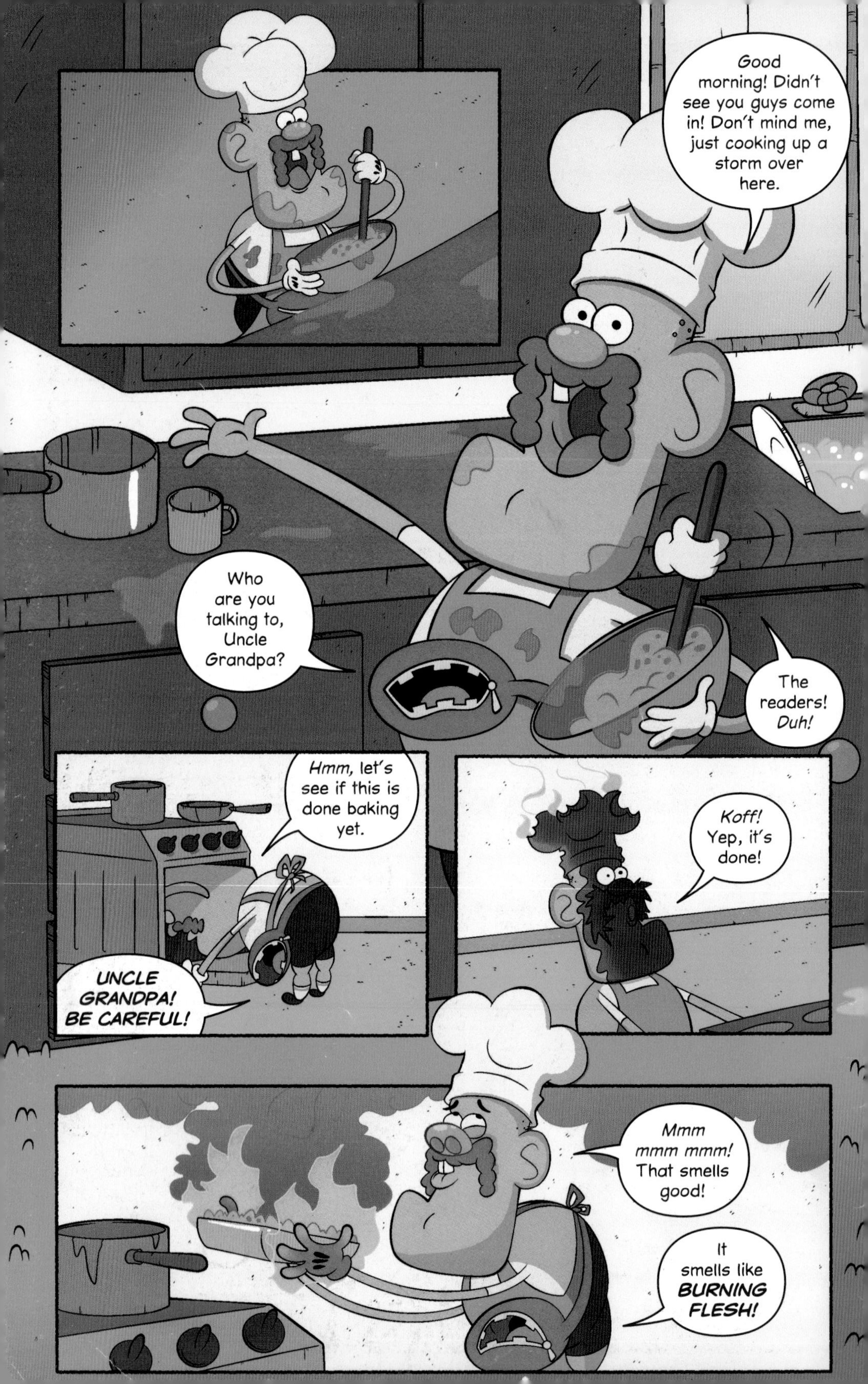
Good morning! Didn't see you guys come in! Don't mind me, just cooking up a storm over here.
Who are you talking to, Uncle Grandpa?
The readers! *Duh!*
Hmm, let's see if this is done baking yet.
UNCLE GRANDPA! BE CAREFUL!
Koff! Yep, it's done!
Mmm mmm mmm! That smells good!
It smells like **BURNING FLESH!**

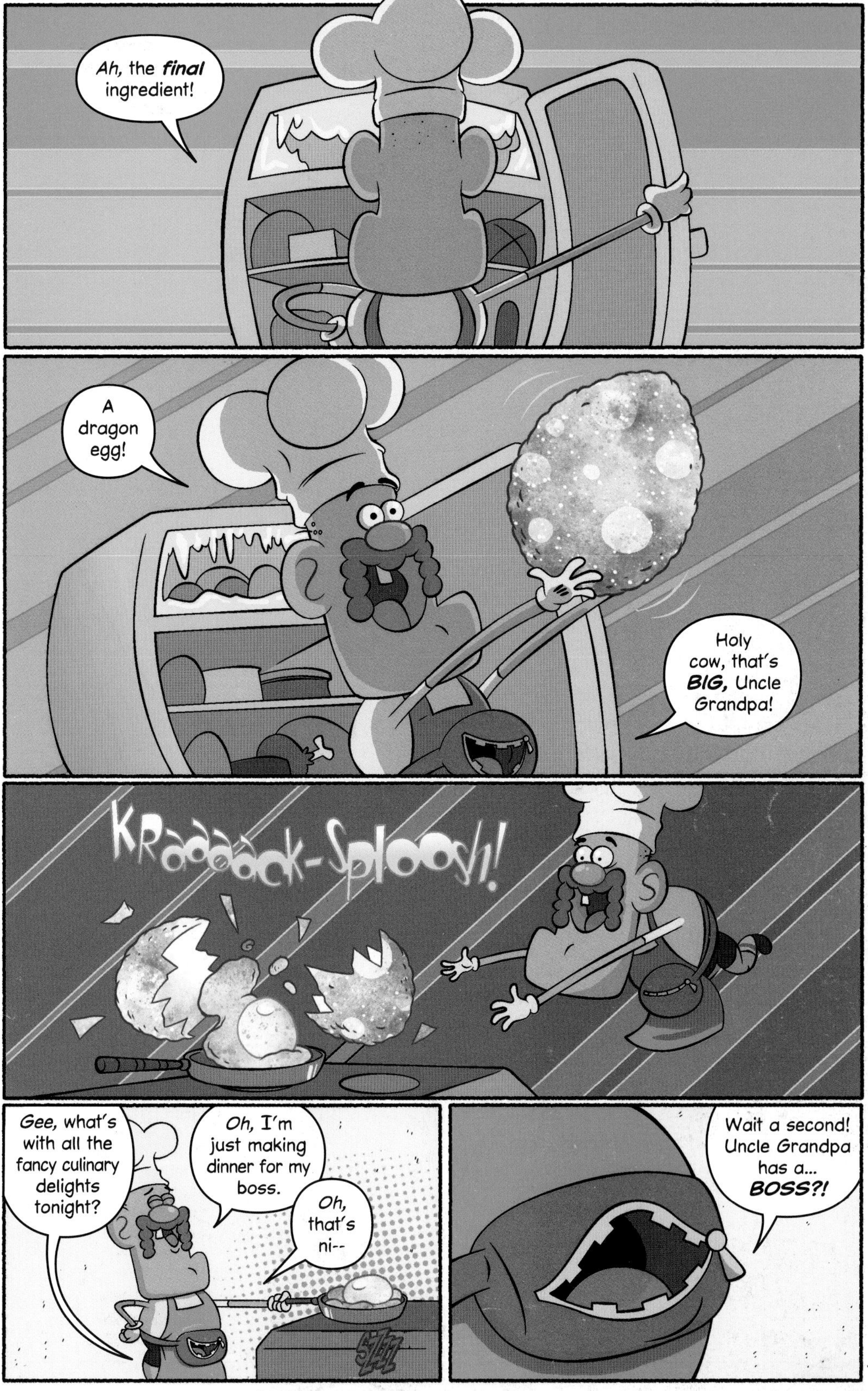
Ah, the ***final*** ingredient!
A dragon egg!
Holy cow, that's ***BIG,*** Uncle Grandpa!
KRaaaack-Sploosh!
Gee, what's with all the fancy culinary delights tonight?
Oh, I'm just making dinner for my boss.
Oh, that's ni--
Wait a second! Uncle Grandpa has a... ***BOSS?!***

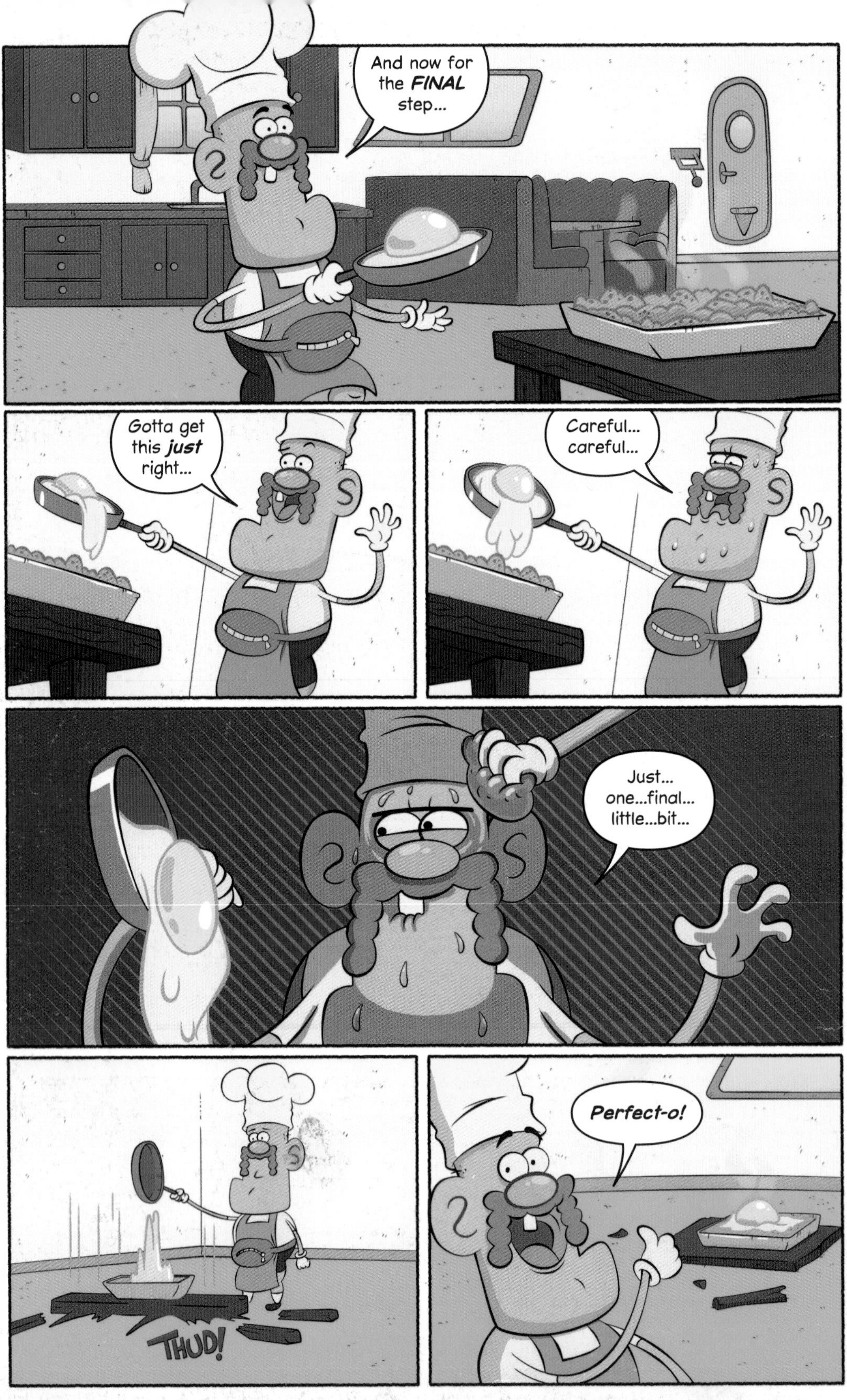
And now for the ***FINAL*** step...
Gotta get this ***just*** right...
Careful... careful...
Just... one...final... little...bit...
THUD!
Perfect-o!

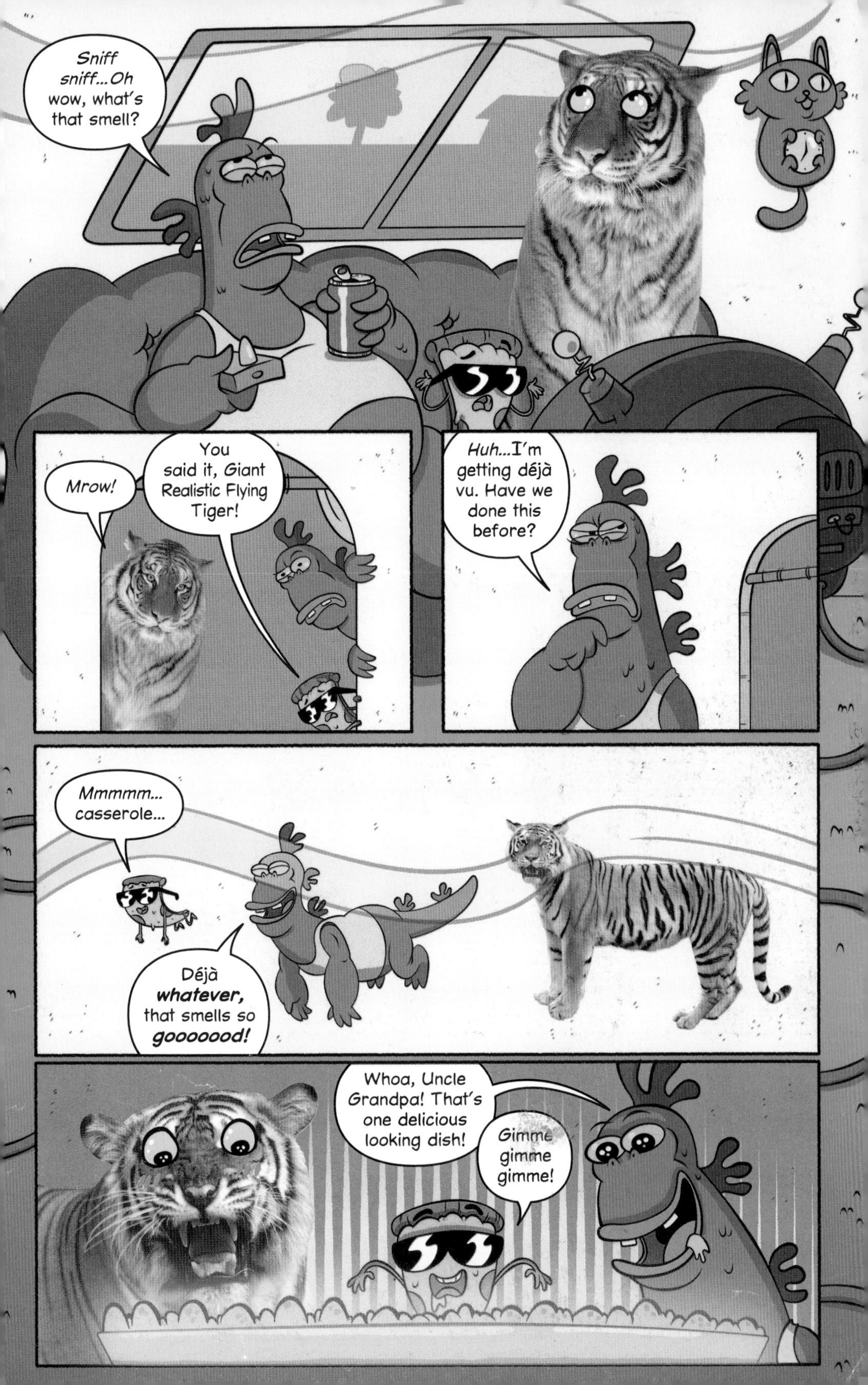
Sniff sniff...Oh wow, what's that smell?
Mrow!
You said it, Giant Realistic Flying Tiger!
Huh...I'm getting déjà vu. Have we done this before?
Mmmmm... casserole...
Déjà **whatever,** that smells so ***goooooood!***
Whoa, Uncle Grandpa! That's one delicious looking dish!
Gimme gimme gimme!

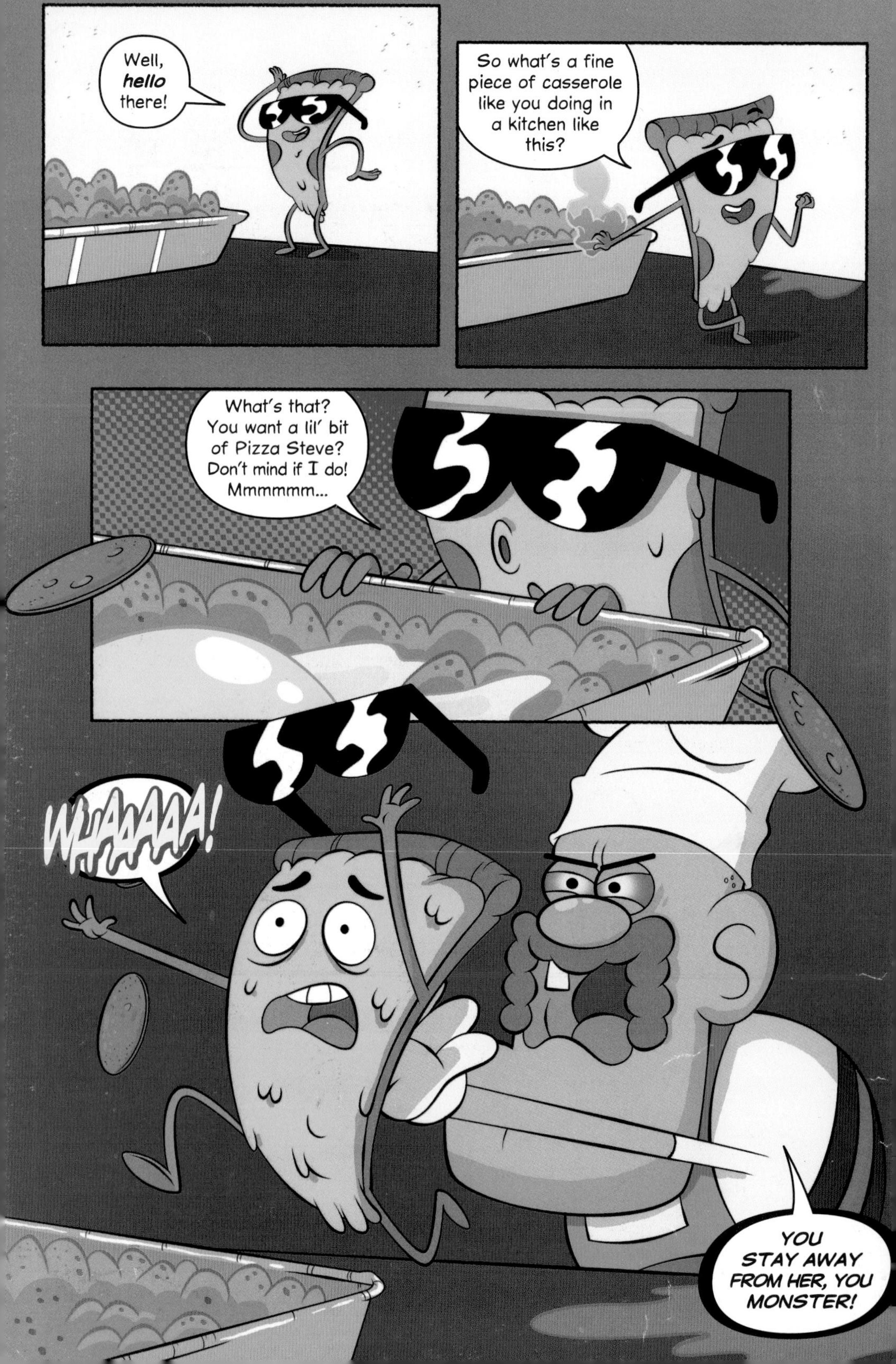
Well, **hello** there!
So what's a fine piece of casserole like you doing in a kitchen like this?
What's that? You want a lil' bit of Pizza Steve? Don't mind if I do! Mmmmmm...
WHAAAAA!
YOU STAY AWAY FROM HER, YOU MONSTER!

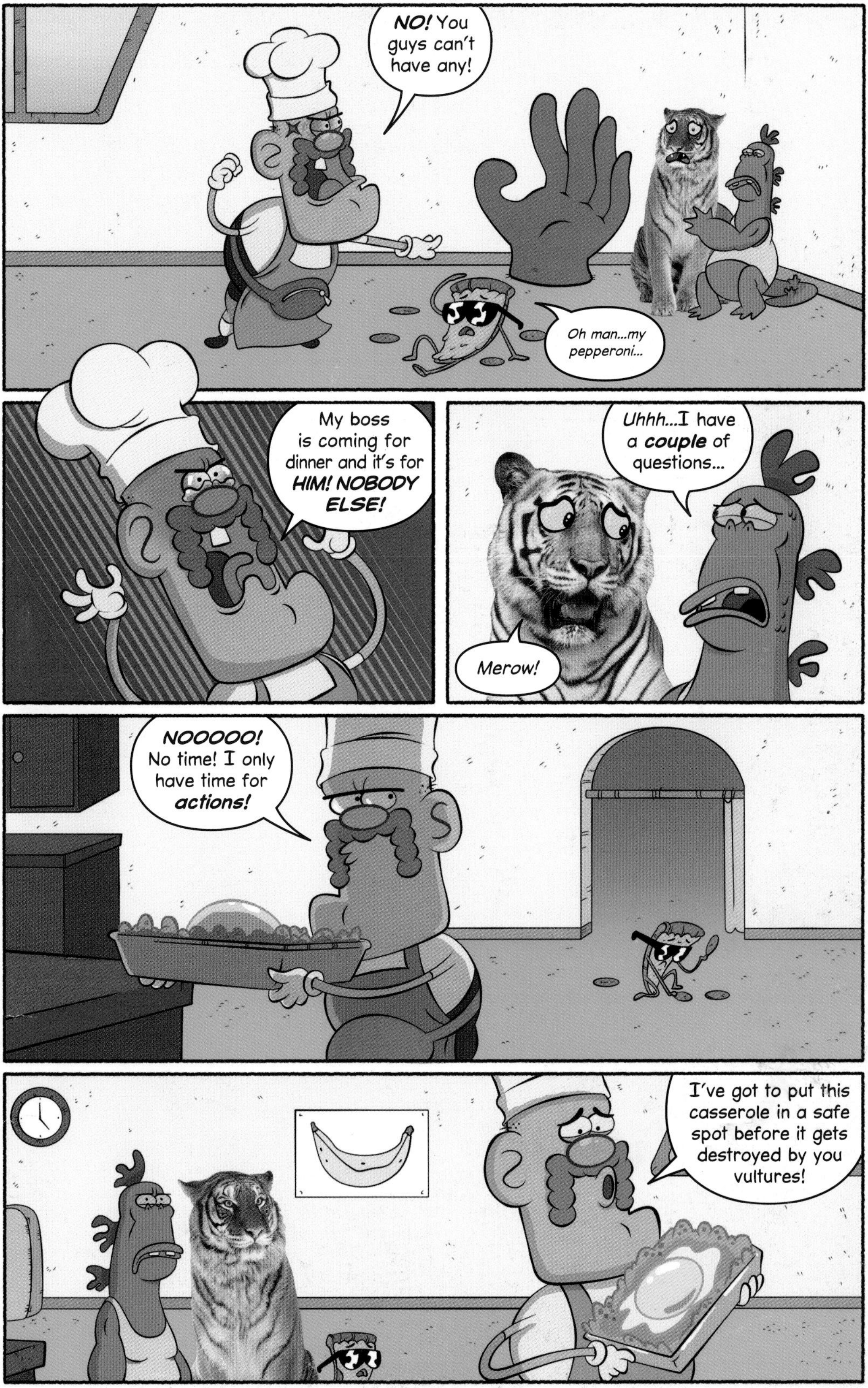
NO! You guys can't have any!
Oh man...my pepperoni...
My boss is coming for dinner and it's for HIM! NOBODY ELSE!
Uhhh...I have a couple of questions...
Merow!
NOOOOO! No time! I only have time for actions!
I've got to put this casserole in a safe spot before it gets destroyed by you vultures!

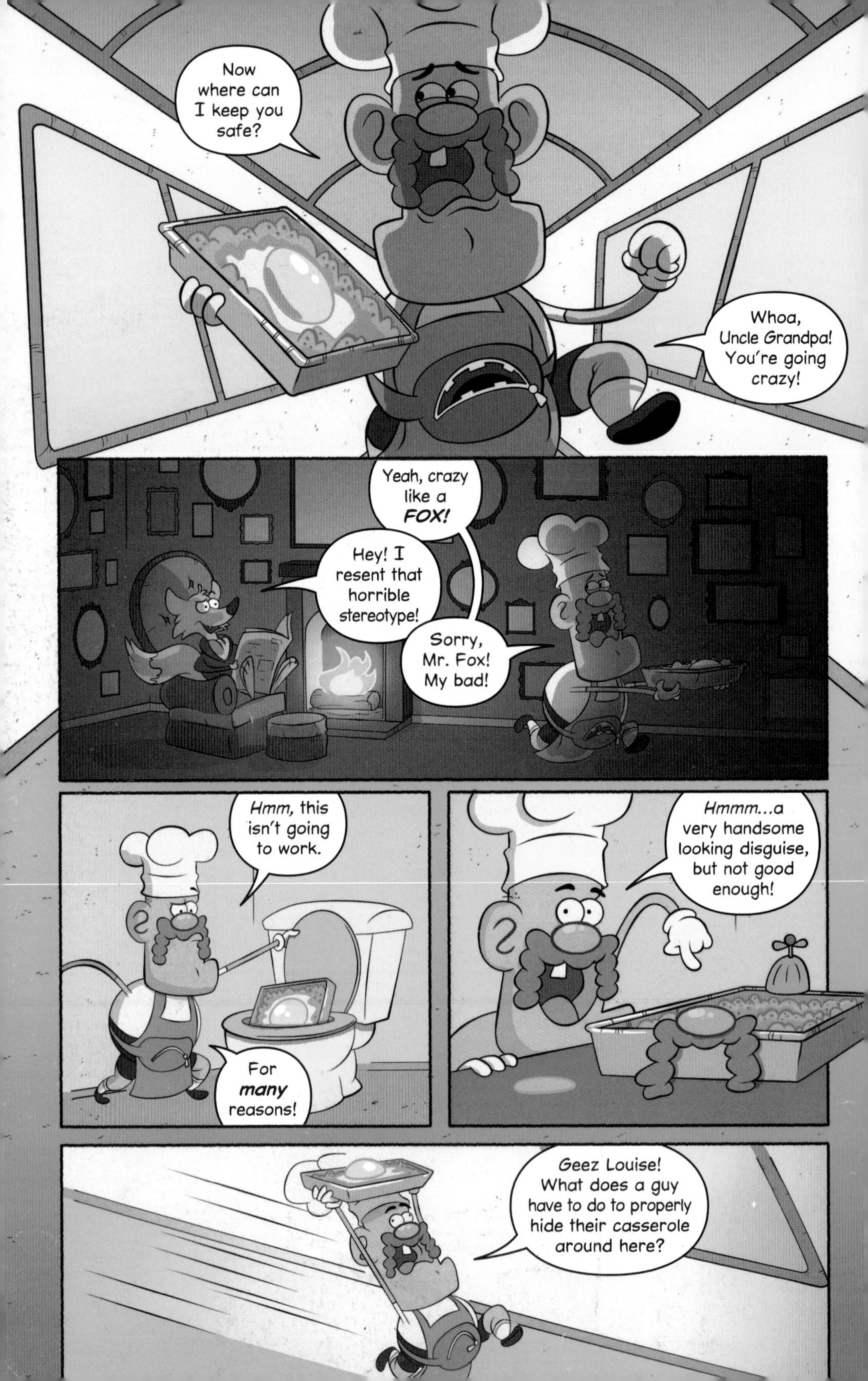
Now where can I keep you safe?
Whoa, Uncle Grandpa! You're going crazy!
Yeah, crazy like a *FOX!*
Hey! I resent that horrible stereotype!
Sorry, Mr. Fox! My bad!
Hmm, this isn't going to work.
For *many* reasons!
*Hmmm...*a very handsome looking disguise, but not good enough!
Geez Louise! What does a guy have to do to properly hide their casserole around here?

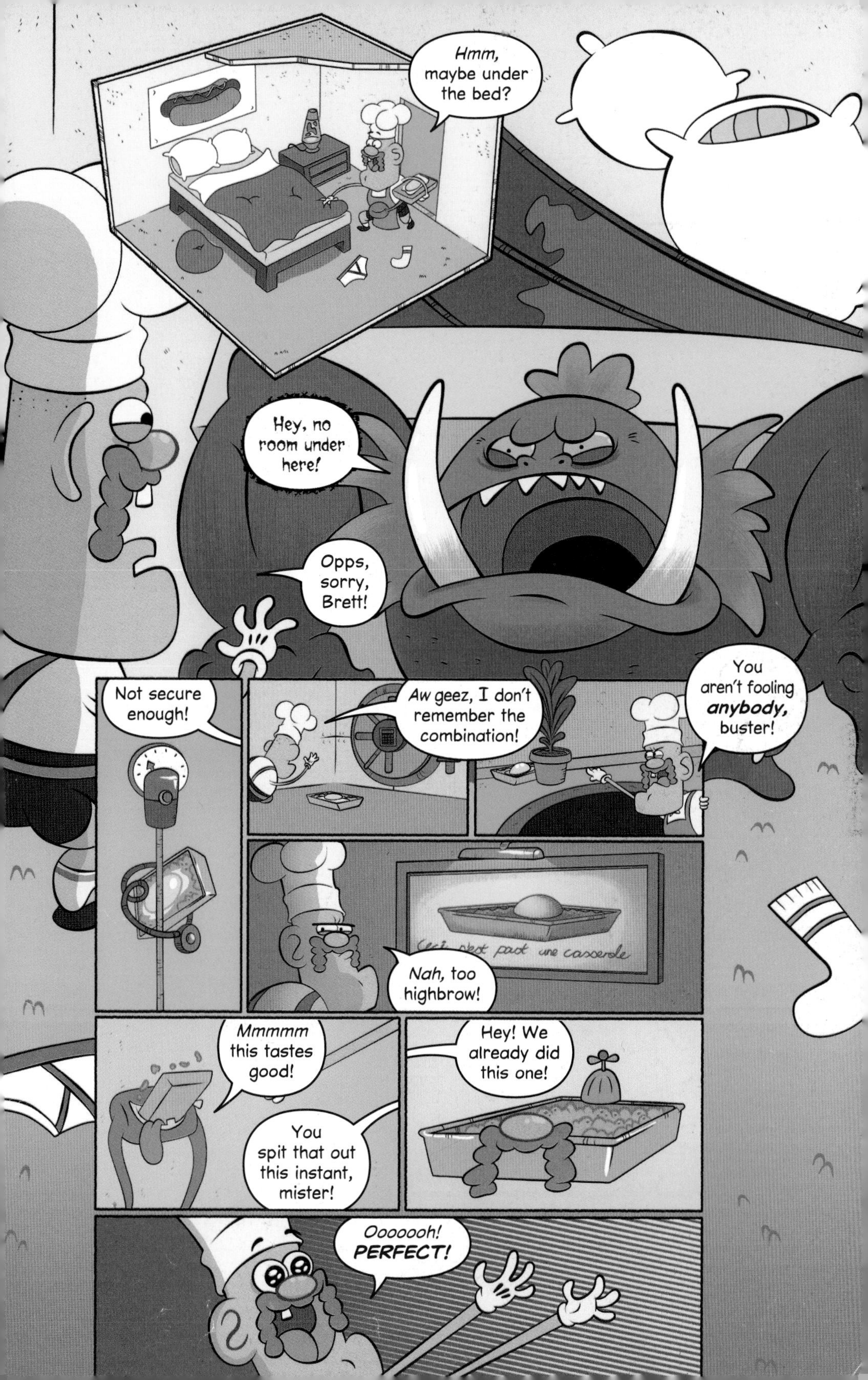
Hmm, maybe under the bed?
Hey, no room under here!
Opps, sorry, Brett!
Not secure enough!
Aw geez, I don't remember the combination!
You aren't fooling **anybody,** buster!
Ceci n'est pas une casserole
Nah, too highbrow!
Mmmmm this tastes good!
You spit that out this instant, mister!
Hey! We already did this one!
Ooooooh! **PERFECT!**

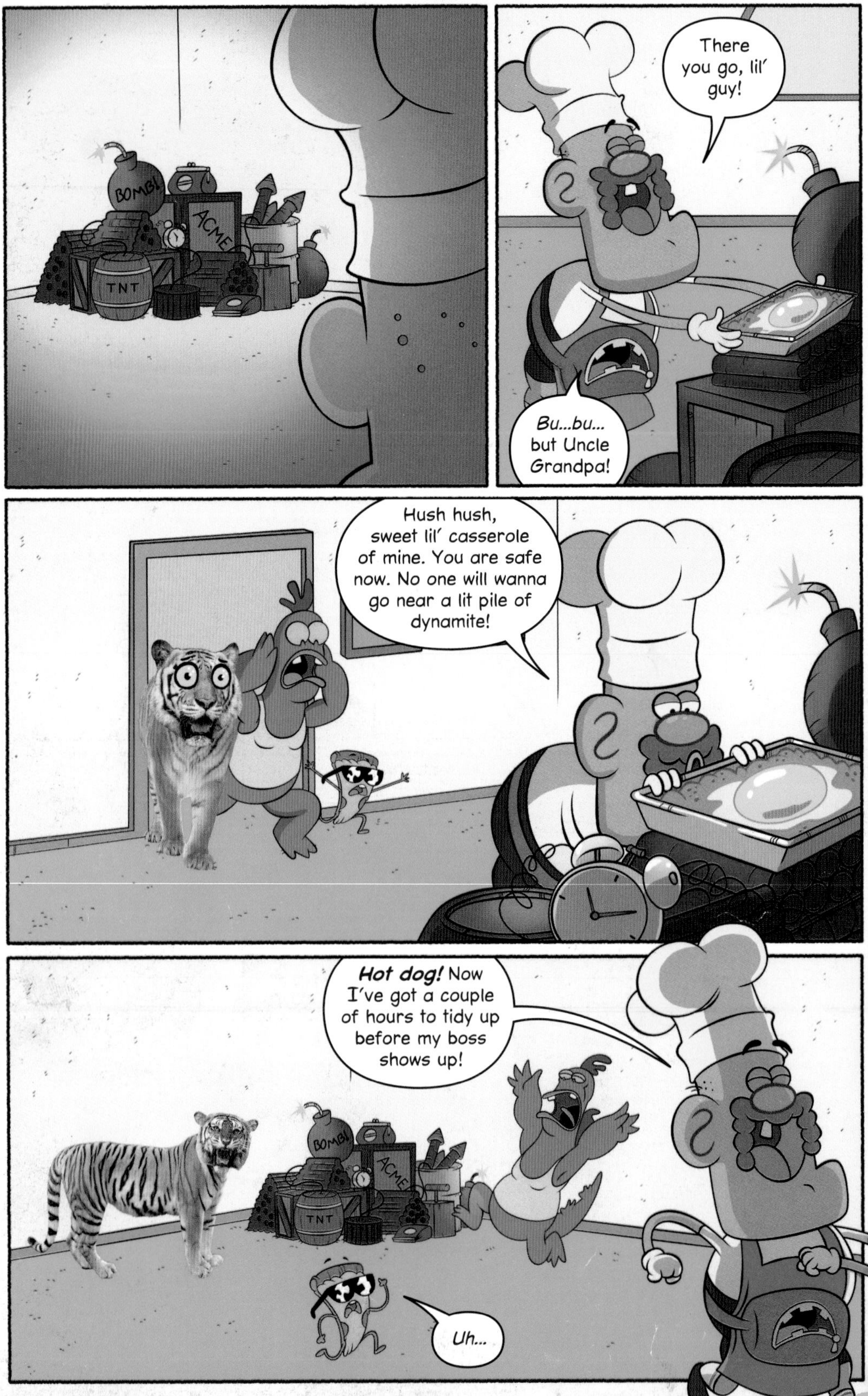
BOMB!
ACME!
TNT
There you go, lil' guy!
Bu...bu... but Uncle Grandpa!
Hush hush, sweet lil' casserole of mine. You are safe now. No one will wanna go near a lit pile of dynamite!
Hot dog! Now I've got a couple of hours to tidy up before my boss shows up!
BOMB!
ACME!
TNT
Uh...

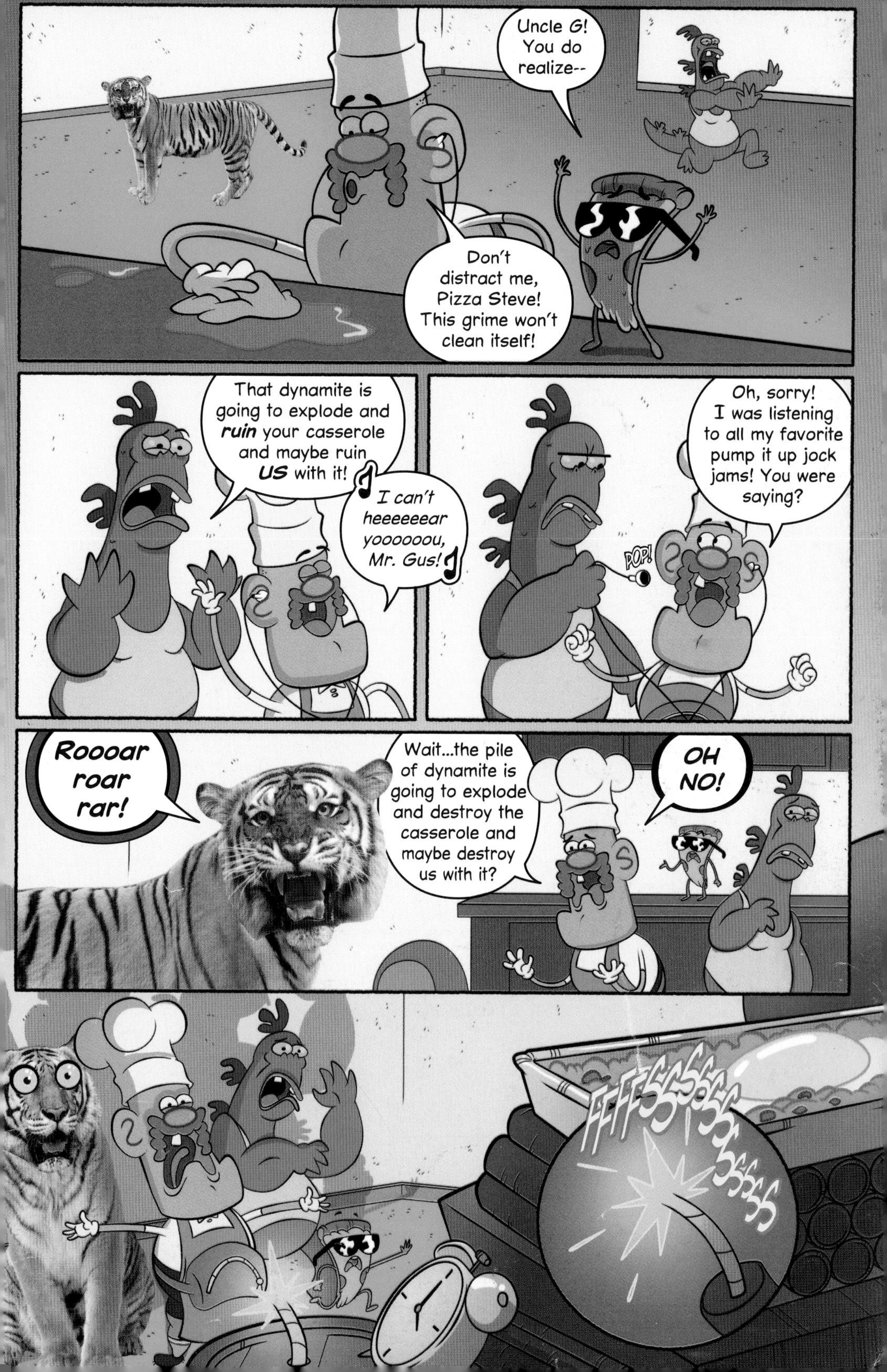
Uncle G! You do realize--
Don't distract me, Pizza Steve! This grime won't clean itself!
That dynamite is going to explode and ruin your casserole and maybe ruin US with it!
I can't heeeeeear yoooooou, Mr. Gus!
POP!
Oh, sorry! I was listening to all my favorite pump it up jock jams! You were saying?
Roooar roar rar!
Wait...the pile of dynamite is going to explode and destroy the casserole and maybe destroy us with it?
OH NO!
FFFFSSSSSSSSSSSS

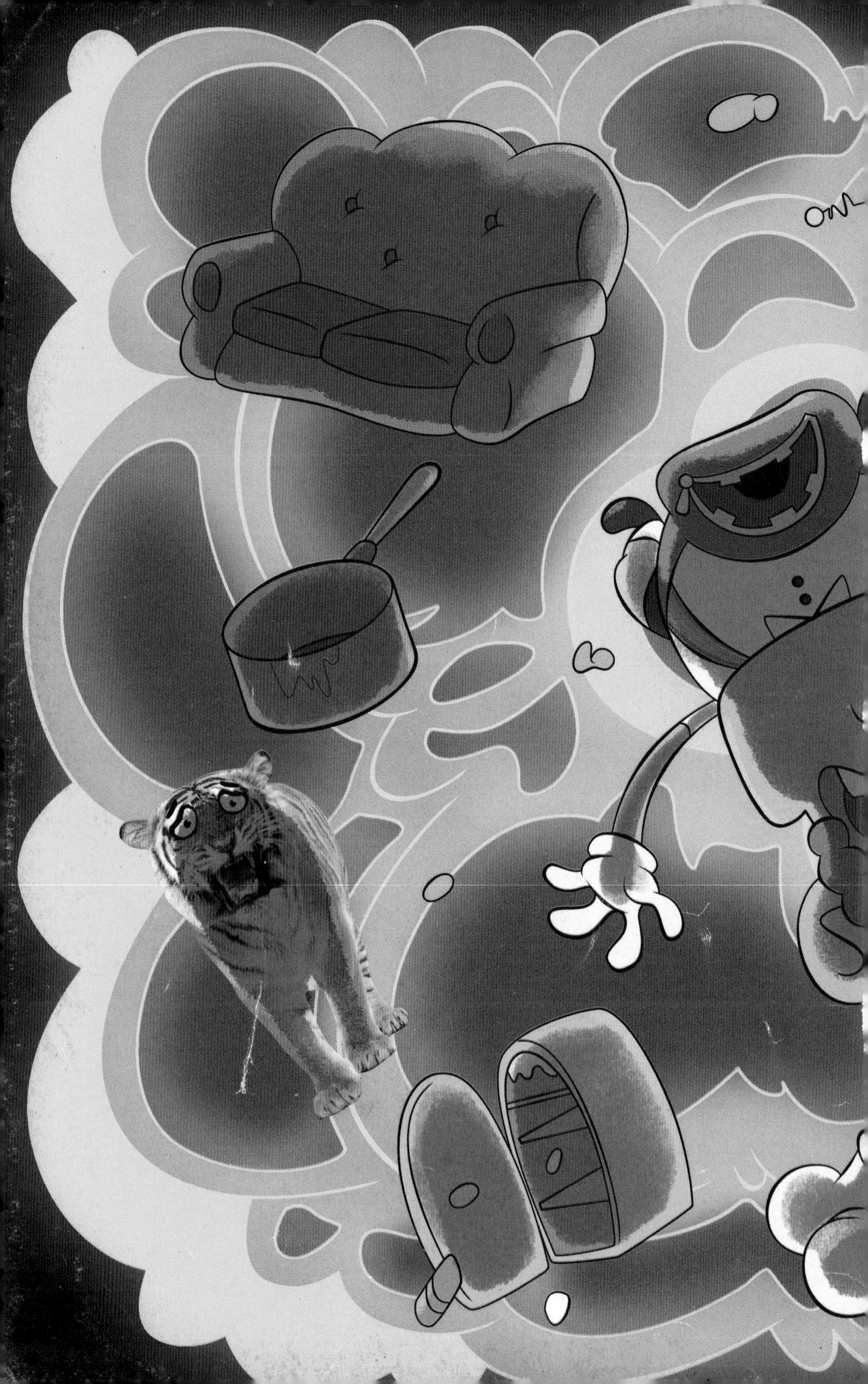

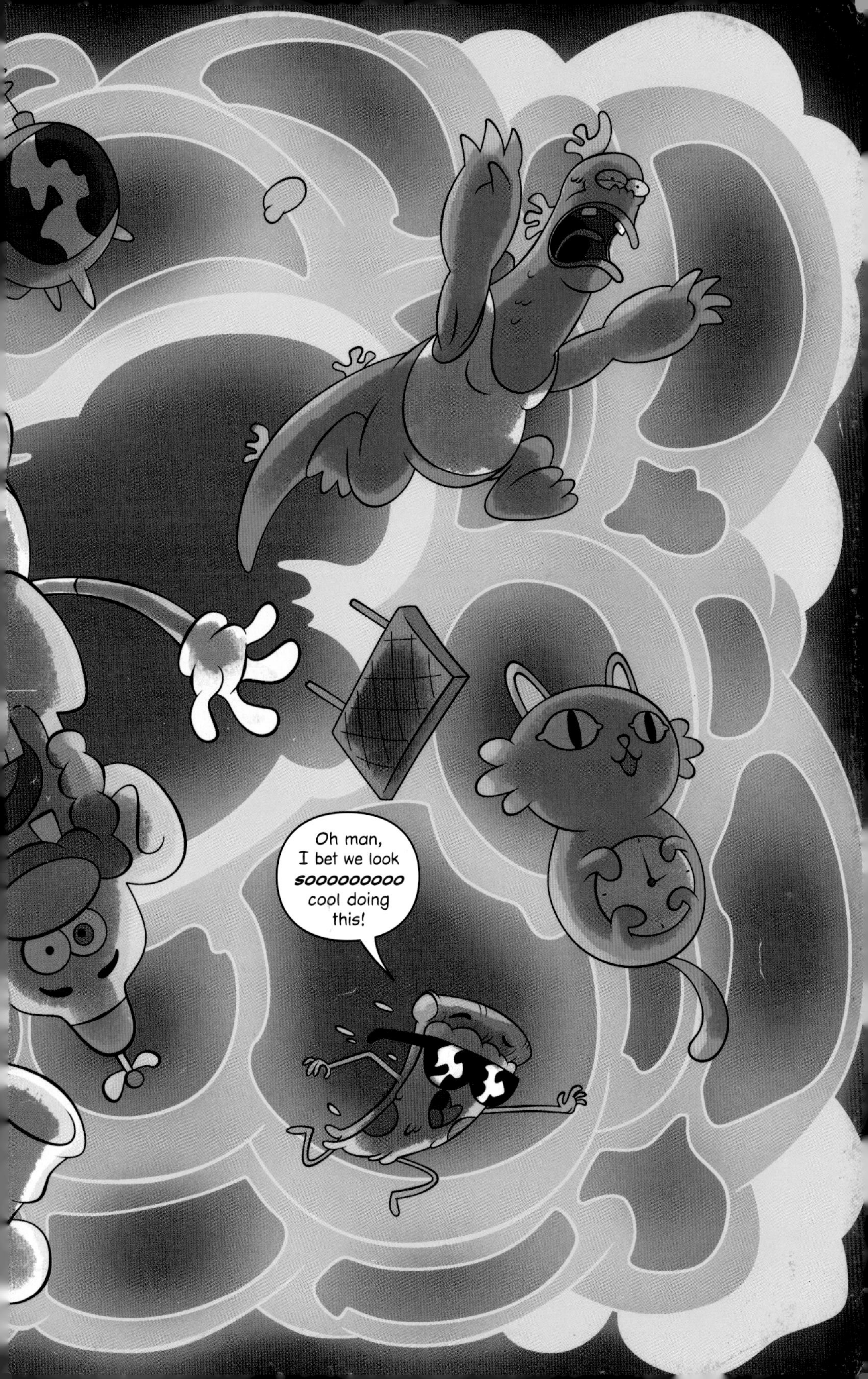
Oh man, I bet we look SOOOOOOOOO cool doing this!

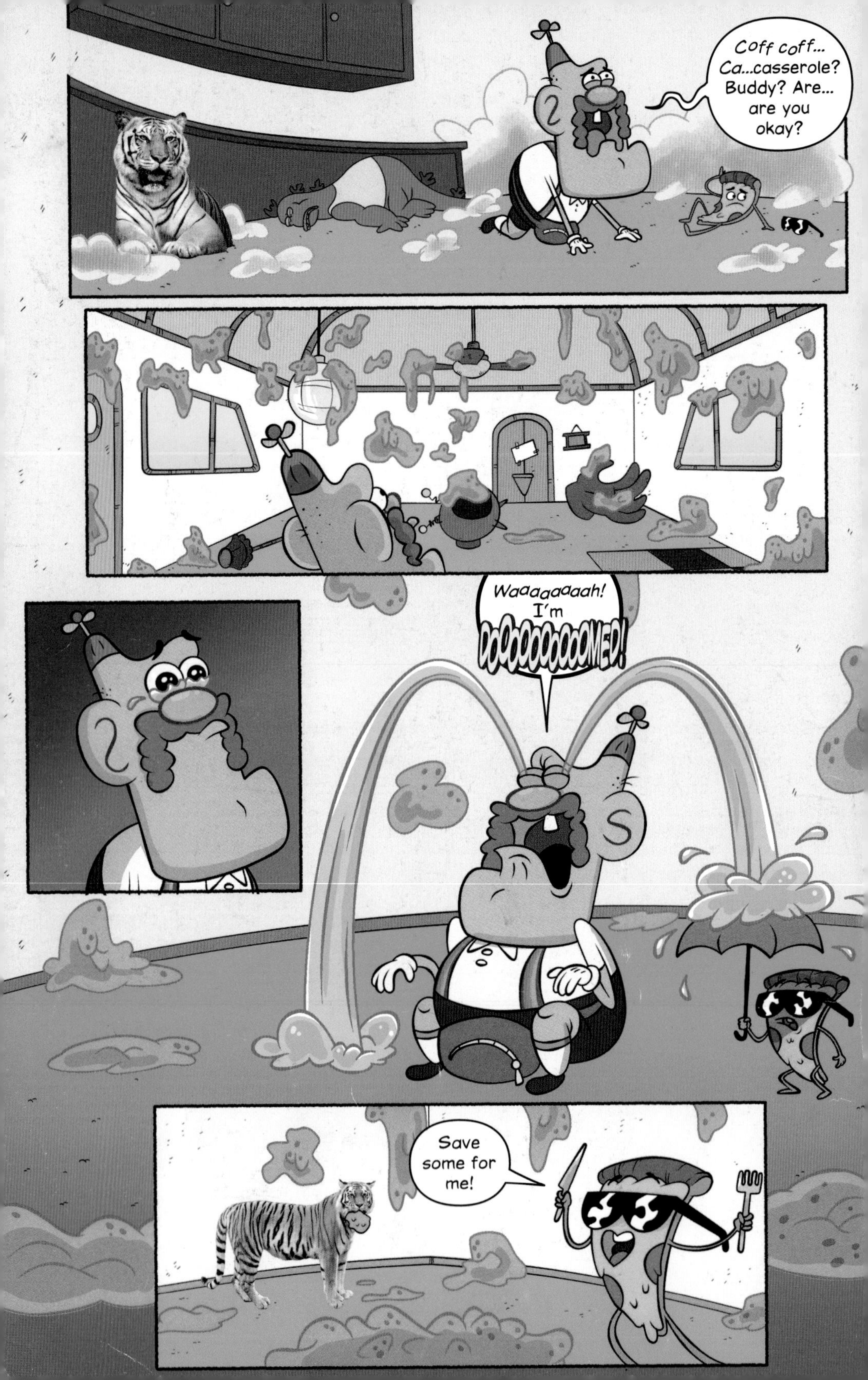
Coff coff... Ca...casserole? Buddy? Are... are you okay?
Waaaaaaaah! I'm DOOOOOOOOOOMED!
Save some for me!

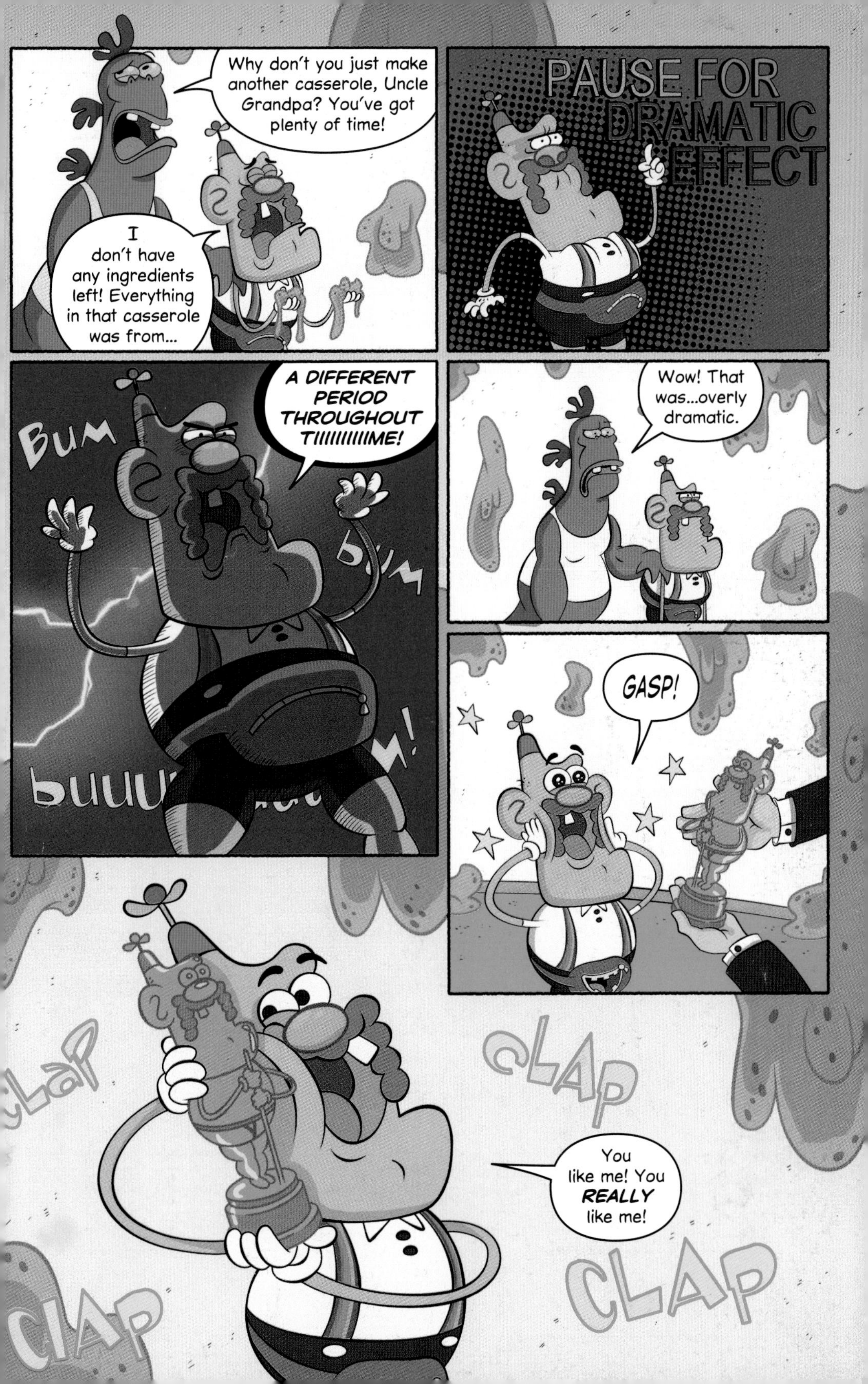

Why don't you just make another casserole, Uncle Grandpa? You've got plenty of time!
I don't have any ingredients left! Everything in that casserole was from...
PAUSE FOR DRAMATIC EFFECT
A DIFFERENT PERIOD THROUGHOUT TIIIIIIIIIIME!
Bum
Wow! That was...overly dramatic.
GASP!
CLAP
CLAP
You like me! You REALLY like me!
CLAP
CLAP

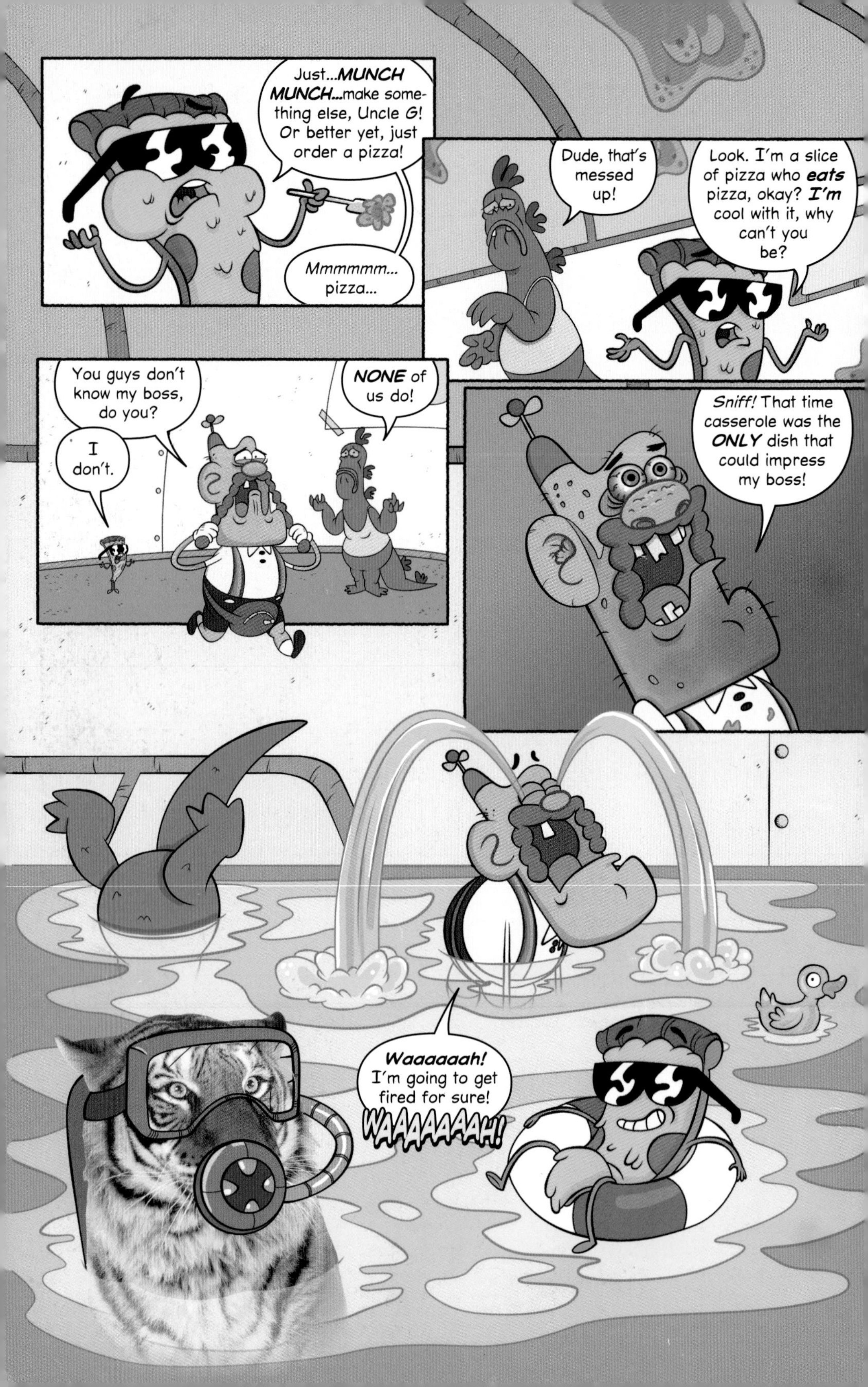
Just...MUNCH MUNCH...make something else, Uncle G! Or better yet, just order a pizza!
Mmmmmm... pizza...
Dude, that's messed up!
Look. I'm a slice of pizza who eats pizza, okay? I'm cool with it, why can't you be?
You guys don't know my boss, do you?
I don't.
NONE of us do!
Sniff! That time casserole was the ONLY dish that could impress my boss!
Waaaaaah! I'm going to get fired for sure!
WAAAAAAAH!

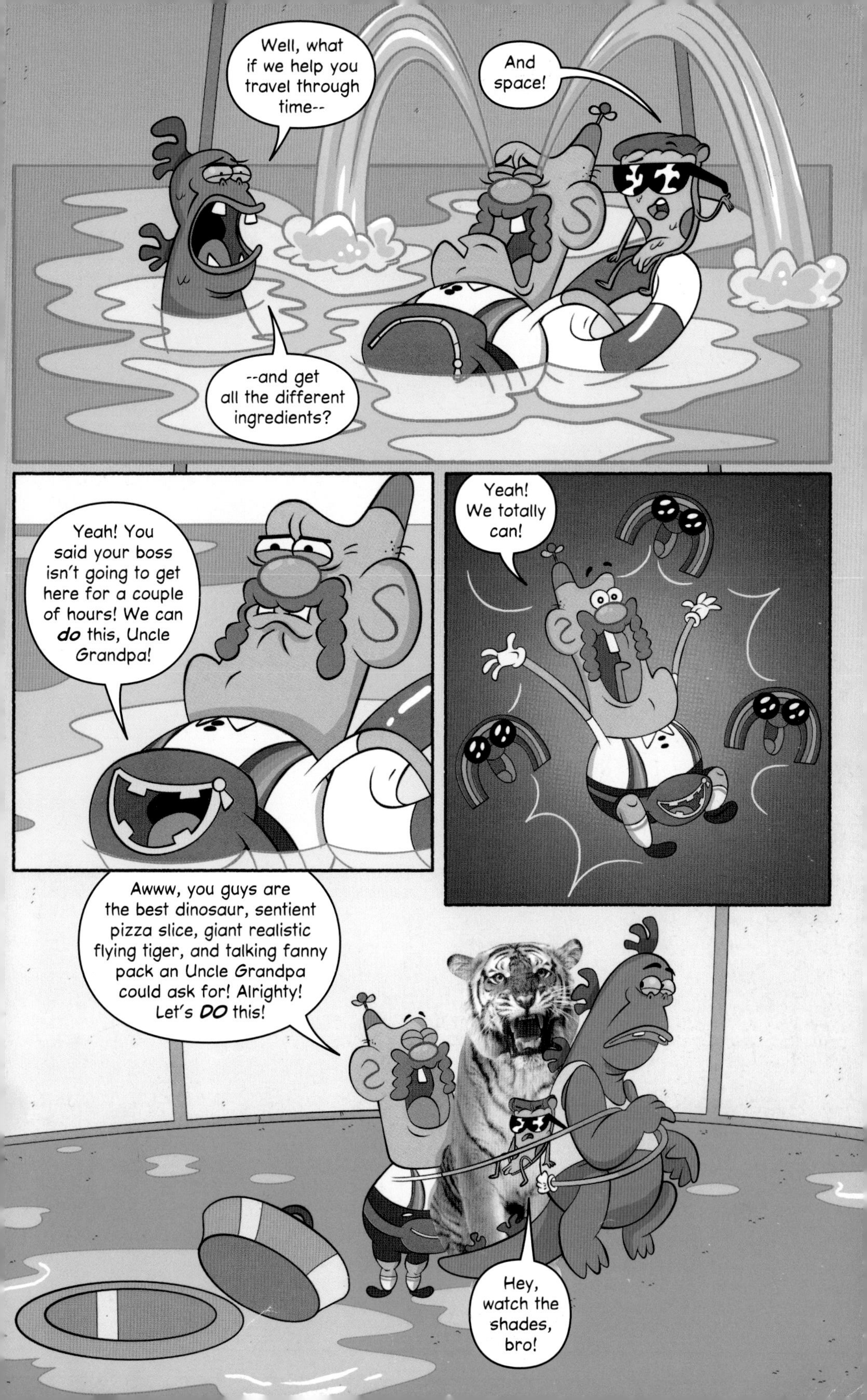
Well, what if we help you travel through time--
And space!
--and get all the different ingredients?
Yeah! You said your boss isn't going to get here for a couple of hours! We can *do* this, Uncle Grandpa!
Yeah! We totally can!
Awww, you guys are the best dinosaur, sentient pizza slice, giant realistic flying tiger, and talking fanny pack an Uncle Grandpa could ask for! Alrighty! Let's *DO* this!
Hey, watch the shades, bro!

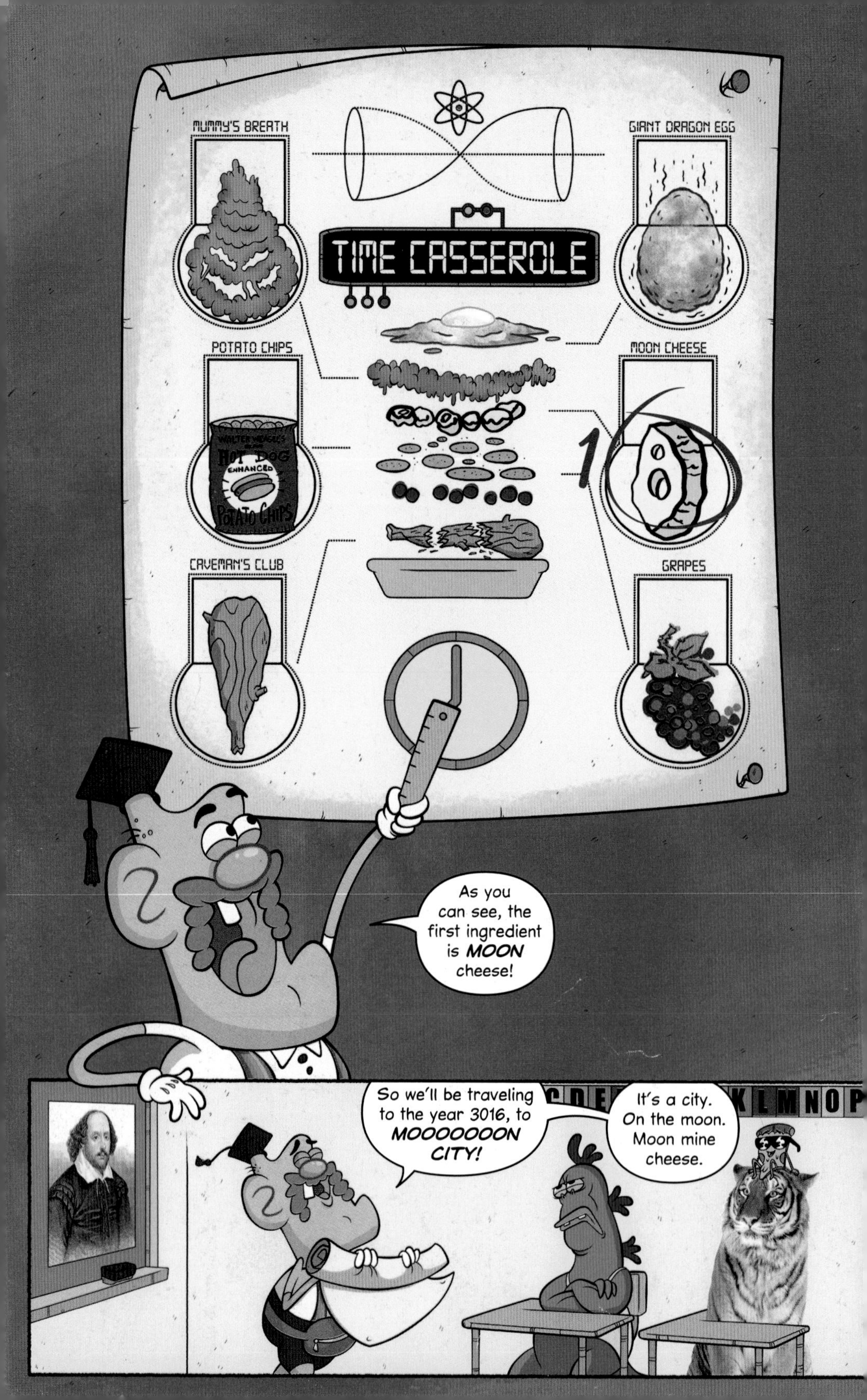
TIME CASSEROLE
MUMMY'S BREATH
GIANT DRAGON EGG
POTATO CHIPS
HOT DOG
ENHANCED
POTATO CHIPS
MOON CHEESE
16
CAVEMAN'S CLUB
GRAPES
As you can see, the first ingredient is *MOON* cheese!
So we'll be traveling to the year 3016, to ***MOOOOOOON CITY!***
It's a city. On the moon. Moon mine cheese.

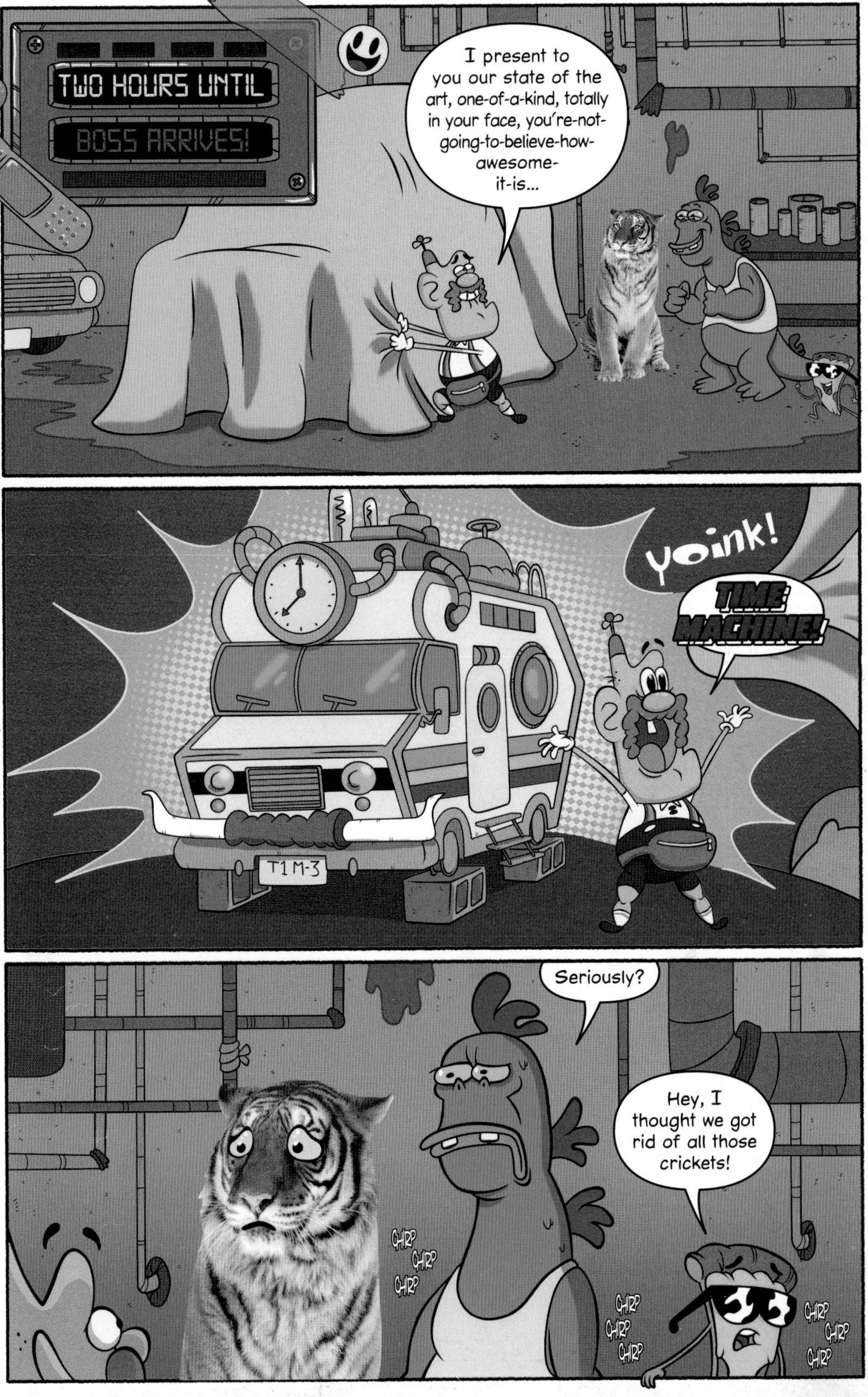
TWO HOURS UNTIL
BOSS ARRIVES!
I present to you our state of the art, one-of-a-kind, totally in your face, you're-not-going-to-believe-how-awesome-it-is...
YOINK!
TIME MACHINE!
T1M-3
Seriously?
Hey, I thought we got rid of all those crickets!
CHIRP CHIRP CHIRP
CHIRP CHIRP CHIRP
CHIRP CHIRP CHIRP

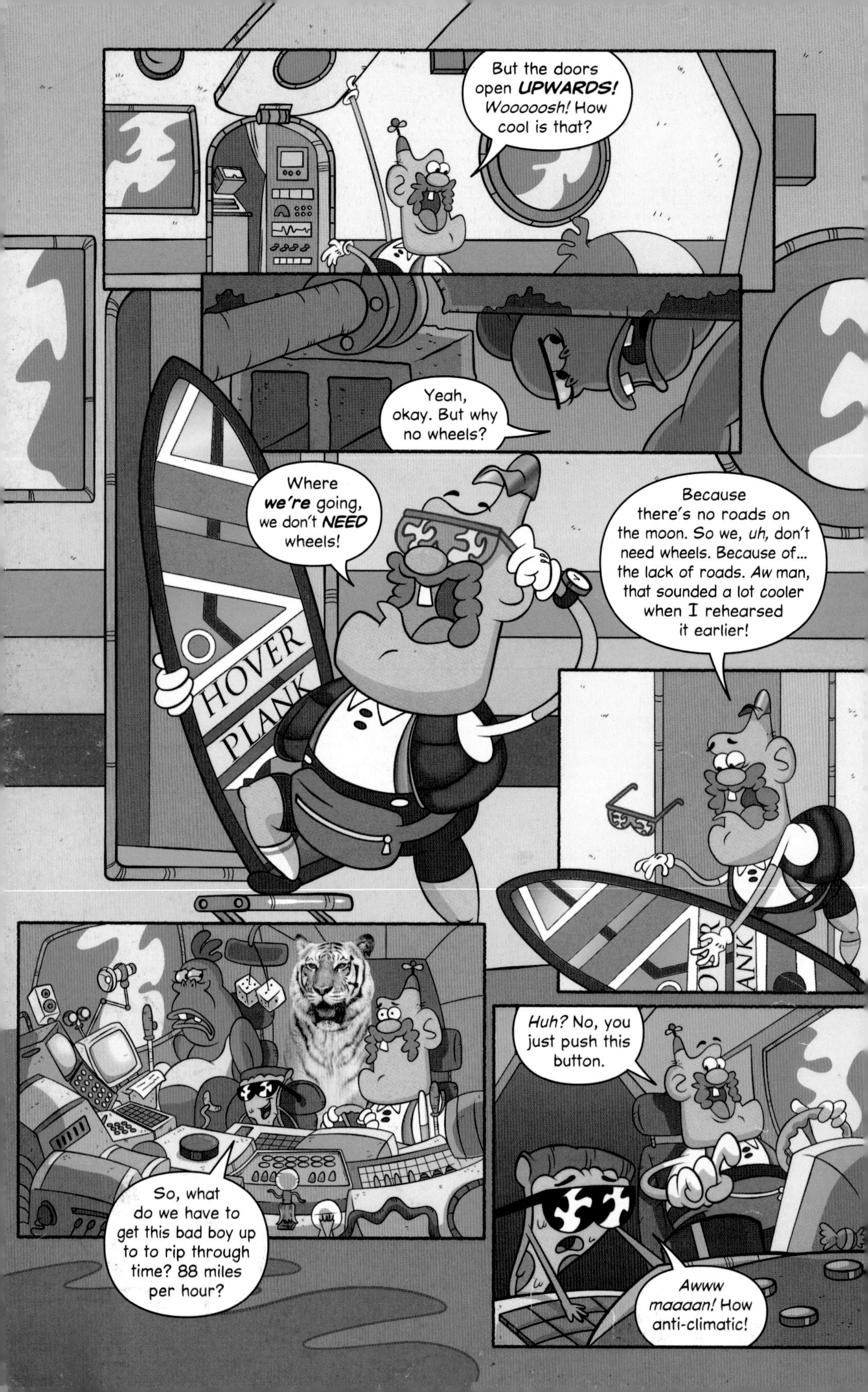

But the doors open **UPWARDS!** *Wooooosh!* How cool is that?
Yeah, okay. But why no wheels?
Where ***we're*** going, we don't ***NEED*** wheels!
Because there's no roads on the moon. So we, *uh,* don't need wheels. Because of... the lack of roads. *Aw* man, that sounded a lot cooler when I rehearsed it earlier!
HOVER PLANK
So, what do we have to get this bad boy up to to rip through time? 88 miles per hour?
Huh? No, you just push this button.
Awww maaaan! How anti-climatic!

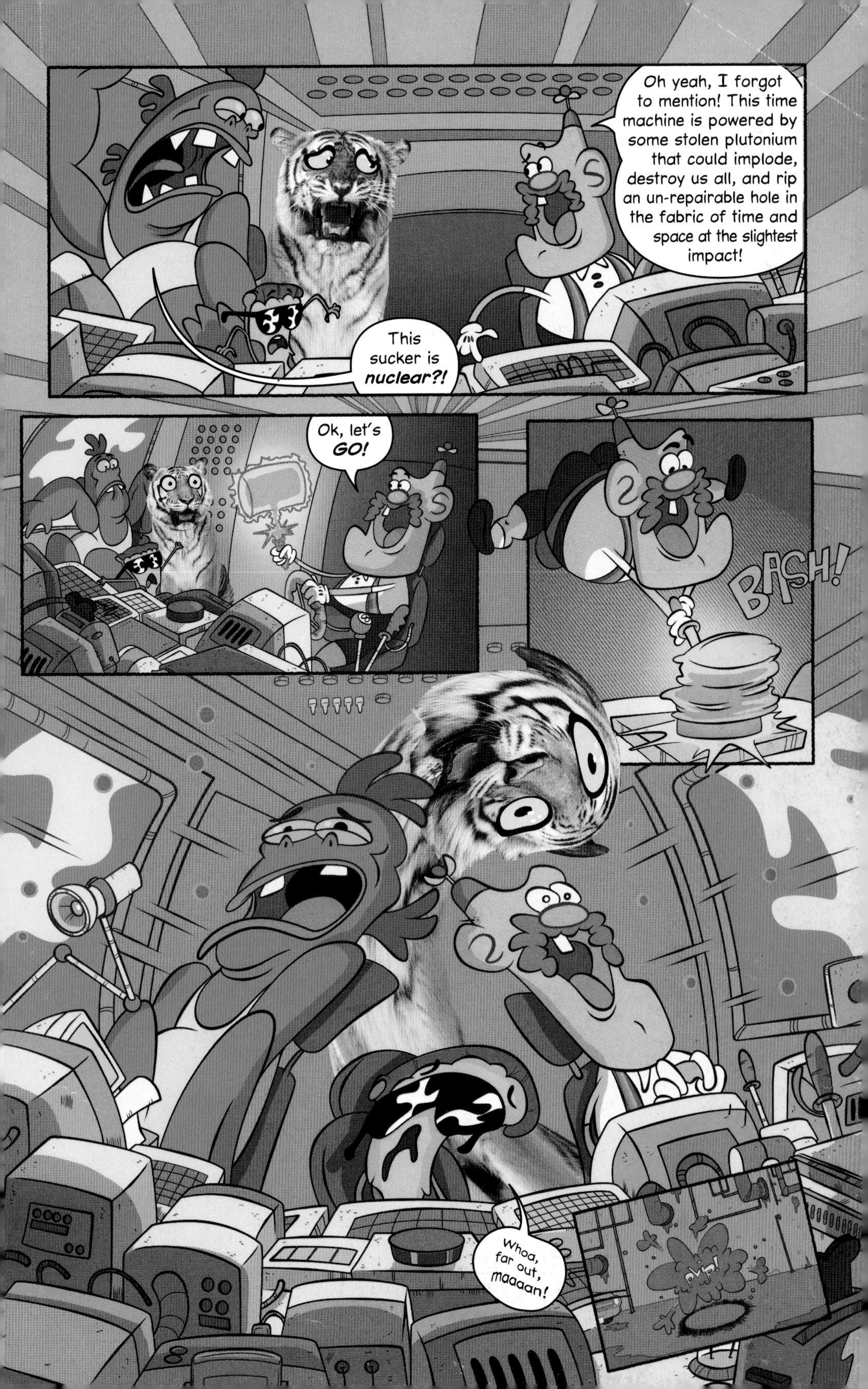

Oh yeah, I forgot to mention! This time machine is powered by some stolen plutonium that could implode, destroy us all, and rip an un-repairable hole in the fabric of time and space at the slightest impact!
This sucker is ***nuclear?!***
Ok, let's ***GO!***
BASH!
Whoa, far out, maaaan!

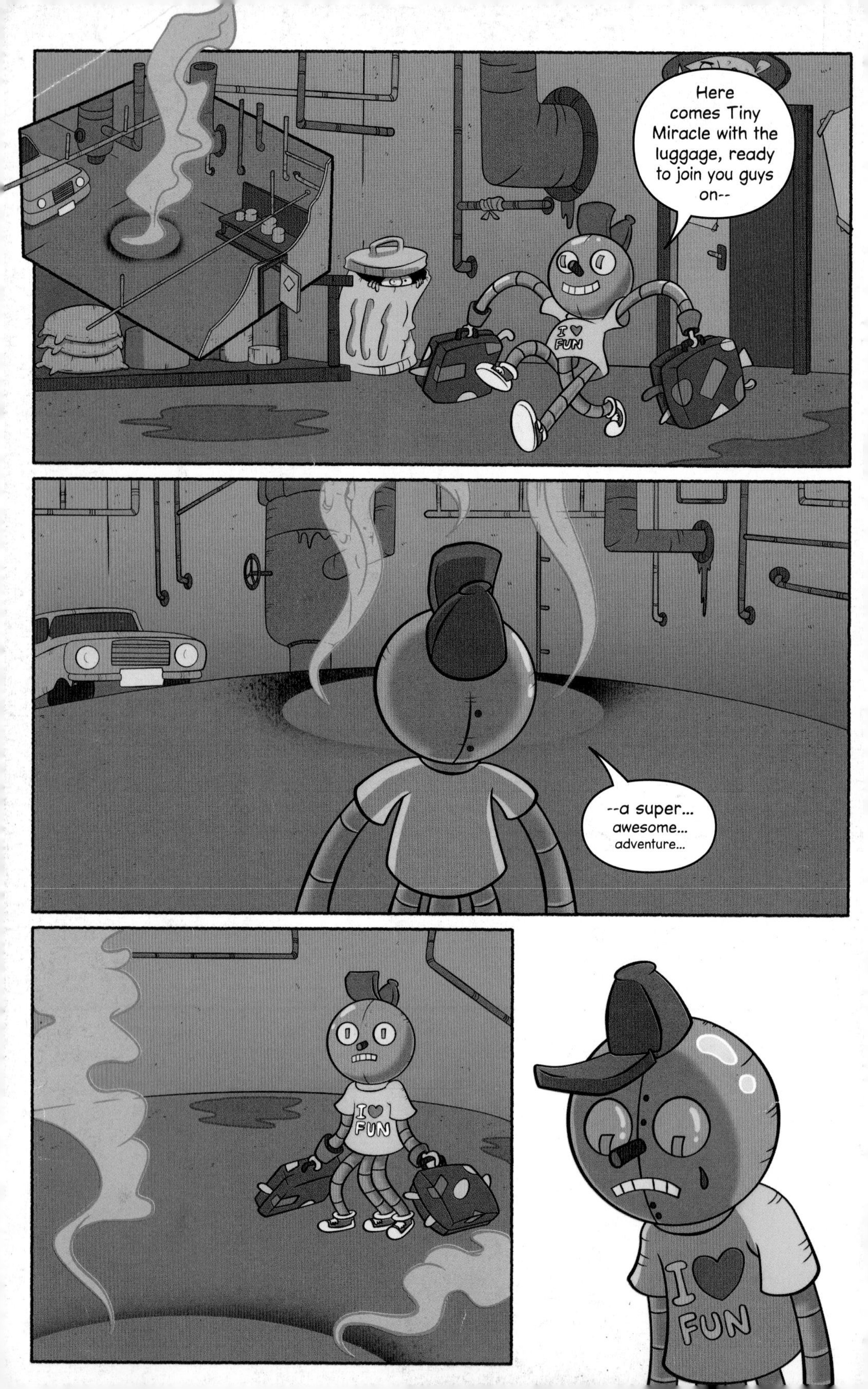
Here comes Tiny Miracle with the luggage, ready to join you guys on--
I ♥ FUN
--a super... awesome... adventure...
I ♥ FUN
I ♥ FUN

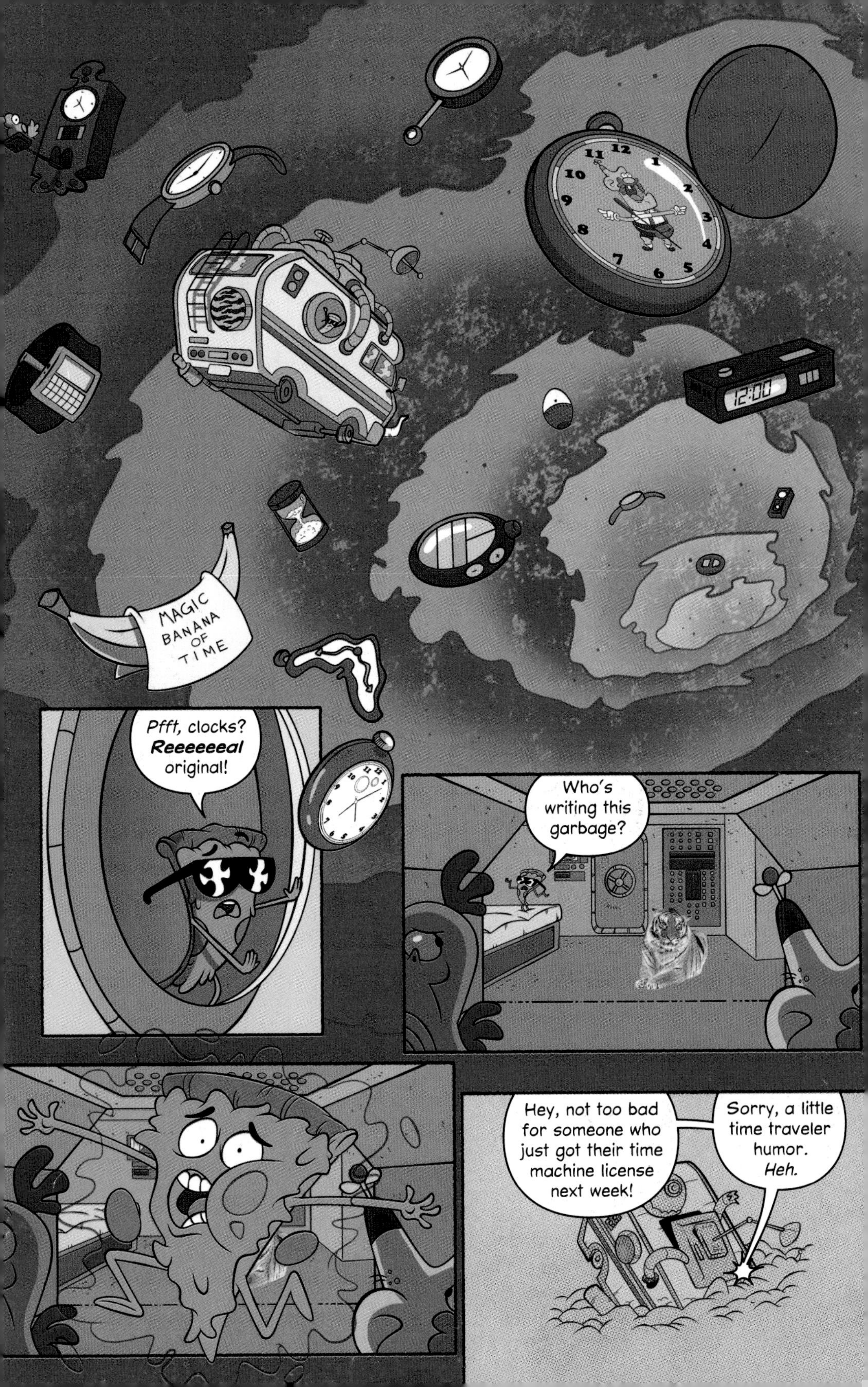

MAGIC BANANA OF TIME
12:00
Pfft, clocks? **Reeeeeeal** original!
Who's writing this garbage?
Hey, not too bad for someone who just got their time machine license next week!
Sorry, a little time traveler humor. *Heh.*

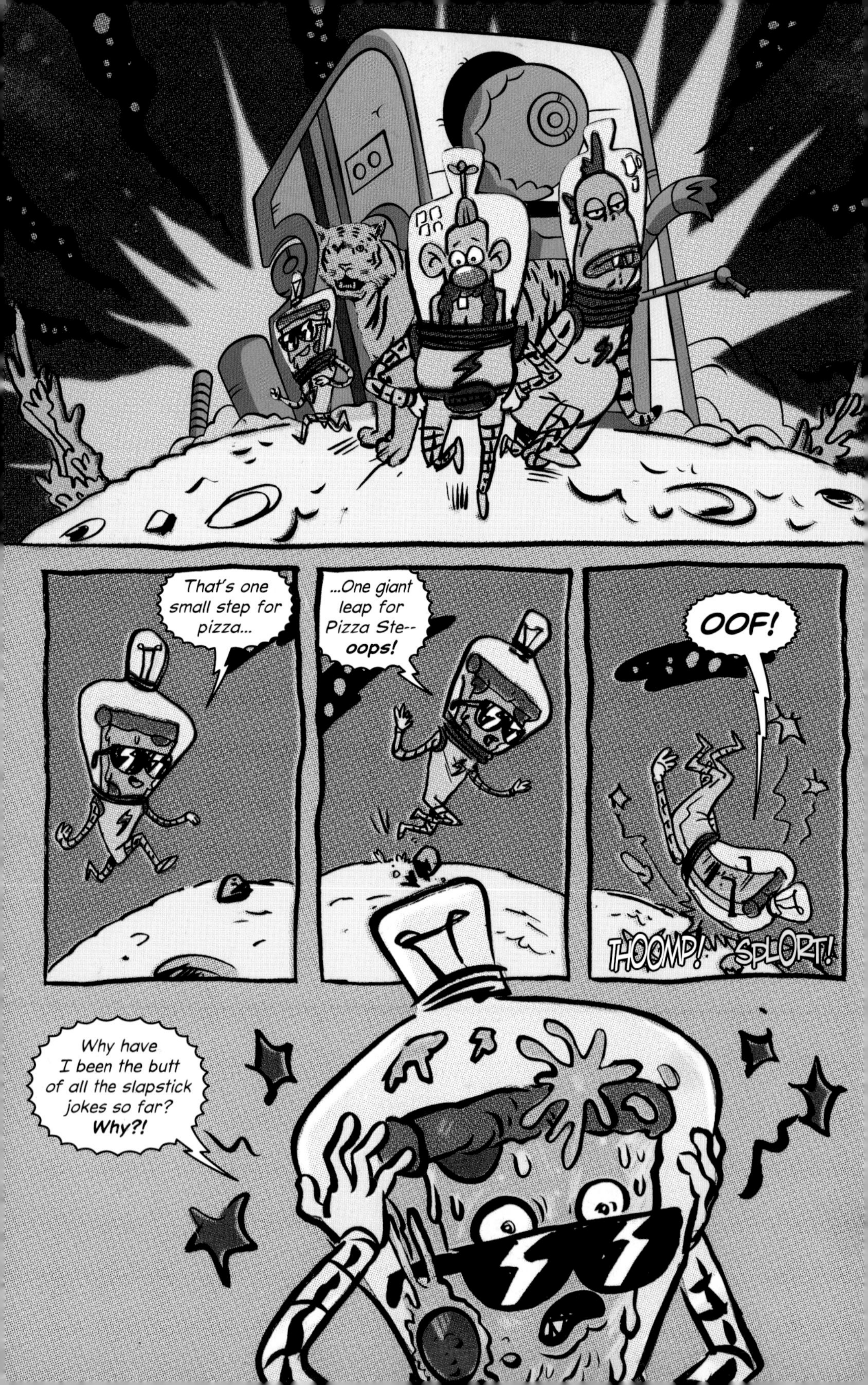
That's one small step for pizza...
...One giant leap for Pizza Ste-- **oops!**
OOF!
THOOMP!
SPLORT!
Why have I been the butt of all the slapstick jokes so far? **Why?!**

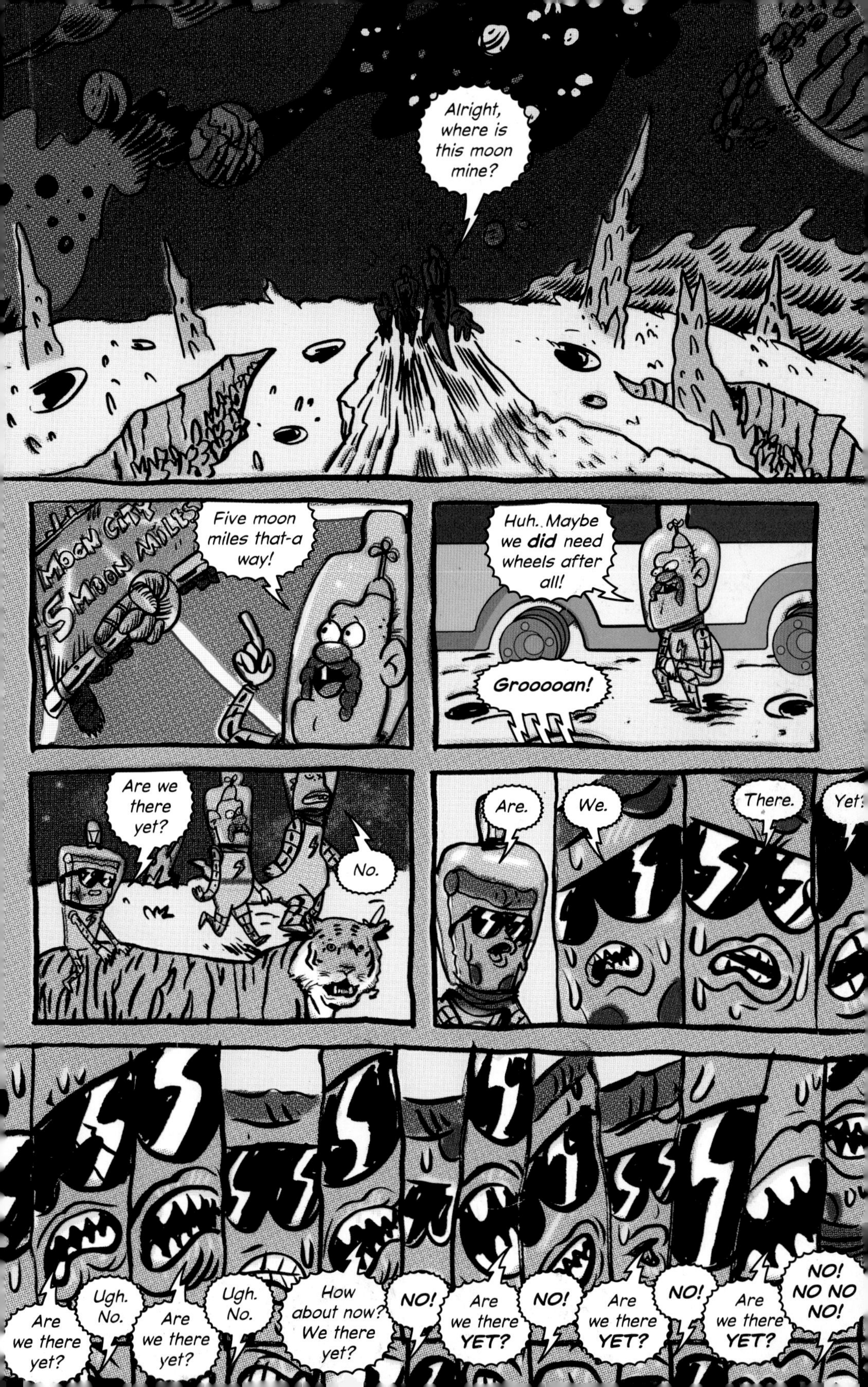
Alright, where is this moon mine?
MOON CITY 5 MOON MILES
Five moon miles that-a way!
Huh.. Maybe we **did** need wheels after all!
Grooooan!
Are we there yet?
No.
Are.
We.
There.
Yet?
Are we there yet?
Ugh. No.
Are we there yet?
Ugh. No.
How about now? We there yet?
NO!
Are we there YET?
NO!
Are we there YET?
NO!
Are we there YET?
NO! NO NO NO!

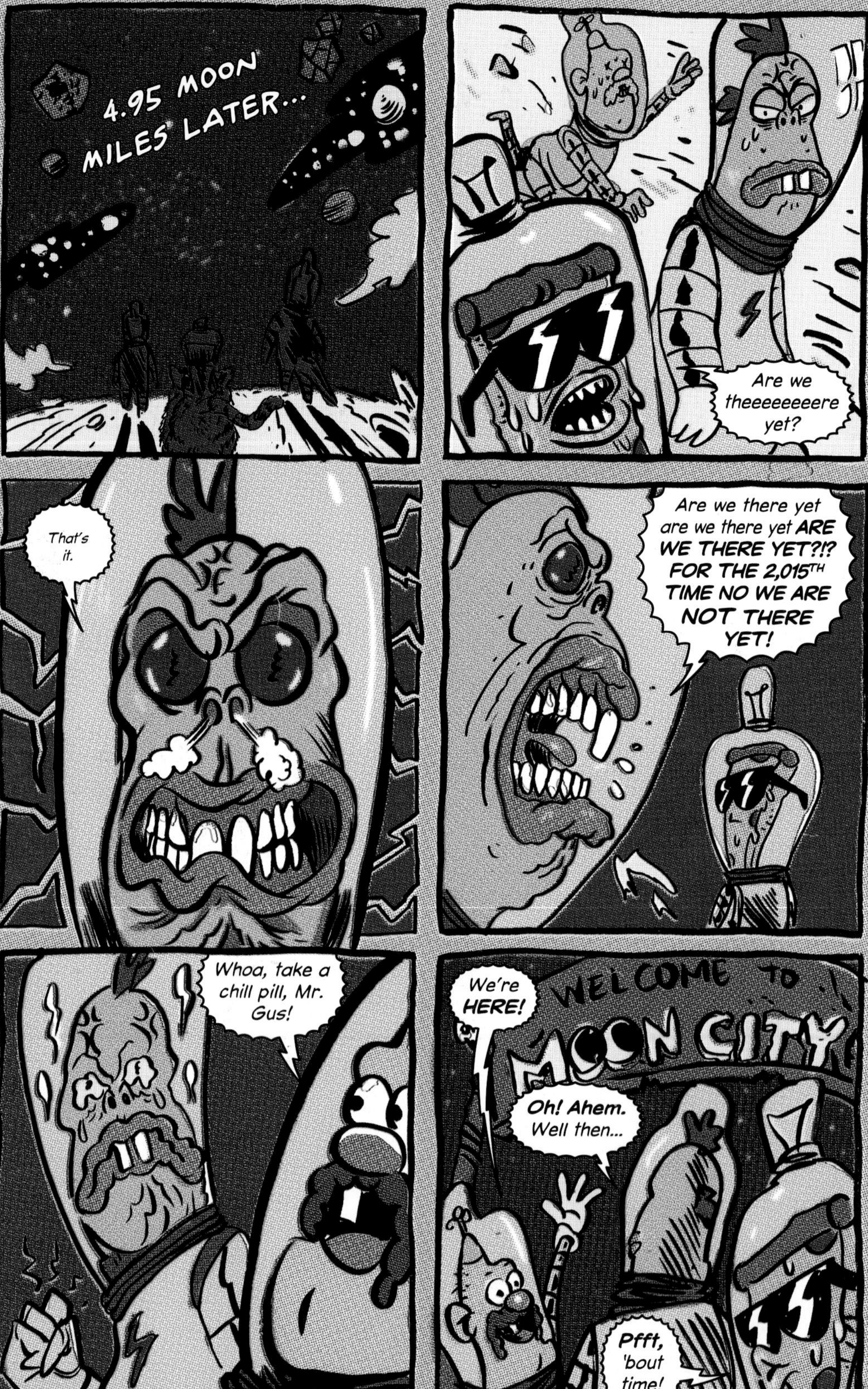
4.95 MOON MILES LATER...
Are we theeeeeeeere yet?
That's it.
Are we there yet are we there yet ARE WE THERE YET?!? FOR THE 2,015TH TIME NO WE ARE NOT THERE YET!
Whoa, take a chill pill, Mr. Gus!
We're HERE!
WELCOME TO MOON CITY
Oh! Ahem. Well then...
Pfft, 'bout time!

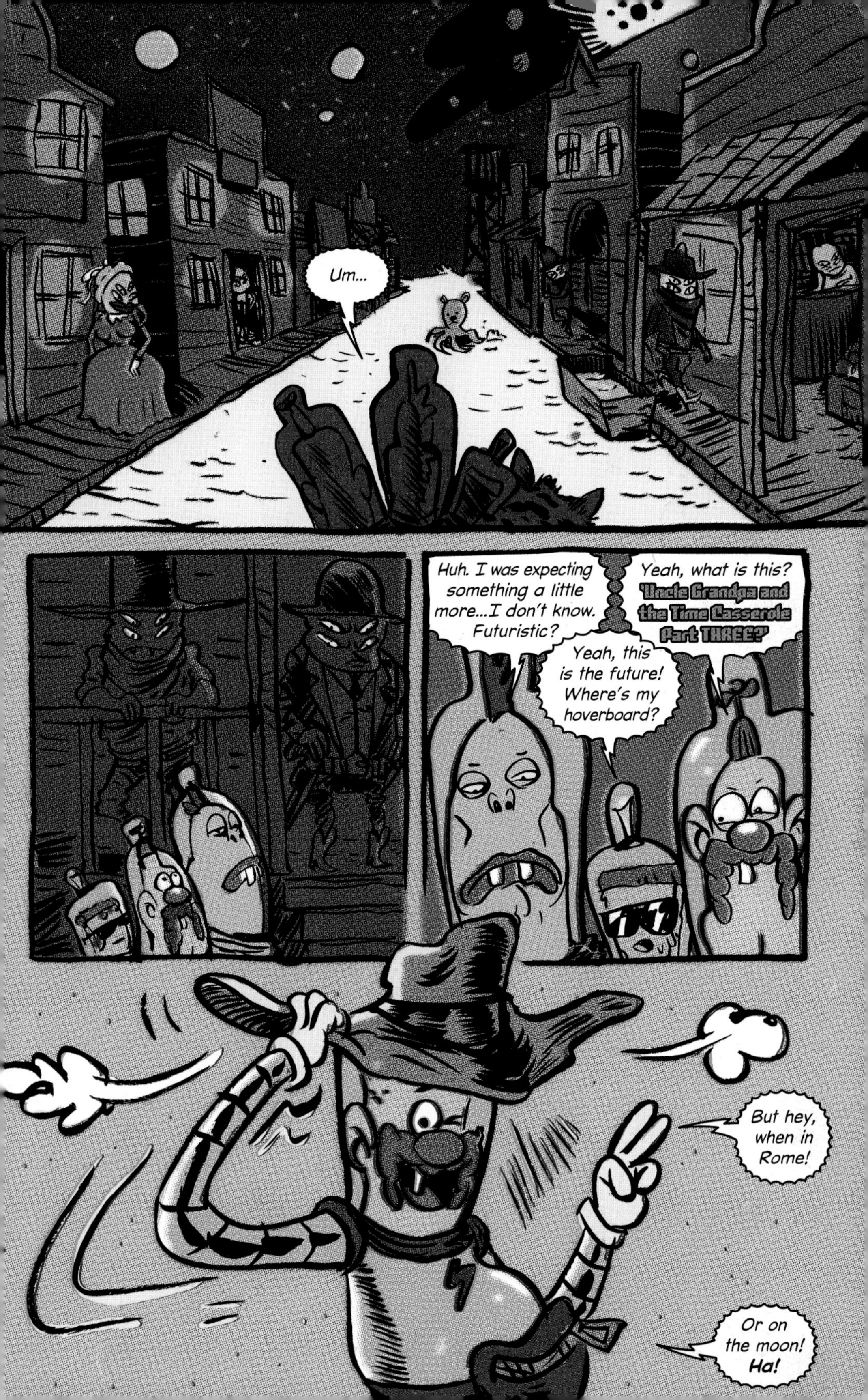
Um...
Huh. I was expecting something a little more...I don't know. Futuristic?
Yeah, what is this? 'Uncle Grandpa and the Time Casserole Part THREE?'
Yeah, this is the future! Where's my hoverboard?
But hey, when in Rome!
Or on the moon! **Ha!**

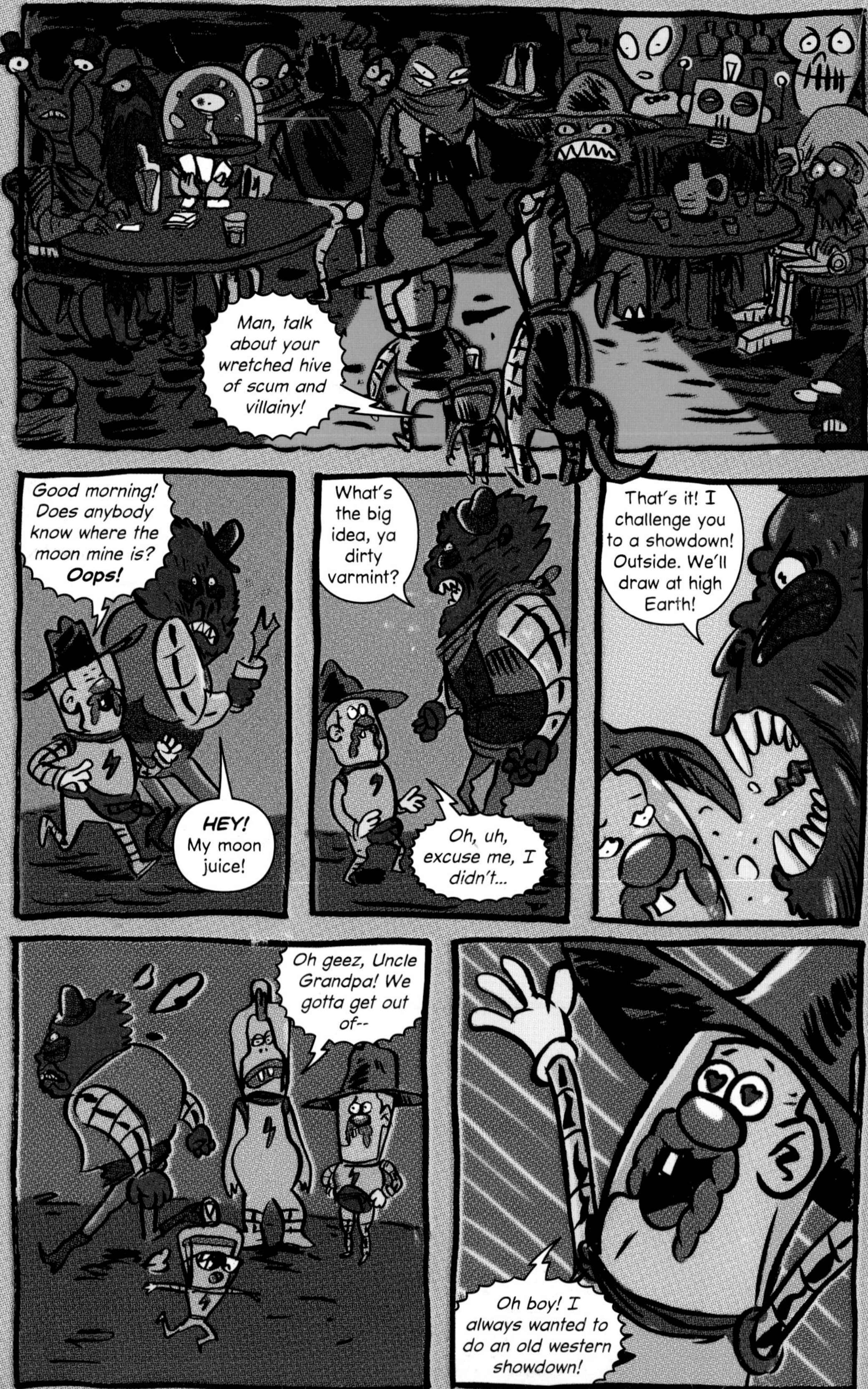

Man, talk about your wretched hive of scum and villainy!
Good morning! Does anybody know where the moon mine is? **Oops!**
HEY! My moon juice!
What's the big idea, ya dirty varmint?
Oh, uh, excuse me, I didn't...
That's it! I challenge you to a showdown! Outside. We'll draw at high Earth!
Oh geez, Uncle Grandpa! We gotta get out of--
Oh boy! I always wanted to do an old western showdown!

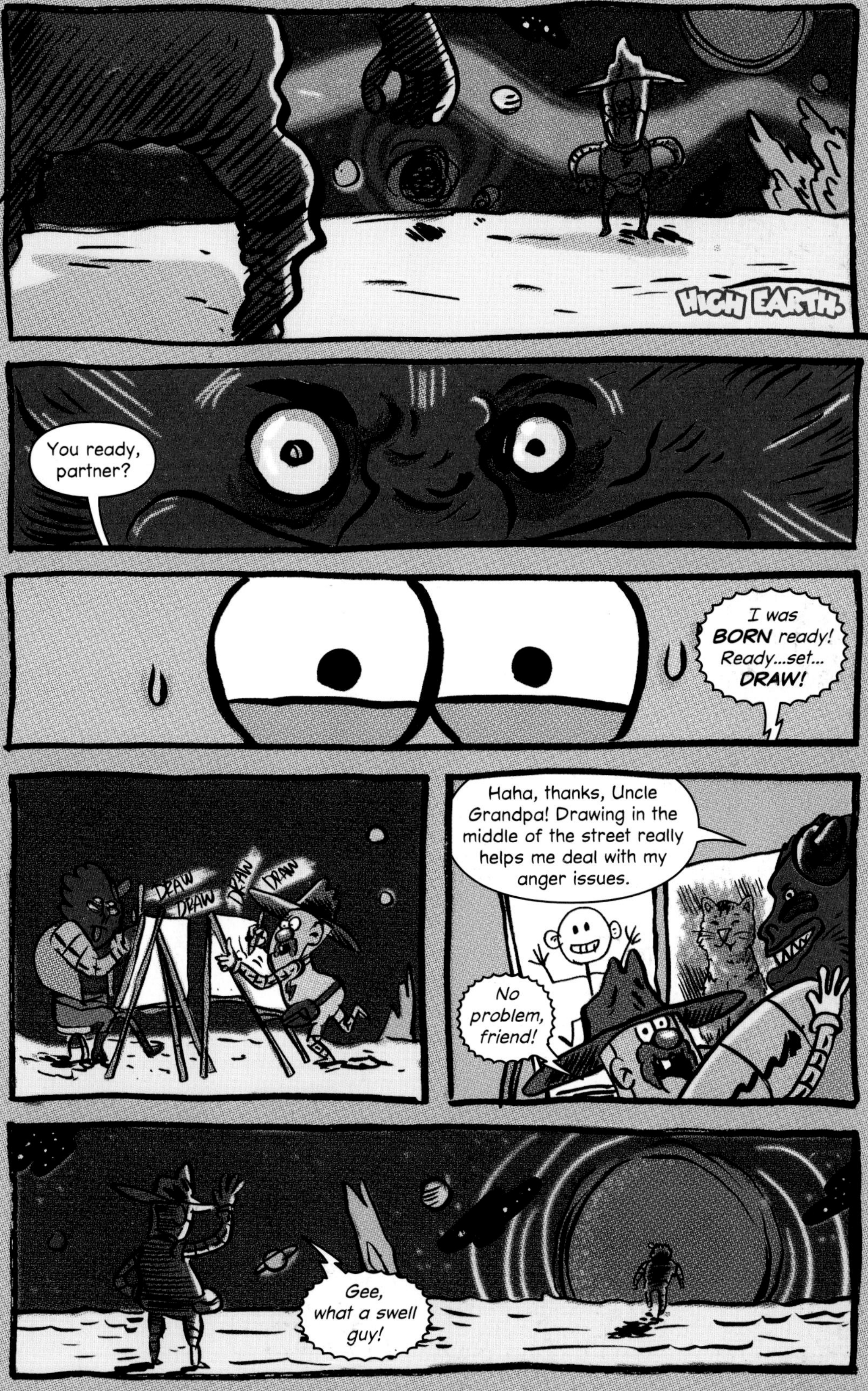
HIGH EARTH.
You ready, partner?
I was BORN ready! Ready...set... DRAW!
DRAW
DRAW
DRAW
DRAW
Haha, thanks, Uncle Grandpa! Drawing in the middle of the street really helps me deal with my anger issues.
No problem, friend!
Gee, what a swell guy!

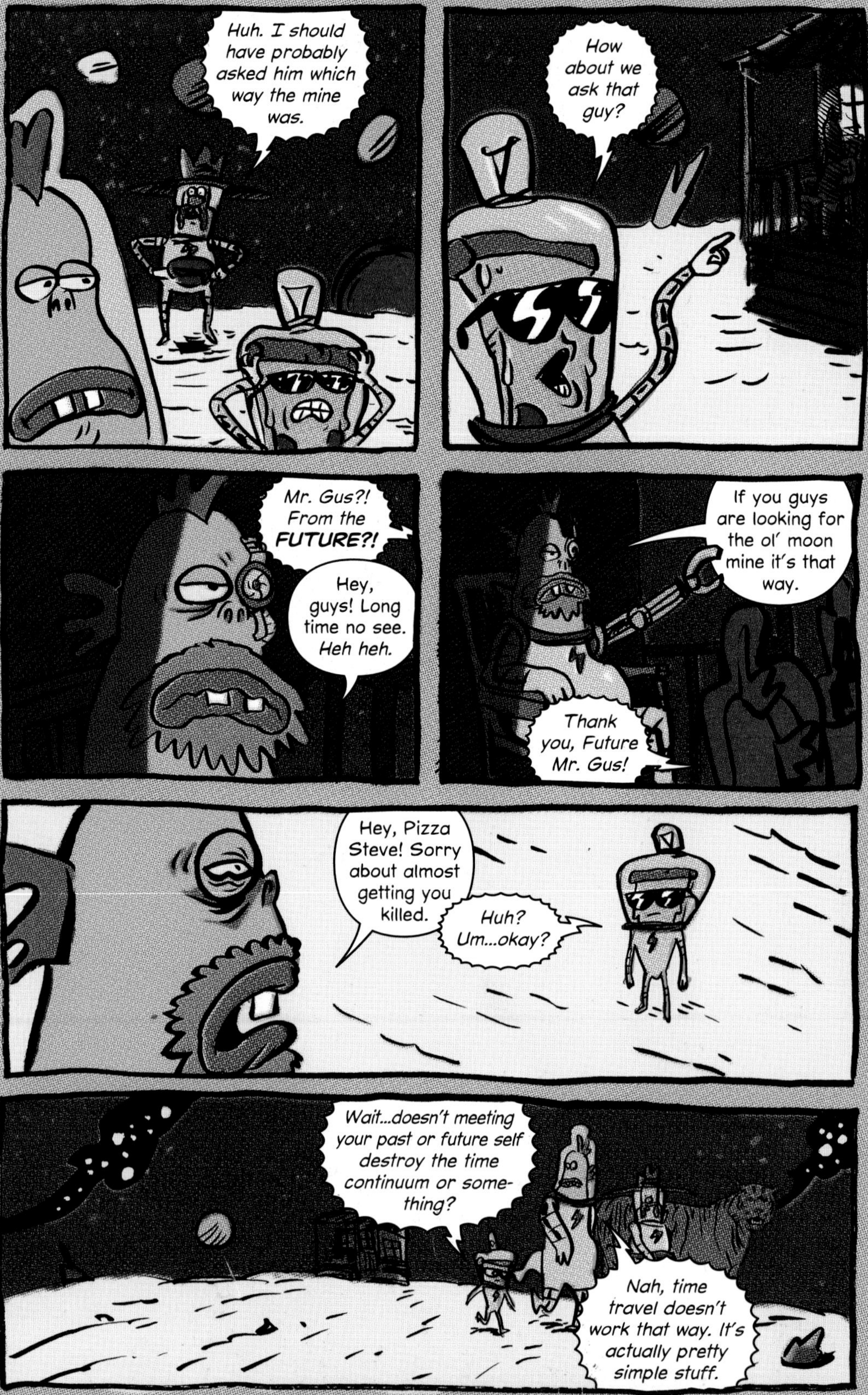
Huh. I should have probably asked him which way the mine was.
How about we ask that guy?
Mr. Gus?! From the **FUTURE?!**
Hey, guys! Long time no see. Heh heh.
If you guys are looking for the ol' moon mine it's that way.
Thank you, Future Mr. Gus!
Hey, Pizza Steve! Sorry about almost getting you killed.
Huh? Um...okay?
Wait...doesn't meeting your past or future self destroy the time continuum or some-thing?
Nah, time travel doesn't work that way. It's actually pretty simple stuff.

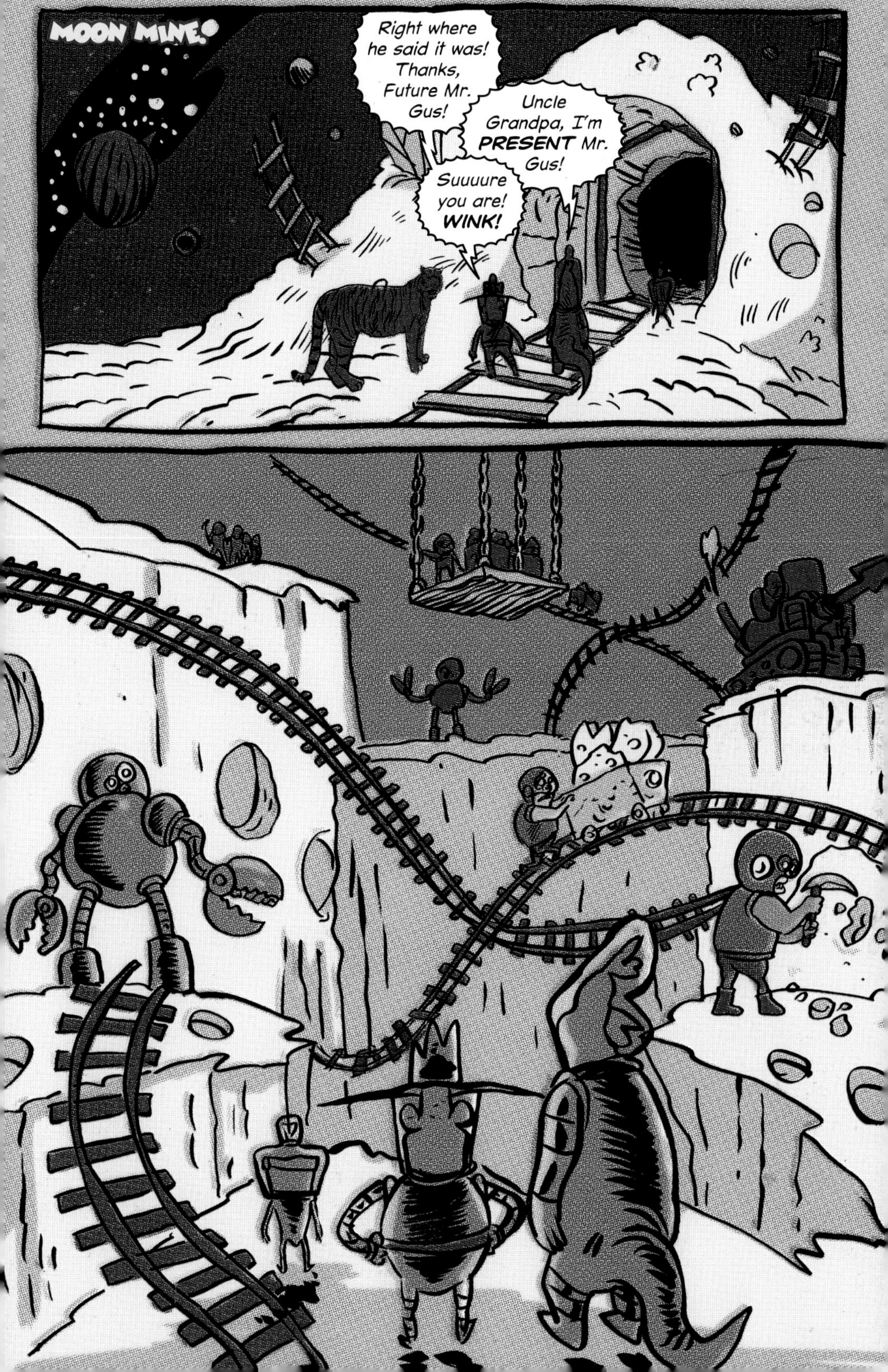
MOON MINE!
Right where he said it was! Thanks, Future Mr. Gus!
Uncle Grandpa, I'm **PRESENT** Mr. Gus!
Suuuure you are! **WINK!**

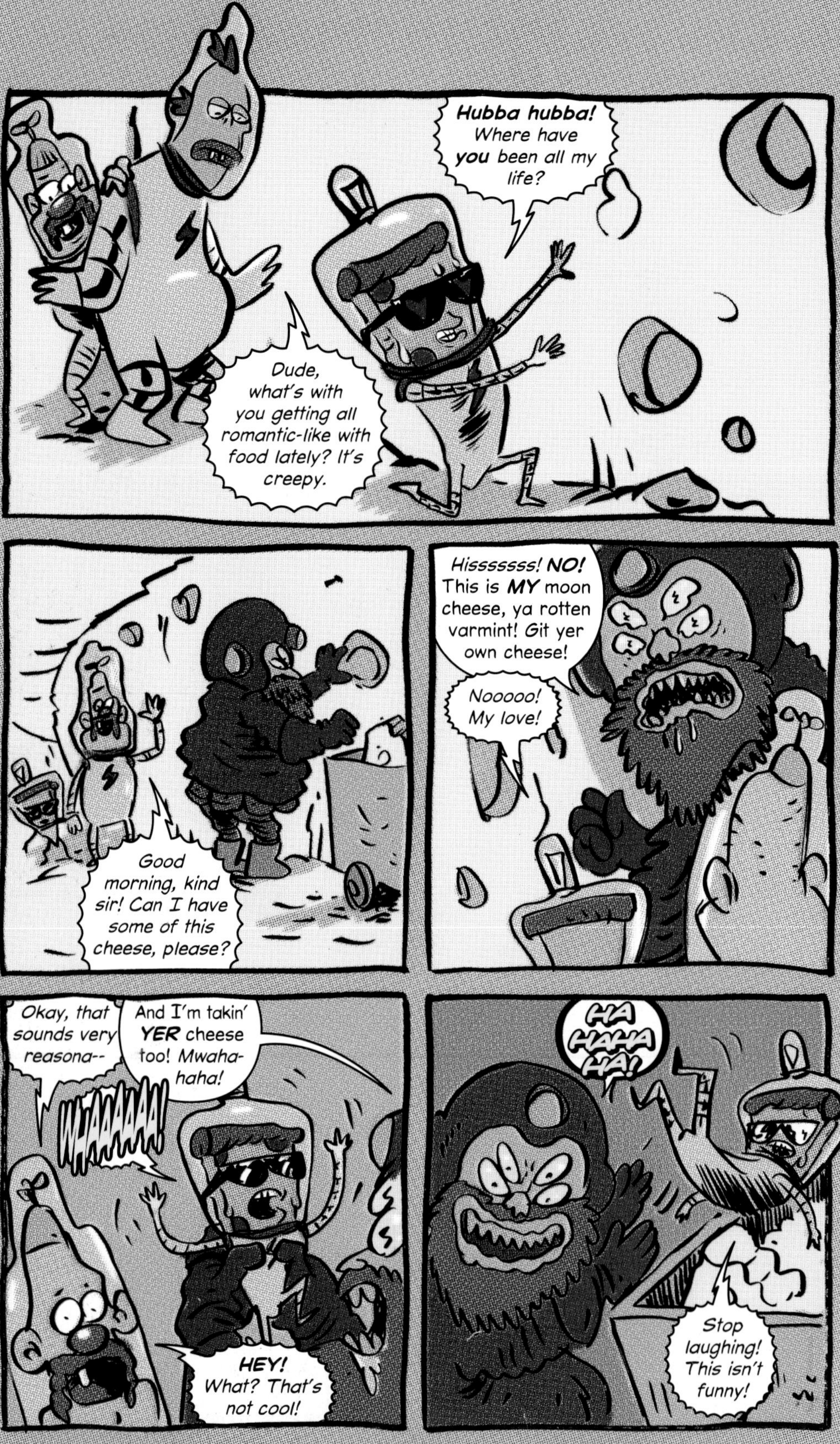
Hubba hubba! Where have you been all my life?
Dude, what's with you getting all romantic-like with food lately? It's creepy.
Good morning, kind sir! Can I have some of this cheese, please?
Hissssss! NO! This is MY moon cheese, ya rotten varmint! Git yer own cheese!
Nooooo! My love!
Okay, that sounds very reasona--
And I'm takin' YER cheese too! Mwaha-haha!
WHAAAAA!
HEY! What? That's not cool!
HA HAHA HA!
Stop laughing! This isn't funny!

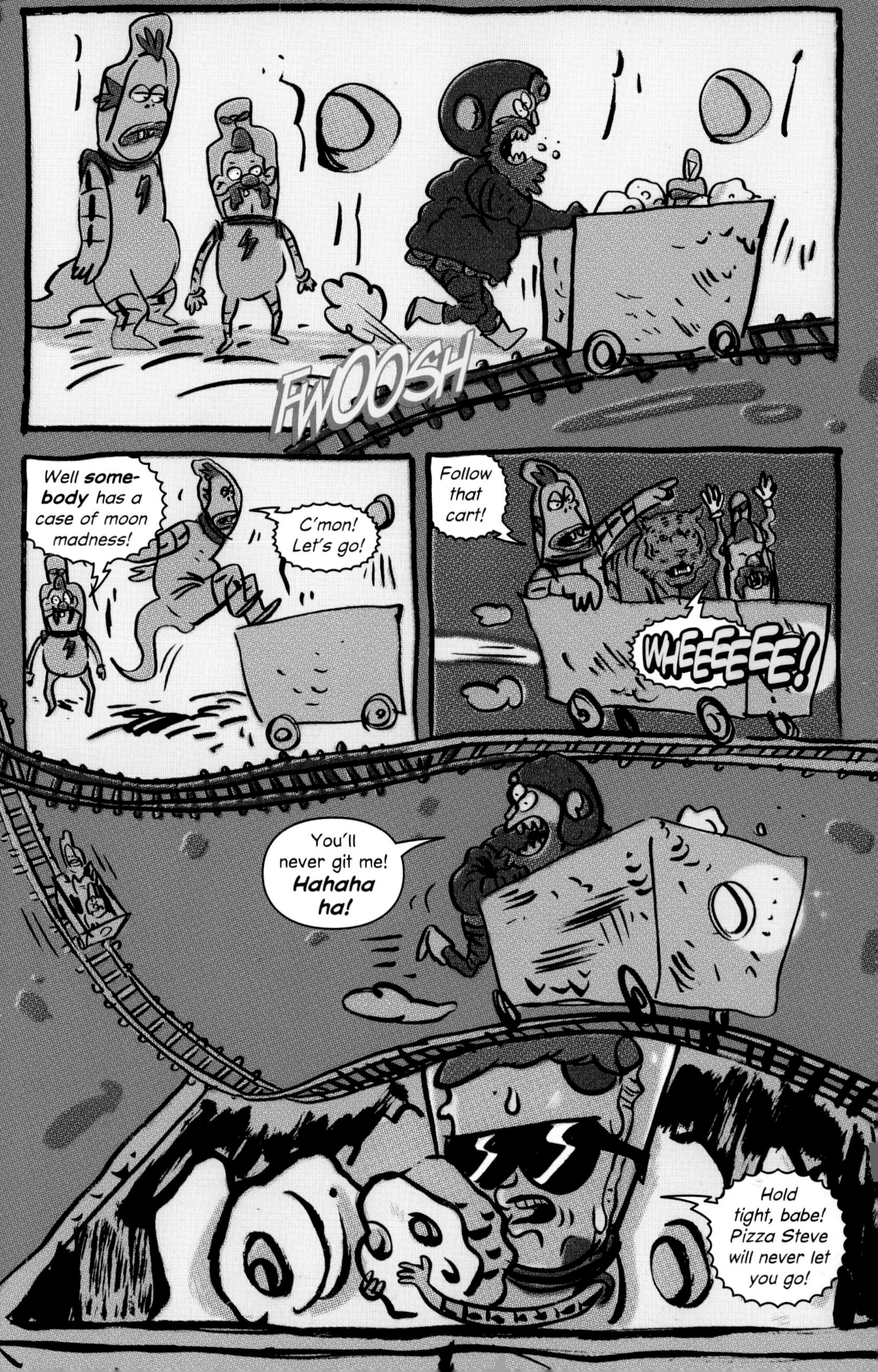
FWOOSH
Well **somebody** has a case of moon madness!
C'mon! Let's go!
Follow that cart!
WHEEEEEE!
You'll never git me! **Hahaha ha!**
Hold tight, babe! Pizza Steve will never let you go!

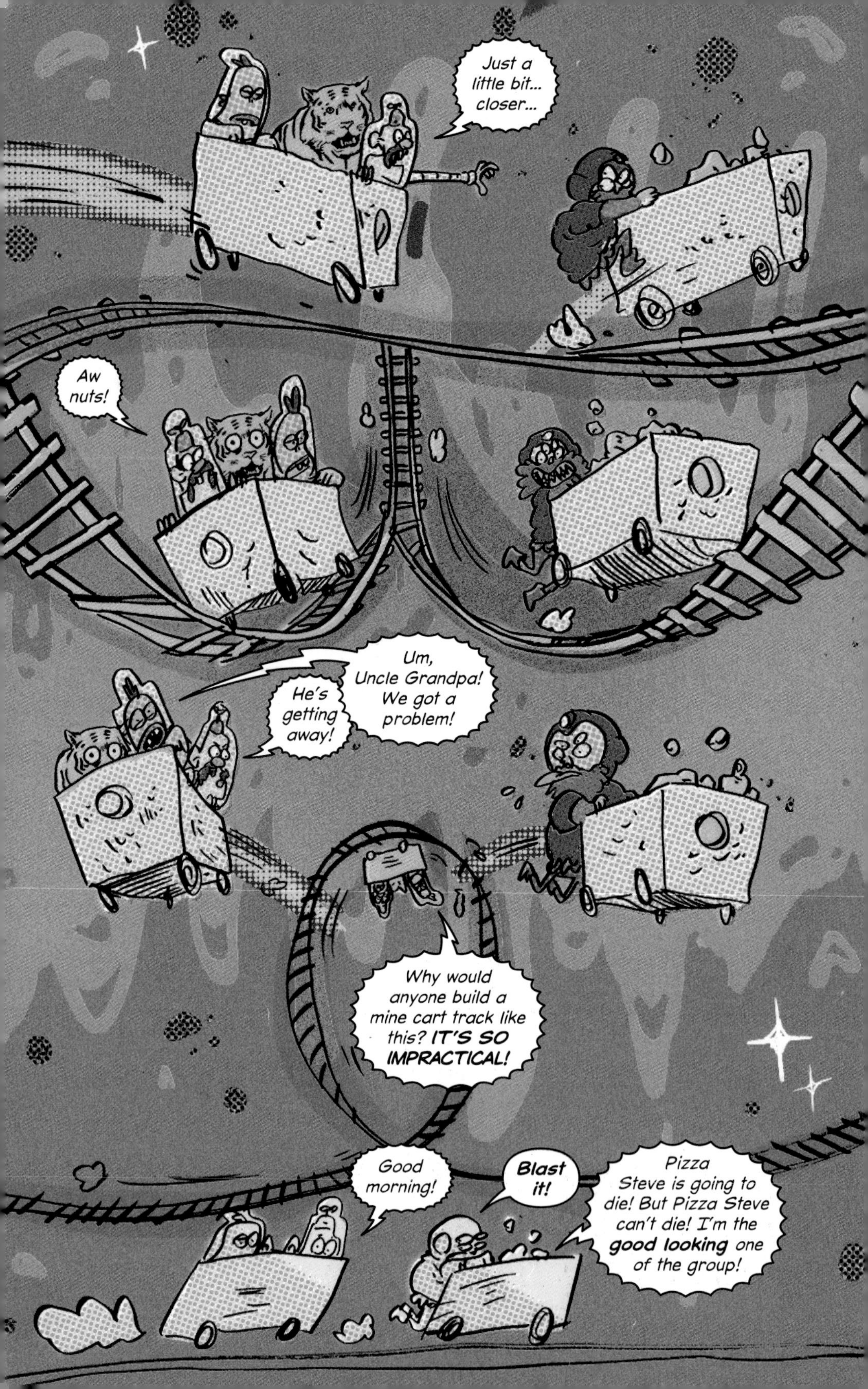
Just a little bit... closer...
Aw nuts!
Um, Uncle Grandpa! We got a problem!
He's getting away!
Why would anyone build a mine cart track like this? IT'S SO IMPRACTICAL!
Good morning!
Blast it!
Pizza Steve is going to die! But Pizza Steve can't die! I'm the good looking one of the group!

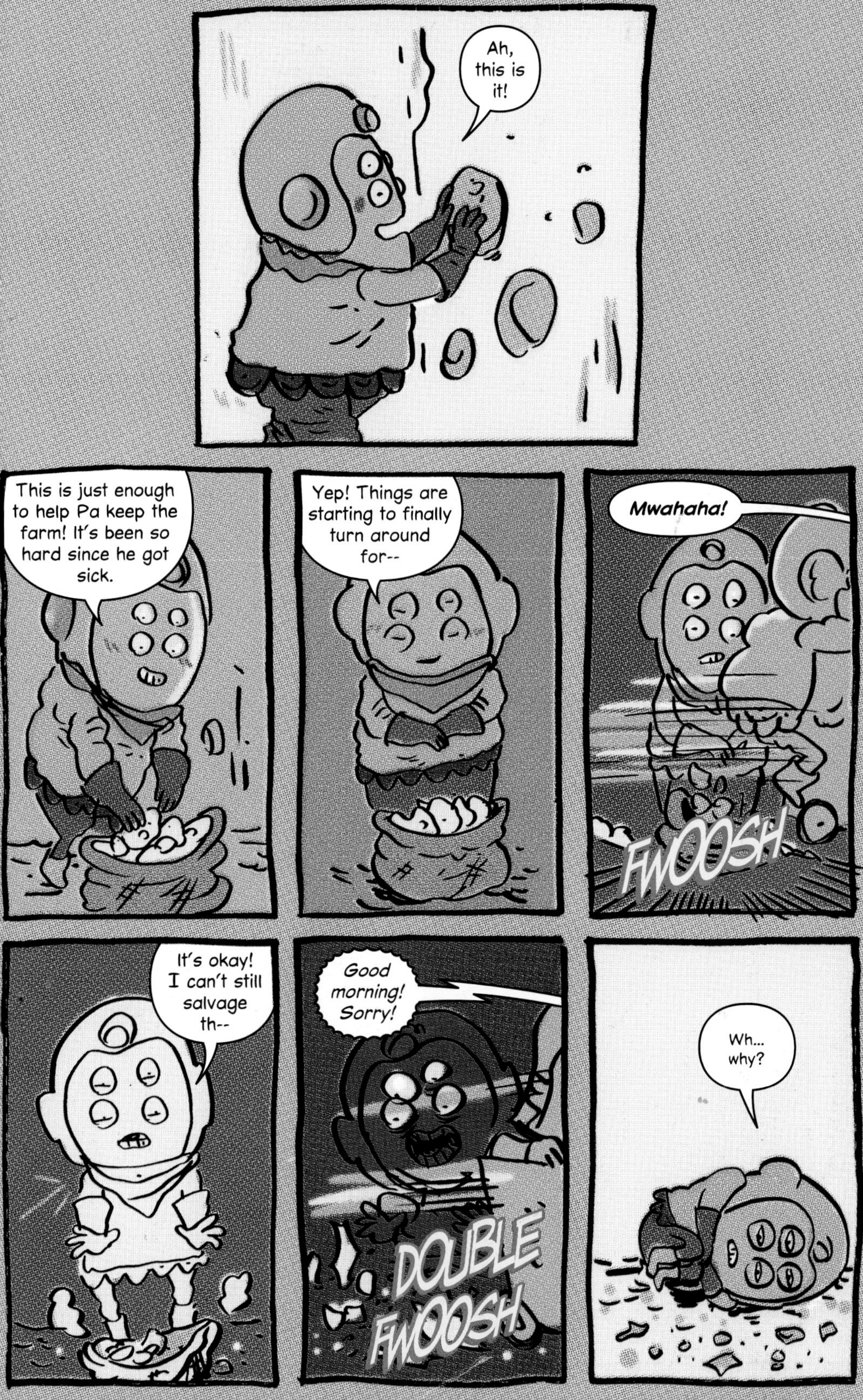
Ah, this is it!
This is just enough to help Pa keep the farm! It's been so hard since he got sick.
Yep! Things are starting to finally turn around for--
Mwahaha!
FWOOSH
It's okay! I can't still salvage th--
Good morning! Sorry!
DOUBLE FWOOSH
Wh... why?

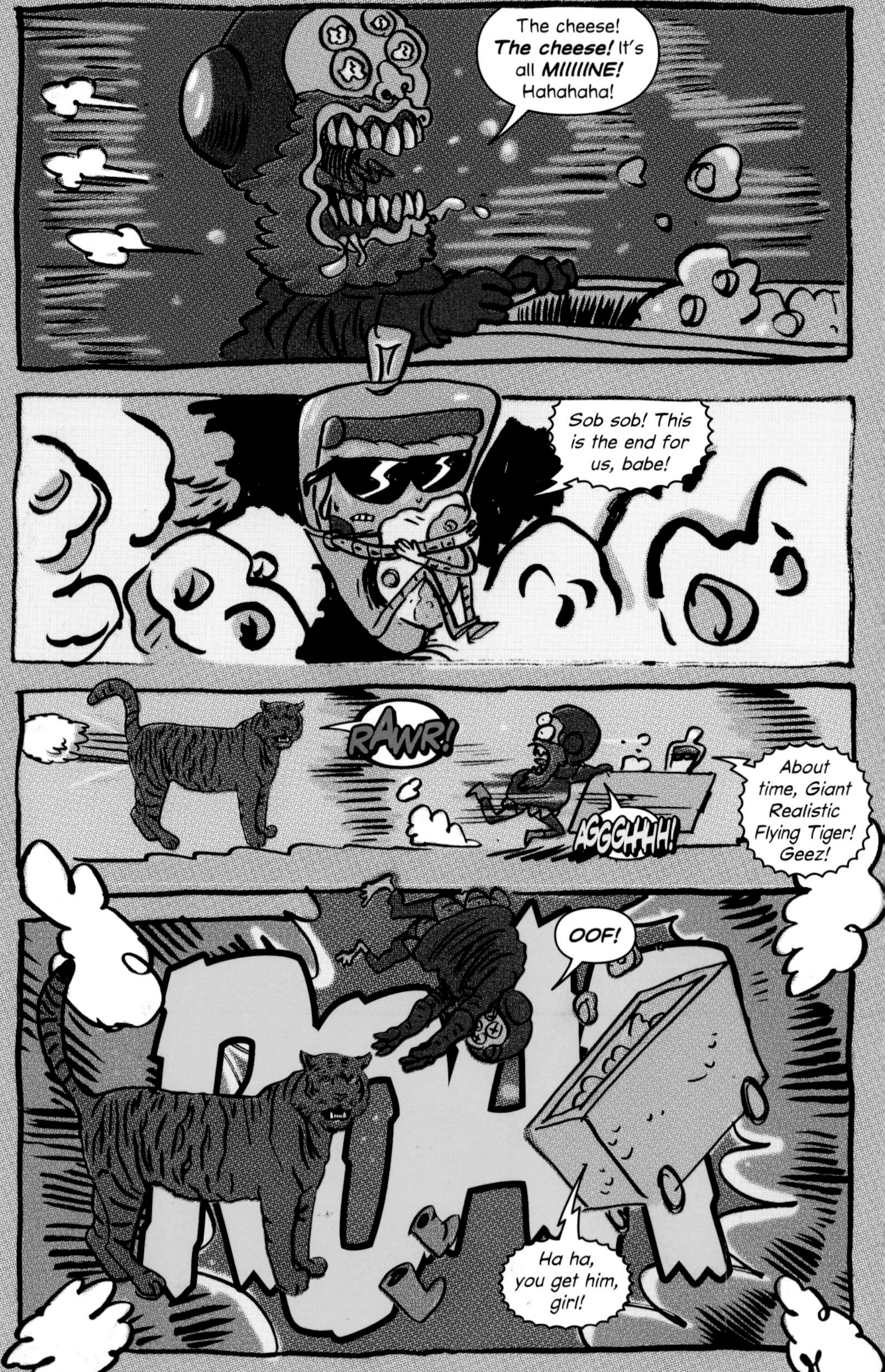
The cheese! The cheese! It's all MIIIIINE! Hahahaha!
Sob sob! This is the end for us, babe!
RAWR!
AGGGHHH!
About time, Giant Realistic Flying Tiger! Geez!
OOF!
Ha ha, you get him, girl!

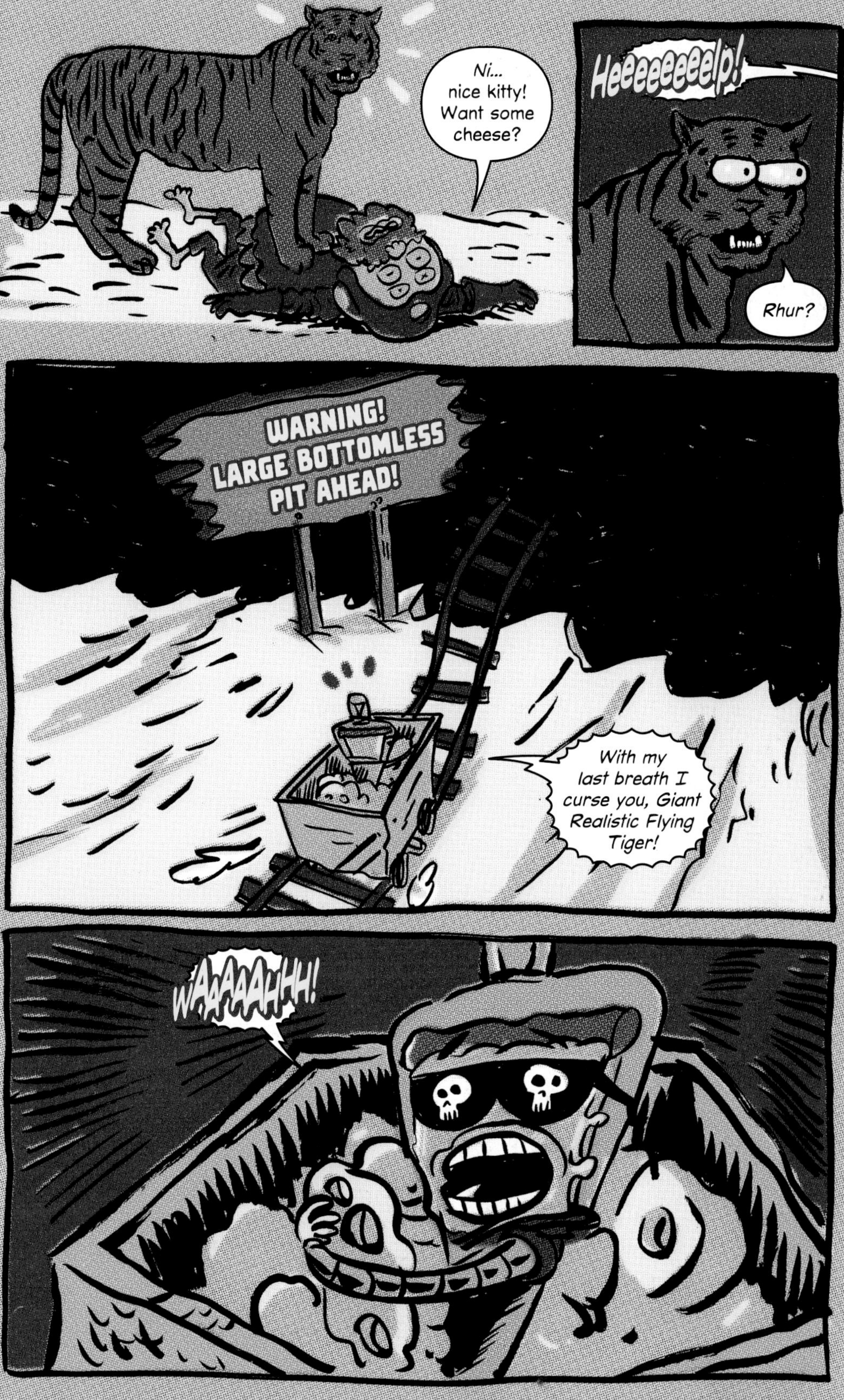
Ni...
nice kitty!
Want some
cheese?
Heeeeeeeeelp!
Rhur?
WARNING!
LARGE BOTTOMLESS
PIT AHEAD!
With my
last breath I
curse you, Giant
Realistic Flying
Tiger!
WAAAAAHHH!

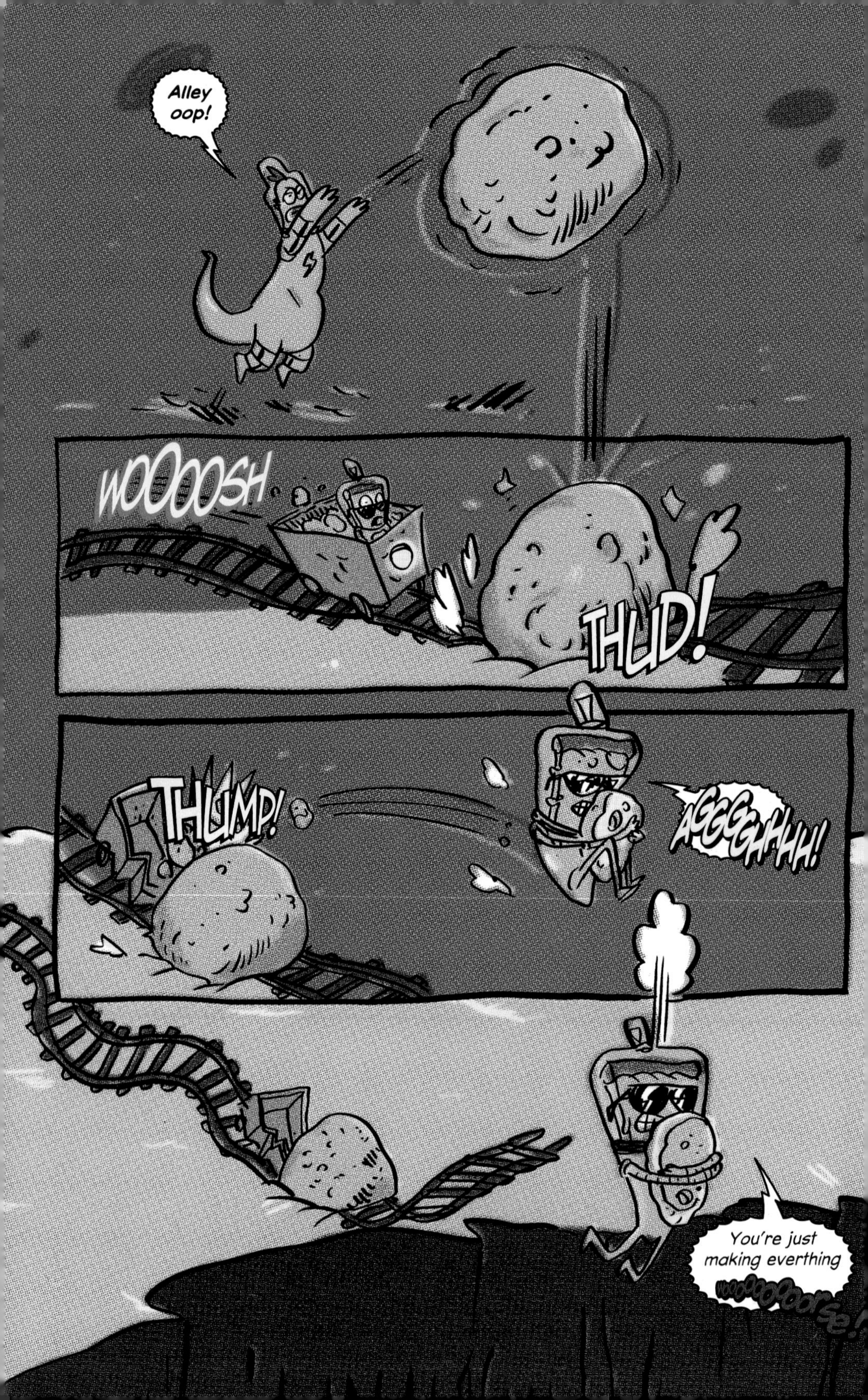
Alley oop!
WOOOOSH
THUD!
THUMP!
AGGGGHHHH!
You're just making everthing
wooOOOOorse!

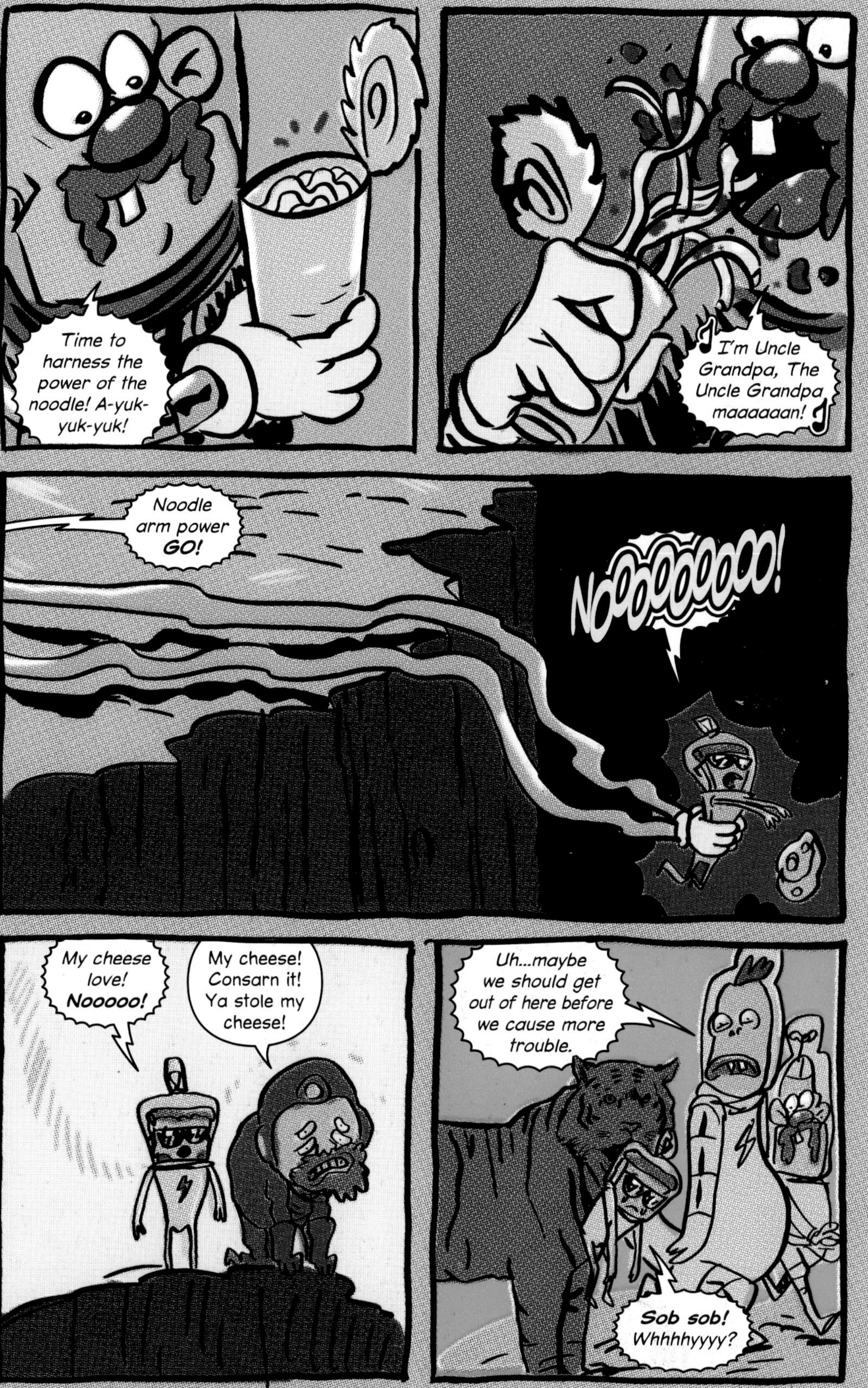
Time to harness the power of the noodle! A-yuk-yuk-yuk!
I'm Uncle Grandpa, The Uncle Grandpa maaaaaan!
Noodle arm power GO!
NOOOOOOOOO!
My cheese love! Nooooo!
My cheese! Consarn it! Ya stole my cheese!
Uh...maybe we should get out of here before we cause more trouble.
Sob sob! Whhhhyyyy?

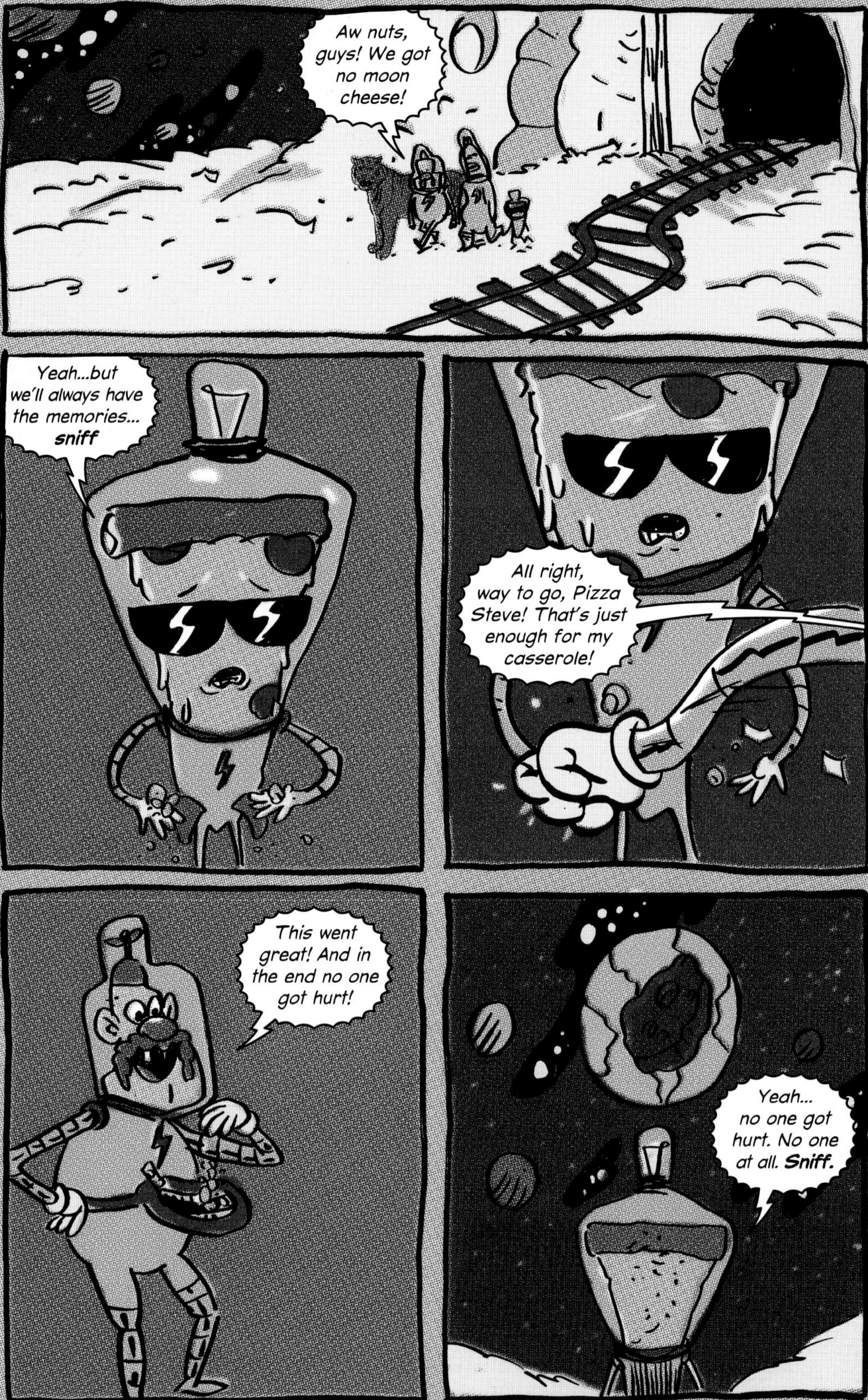
Aw nuts, guys! We got no moon cheese!
Yeah...but we'll always have the memories... **sniff**
All right, way to go, Pizza Steve! That's just enough for my casserole!
This went great! And in the end no one got hurt!
Yeah... no one got hurt. No one at all. **Sniff.**

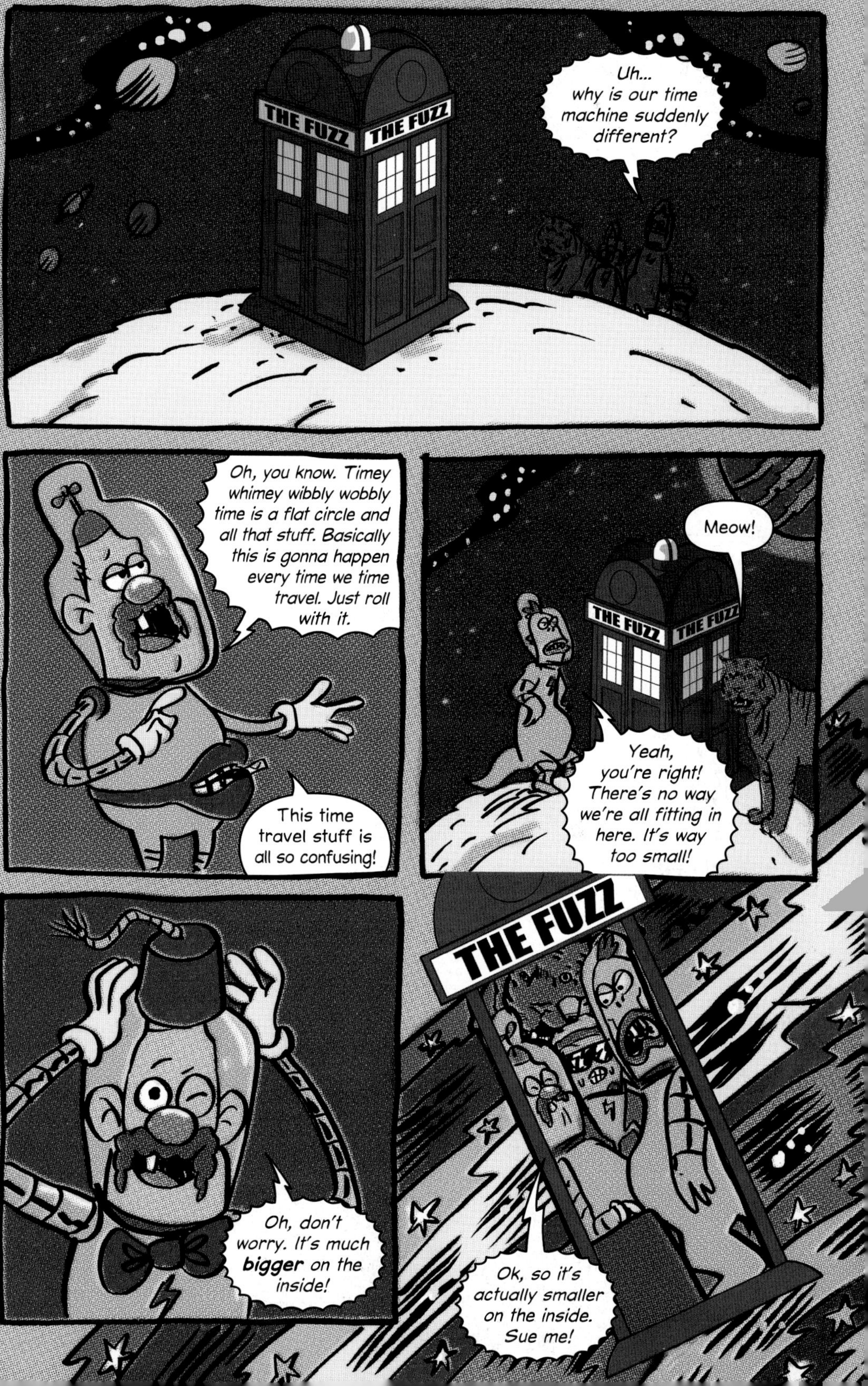

THE FUZZ
THE FUZZ
Uh... why is our time machine suddenly different?
Oh, you know. Timey whimey wibbly wobbly time is a flat circle and all that stuff. Basically this is gonna happen every time we time travel. Just roll with it.
This time travel stuff is all so confusing!
Meow!
THE FUZZ
THE FUZZ
Yeah, you're right! There's no way we're all fitting in here. It's way too small!
Oh, don't worry. It's much **bigger** on the inside!
THE FUZZ
Ok, so it's actually smaller on the inside. Sue me!

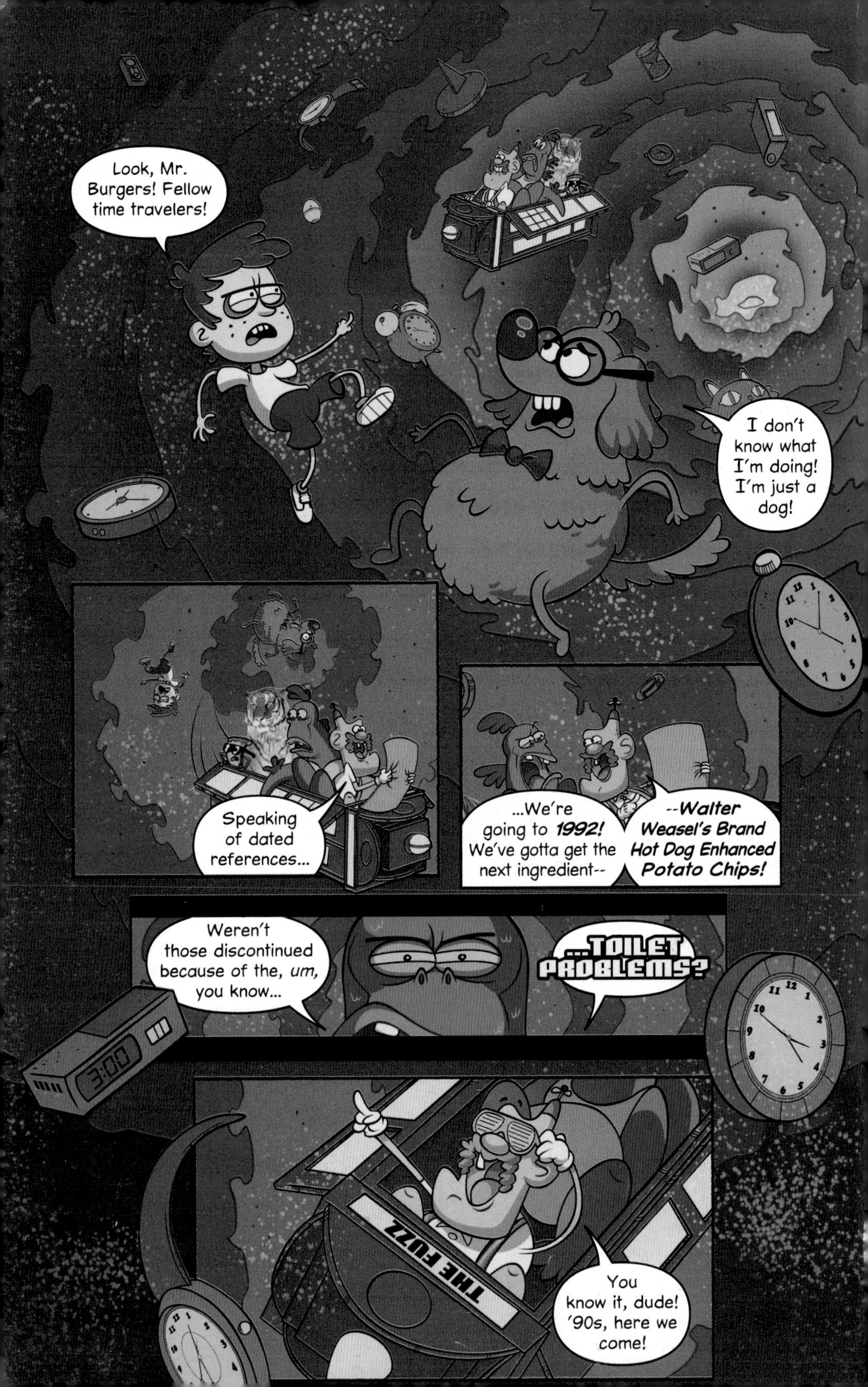
Look, Mr. Burgers! Fellow time travelers!
I don't know what I'm doing! I'm just a dog!
Speaking of dated references...
...We're going to *1992!* We've gotta get the next ingredient--
--Walter Weasel's Brand Hot Dog Enhanced Potato Chips!
Weren't those discontinued because of the, *um*, you know...
...TOILET PROBLEMS?
3:00
THE FUZZ
You know it, dude! '90s, here we come!

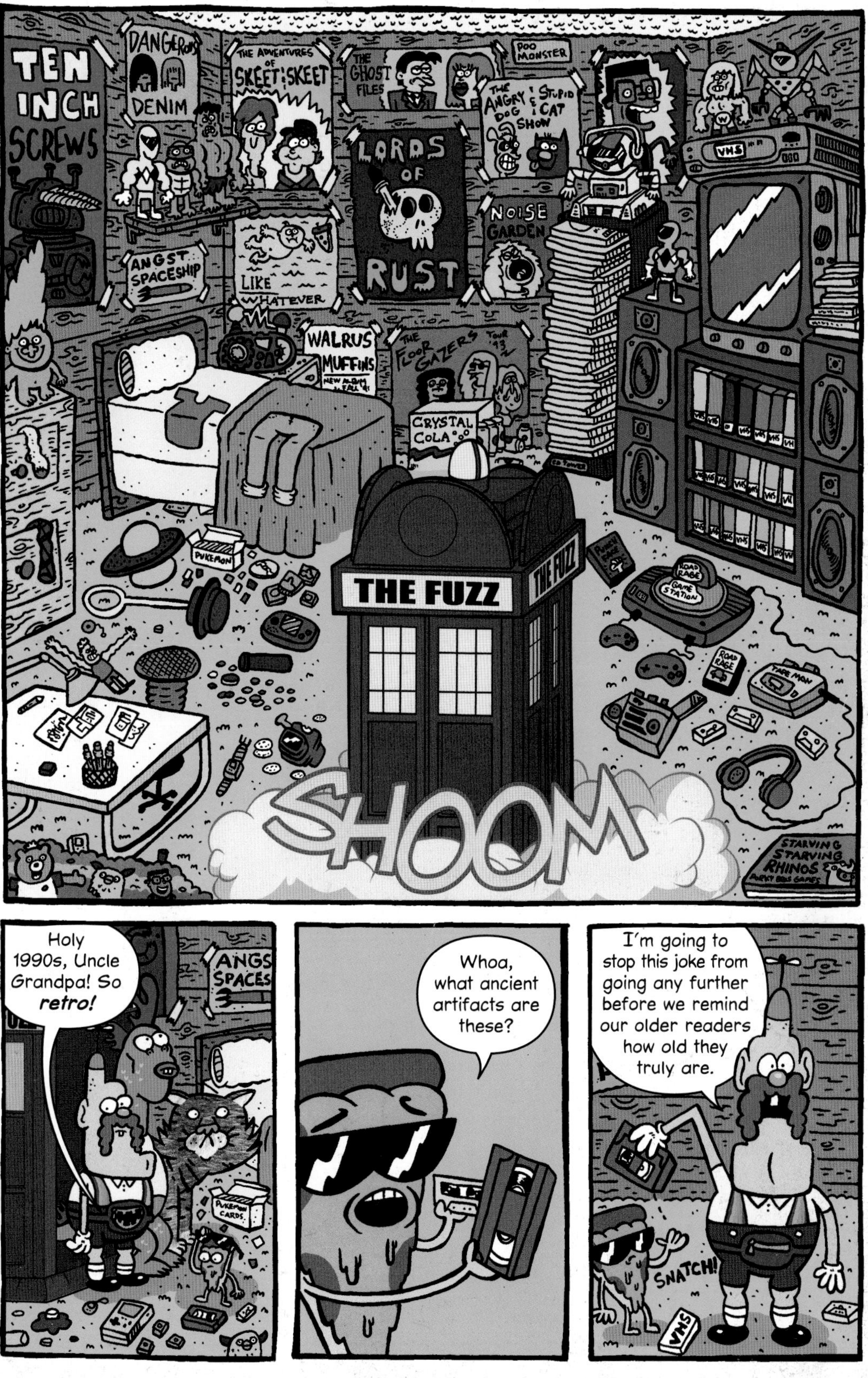
TEN INCH SCREWS
DANGEROUS DENIM
THE ADVENTURES OF SKEET & SKEET
THE GHOST FILES
POO MONSTER
THE ANGRY DOG & STUPID CAT SHOW
LORDS OF RUST
NOISE GARDEN
ANGST SPACESHIP
LIKE WHATEVER
WALRUS MUFFINS
THE FLOOR GAZERS
CRYSTAL COLA
VHS
PUKEMON
THE FUZZ
ROAD RAGE
GAME STATION
TAPE MON
STARVING STARVING RHINOS
SHOOM
Holy 1990s, Uncle Grandpa! So *retro!*
Whoa, what ancient artifacts are these?
I'm going to stop this joke from going any further before we remind our older readers how old they truly are.
SNATCH!

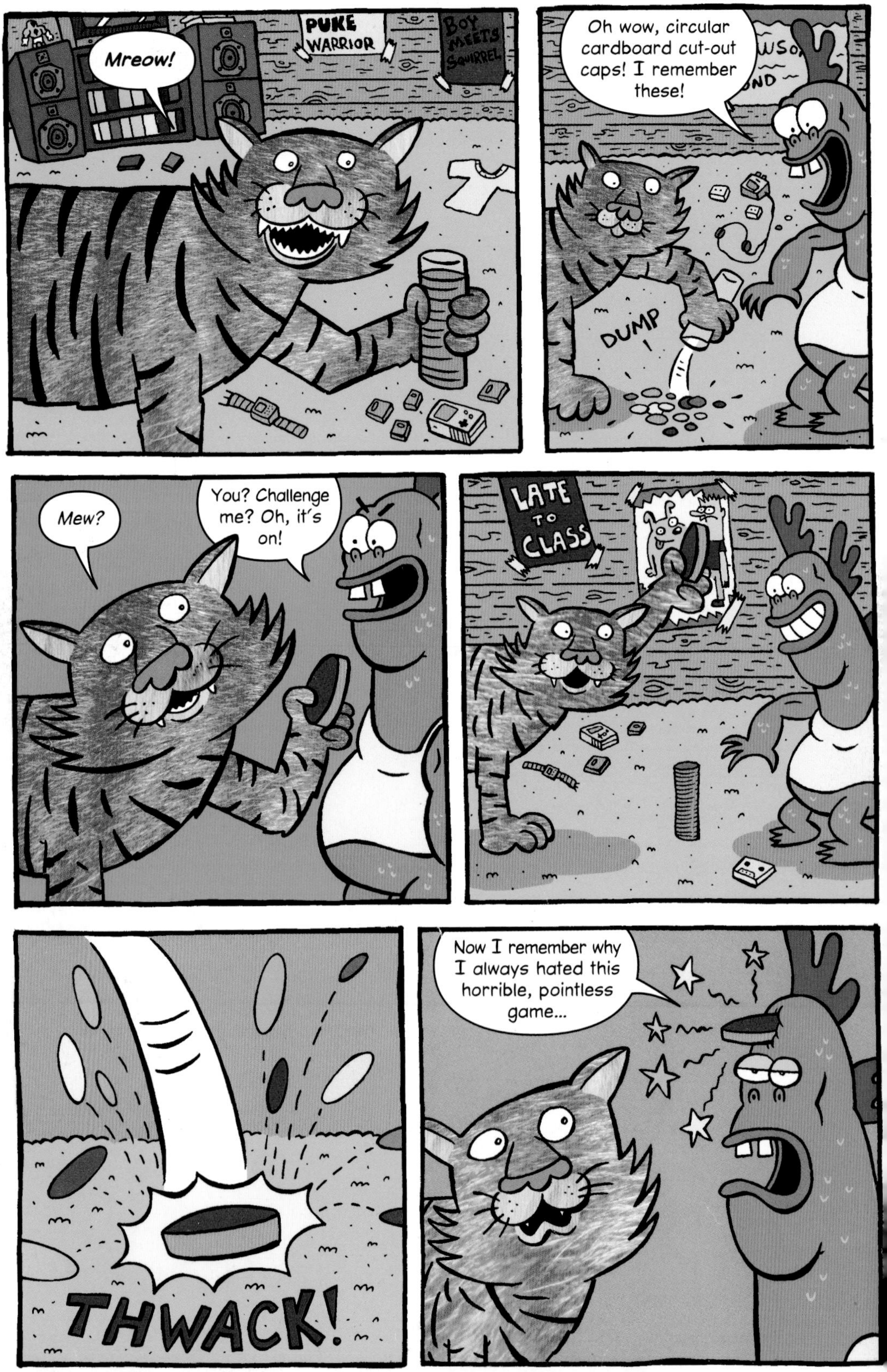
PUKE WARRIOR
BOY MEETS SQUIRREL
Mreow!
Oh wow, circular cardboard cut-out caps! I remember these!
DUMP
Mew?
You? Challenge me? Oh, it's on!
LATE TO CLASS
THWACK!
Now I remember why I always hated this horrible, pointless game...

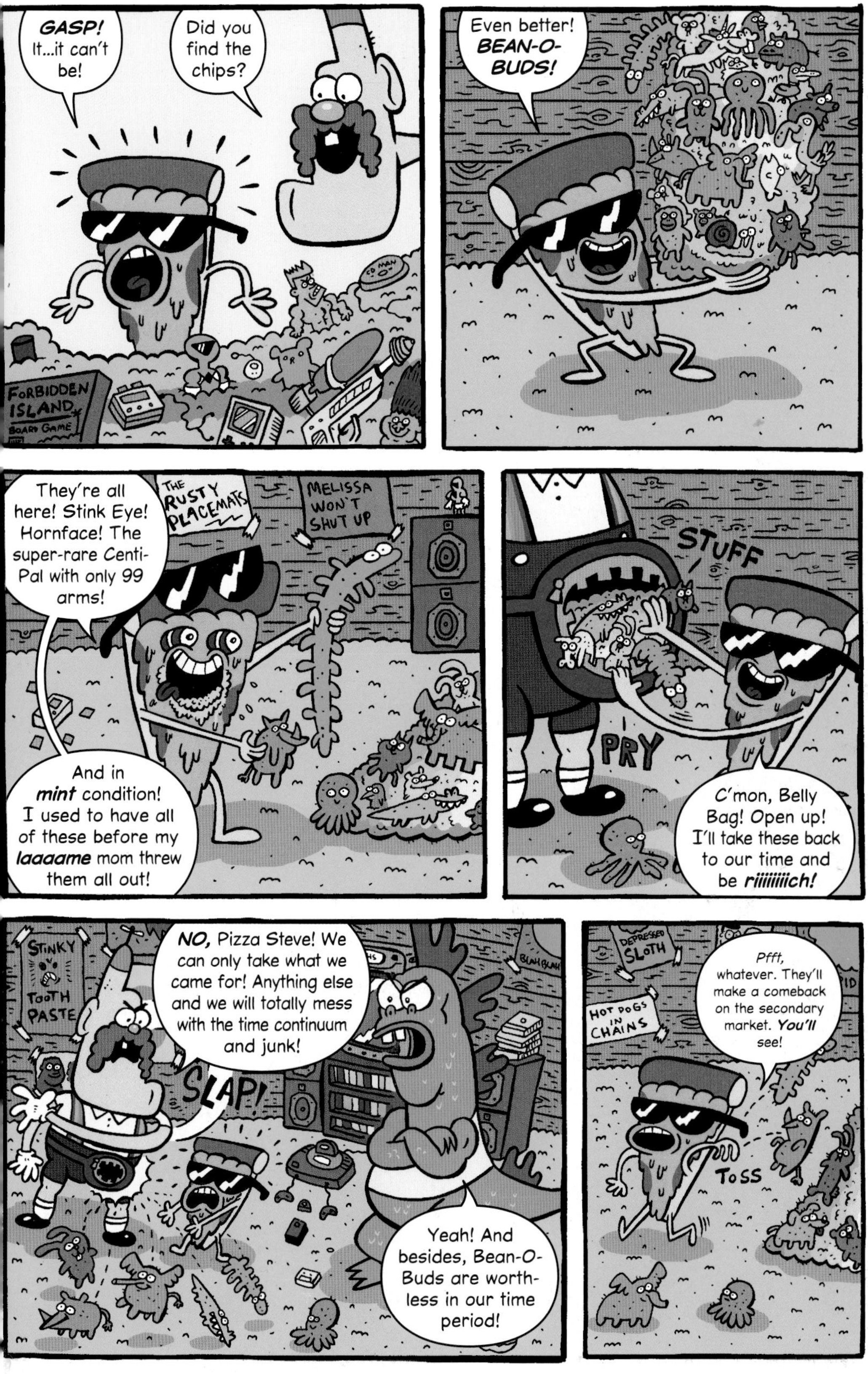
GASP! It...it can't be!
Did you find the chips?
FORBIDDEN ISLAND BOARD GAME
Even better! BEAN-O-BUDS!
They're all here! Stink Eye! Hornface! The super-rare Centi-Pal with only 99 arms!
THE RUSTY PLACEMATS
MELISSA WON'T SHUT UP
And in mint condition! I used to have all of these before my laaaame mom threw them all out!
STUFF
PRY
C'mon, Belly Bag! Open up! I'll take these back to our time and be riiiiiiich!
STINKY TOOTH PASTE
BLAH BLAH
NO, Pizza Steve! We can only take what we came for! Anything else and we will totally mess with the time continuum and junk!
SLAP!
Yeah! And besides, Bean-O-Buds are worthless in our time period!
DEPRESSED SLOTH
HOT DOGS IN CHAINS
Pfft, whatever. They'll make a comeback on the secondary market. You'll see!
TOSS

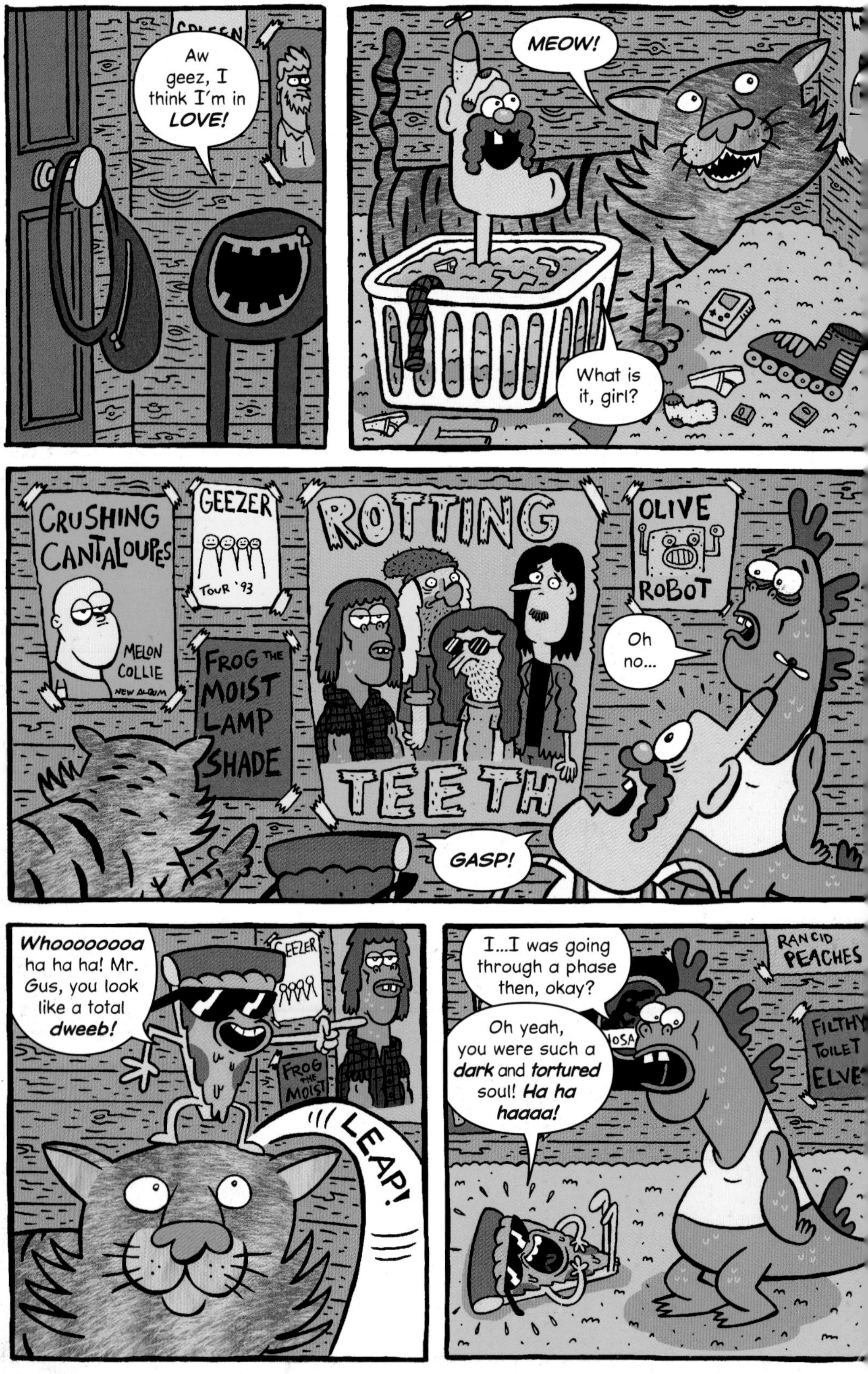
Aw geez, I think I'm in *LOVE!*
MEOW!
What is it, girl?
CRUSHING CANTALOUPES
MELON COLLIE
NEW ALBUM
GEEZER
TOUR '93
ROTTING TEETH
OLIVE ROBOT
FROG THE MOIST LAMP SHADE
Oh no...
GASP!
Whoooooooa ha ha ha! Mr. Gus, you look like a total *dweeb!*
LEAP!
I...I was going through a phase then, okay?
RANCID PEACHES
Oh yeah, you were such a *dark* and *tortured* soul! *Ha ha haaaa!*

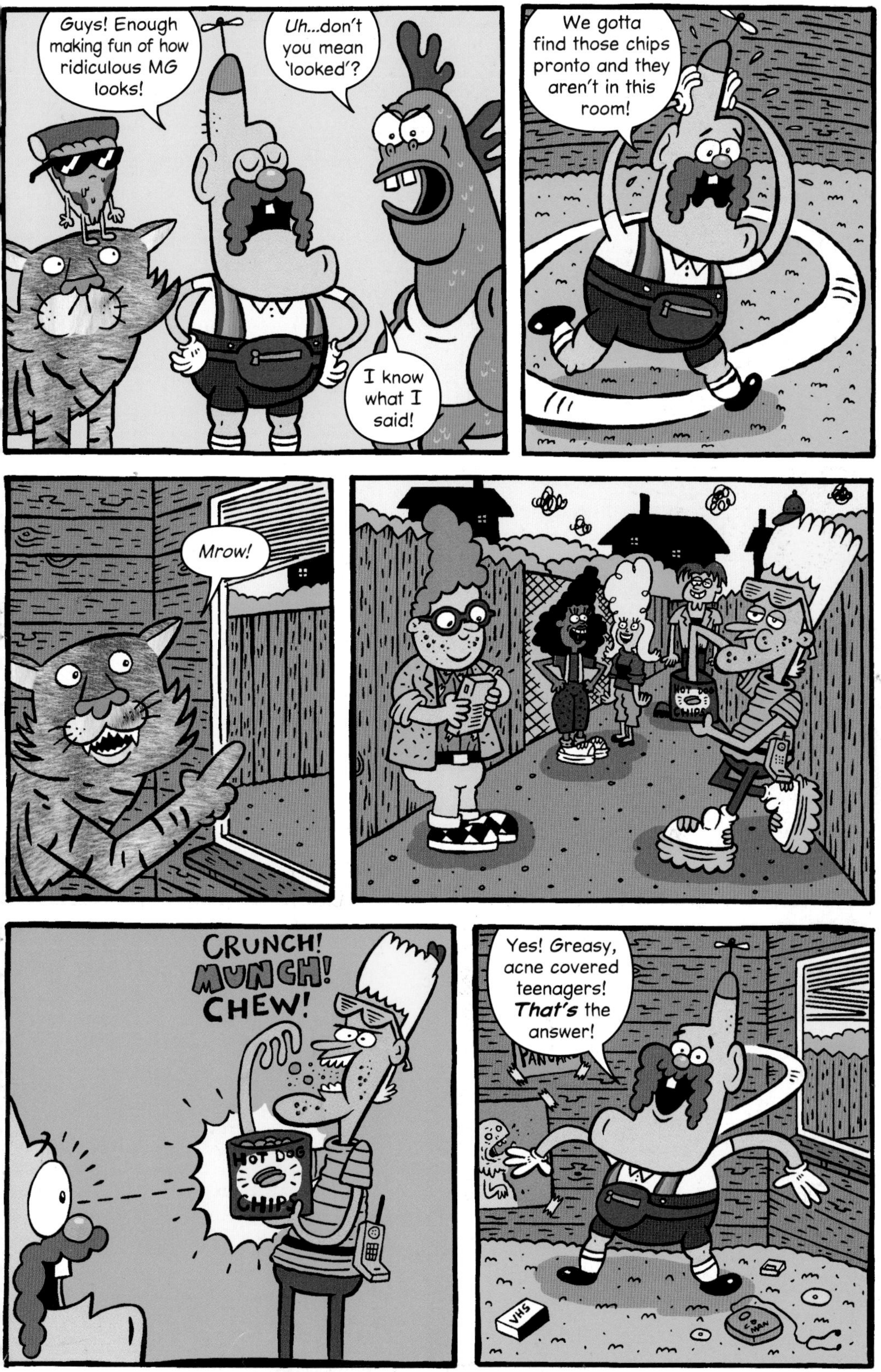
Guys! Enough making fun of how ridiculous MG looks!
Uh...don't you mean 'looked'?
I know what I said!
We gotta find those chips pronto and they aren't in this room!
Mrow!
HOT DOG CHIPS
CRUNCH! MUNCH! CHEW!
HOT DOG CHIPS
Yes! Greasy, acne covered teenagers! That's the answer!
VHS

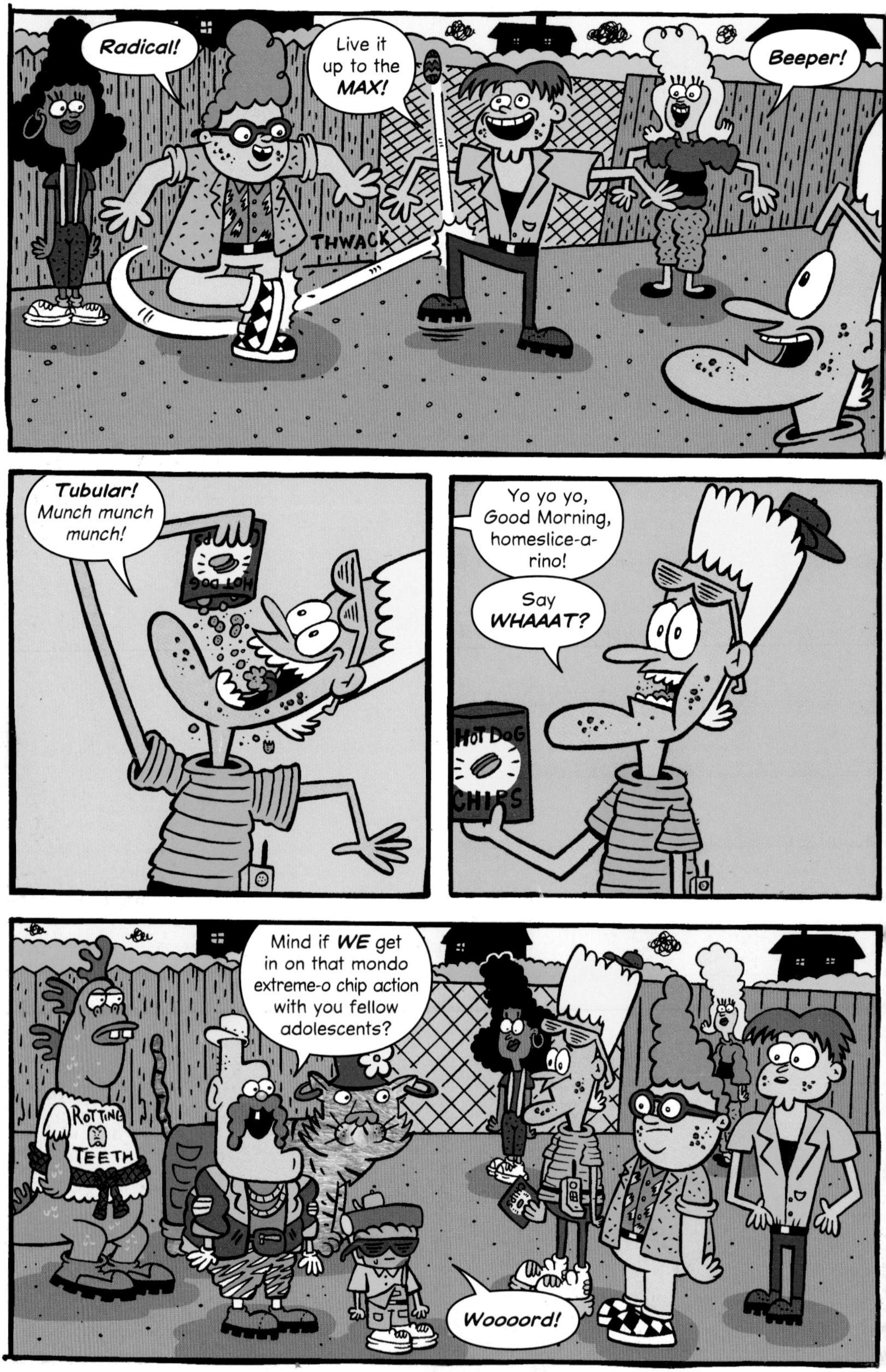
Radical!
Live it up to the *MAX!*
THWACK
Beeper!
Tubular! Munch munch munch!
Yo yo yo, Good Morning, homeslice-a-rino!
Say *WHAAAT?*
HOT DOG CHIPS
ROTTING TEETH
Mind if *WE* get in on that mondo extreme-o chip action with you fellow adolescents?
Wooooord!

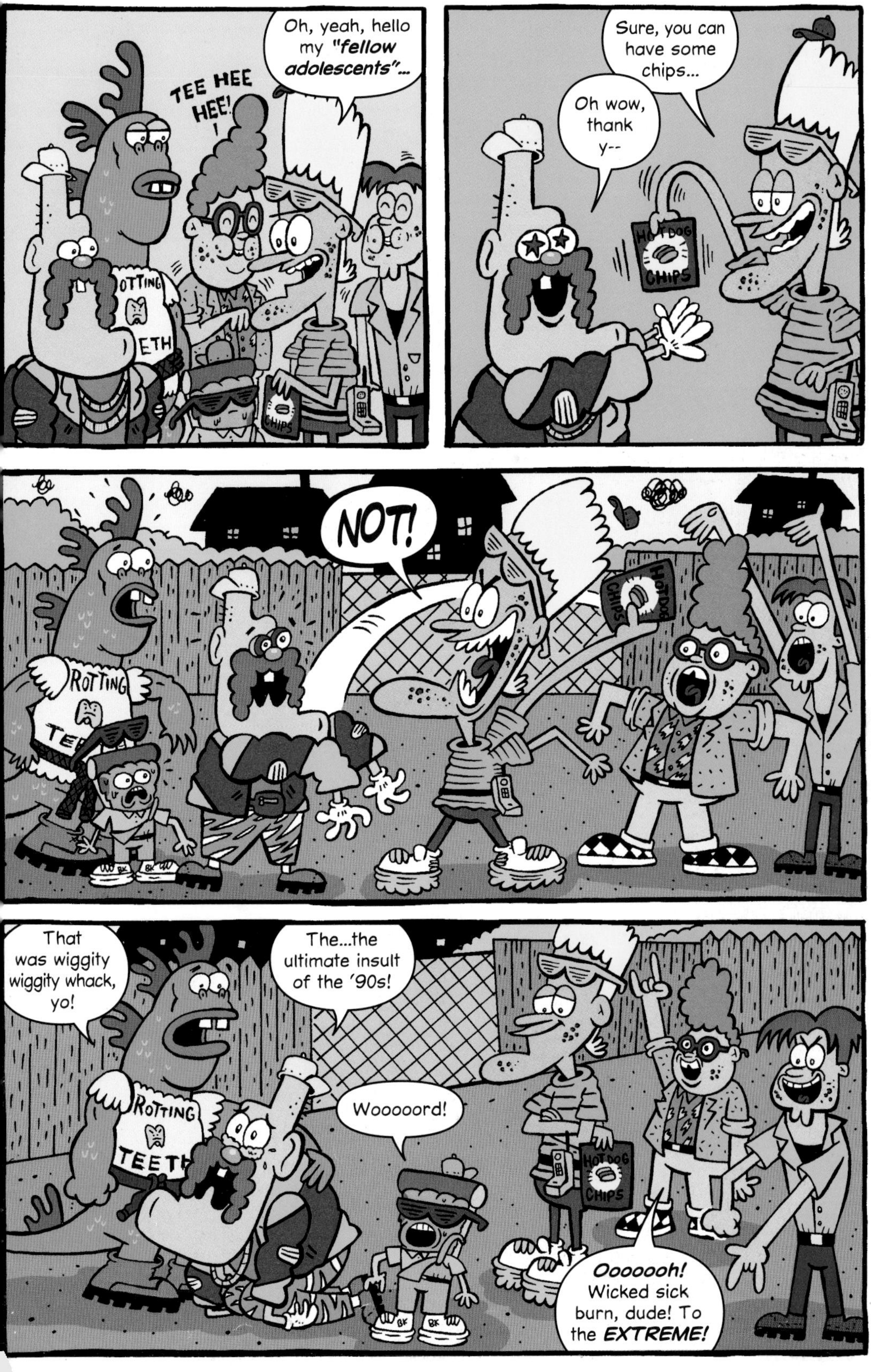
Oh, yeah, hello my *"fellow adolescents"...*
TEE HEE HEE!
Sure, you can have some chips...
Oh wow, thank y--
HOT DOG CHIPS
NOT!
HOT DOG CHIPS
That was wiggity wiggity whack, yo!
The...the ultimate insult of the '90s!
ROTTING TEETH
Wooooord!
HOT DOG CHIPS
Ooooooh! Wicked sick burn, dude! To the ***EXTREME!***

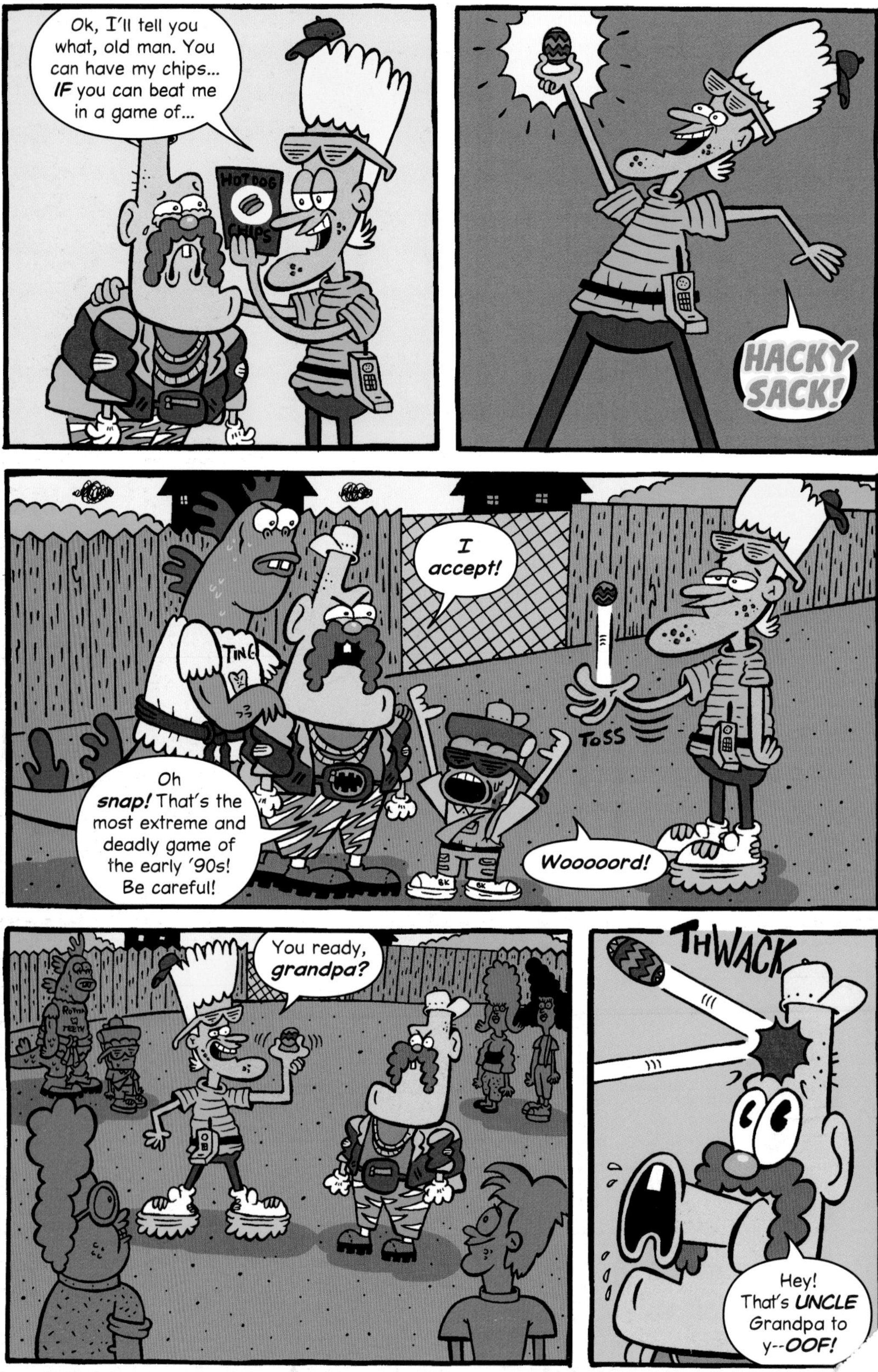

Ok, I'll tell you what, old man. You can have my chips... IF you can beat me in a game of...
HOT DOG CHIPS
HACKY SACK!
I accept!
TING
TOSS
Oh snap! That's the most extreme and deadly game of the early '90s! Be careful!
Wooooord!
You ready, grandpa?
THWACK
Hey! That's UNCLE Grandpa to y--OOF!

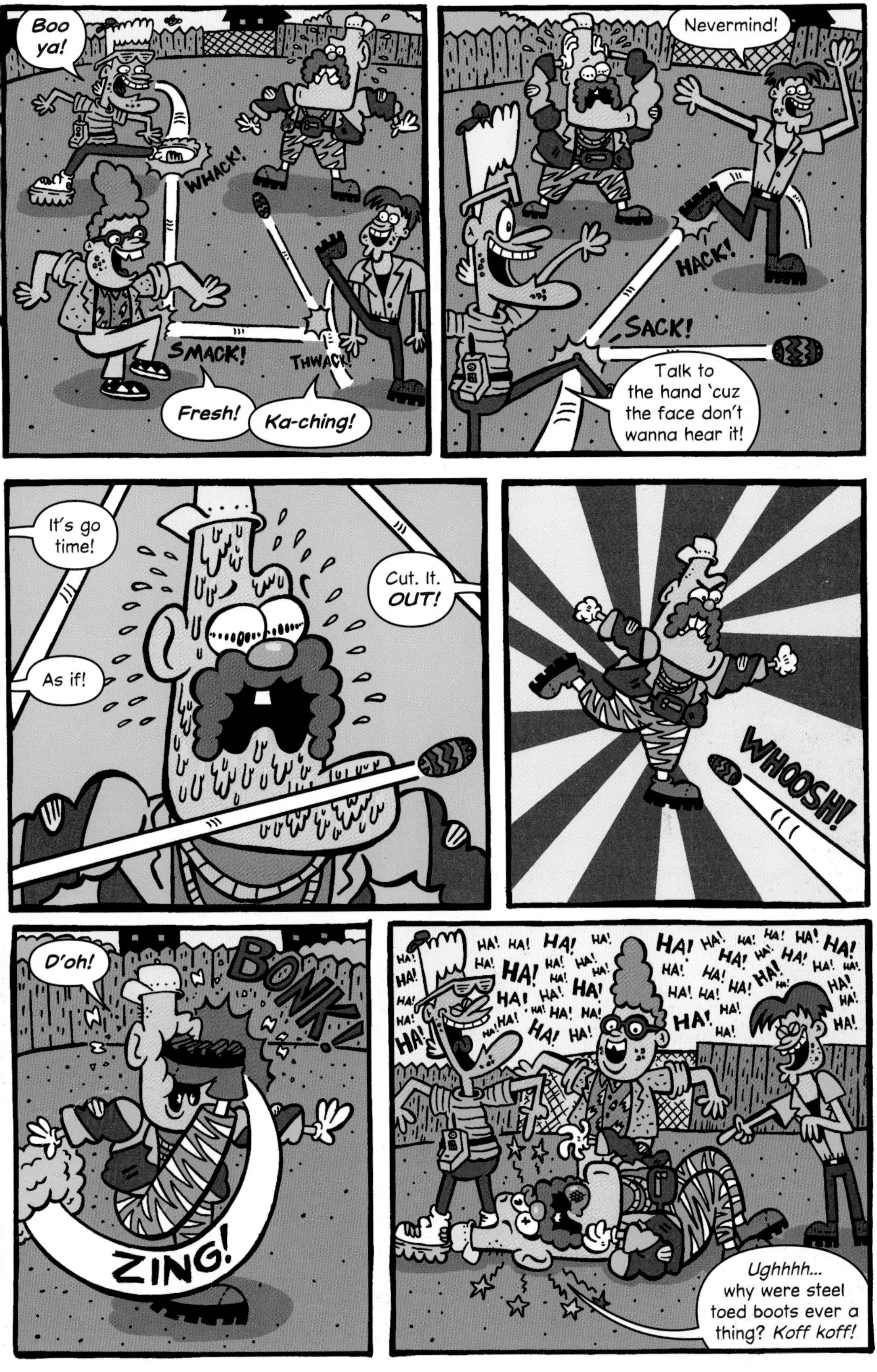
Boo ya!
WHACK!
SMACK!
THWACK!
Fresh!
Ka-ching!
Nevermind!
HACK!
SACK!
Talk to the hand 'cuz the face don't wanna hear it!
It's go time!
Cut. It. OUT!
As if!
WHOOSH!
D'oh!
BONK!
ZING!
HA! HA! HA! HA! HA! HA! HA! HA! HA! HA! HA! HA!
Ughhhh... why were steel toed boots ever a thing? Koff koff!

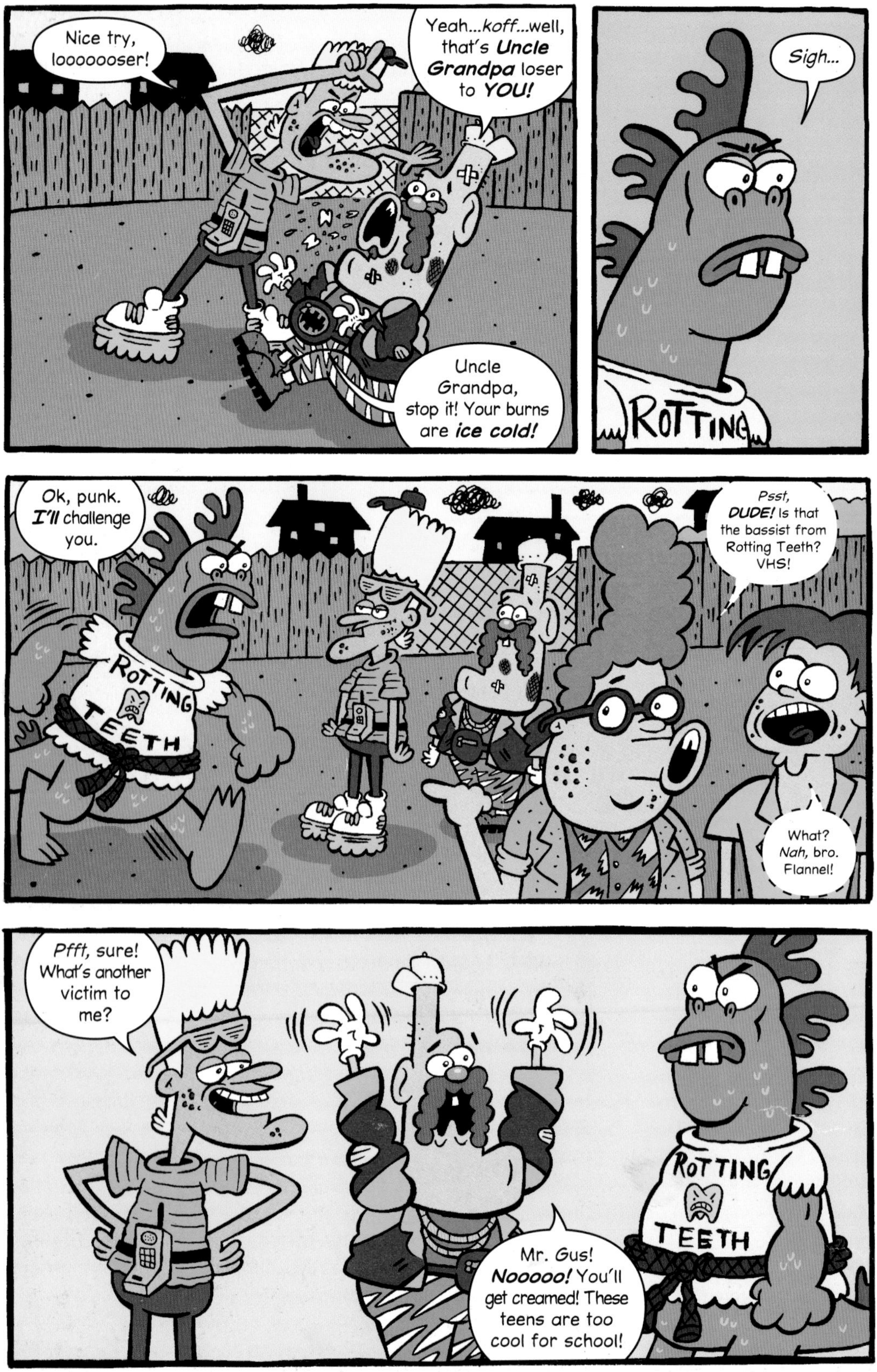
Nice try, looooooser!
Yeah...*koff*...well, that's **Uncle Grandpa** loser to **YOU!**
Uncle Grandpa, stop it! Your burns are ***ice cold!***
Sigh...
ROTTING
Ok, punk. ***I'll*** challenge you.
ROTTING TEETH
Psst, ***DUDE!*** Is that the bassist from Rotting Teeth? VHS!
What? *Nah,* bro. Flannel!
Pfft, sure! What's another victim to me?
Mr. Gus! ***Nooooo!*** You'll get creamed! These teens are too cool for school!
ROTTING TEETH

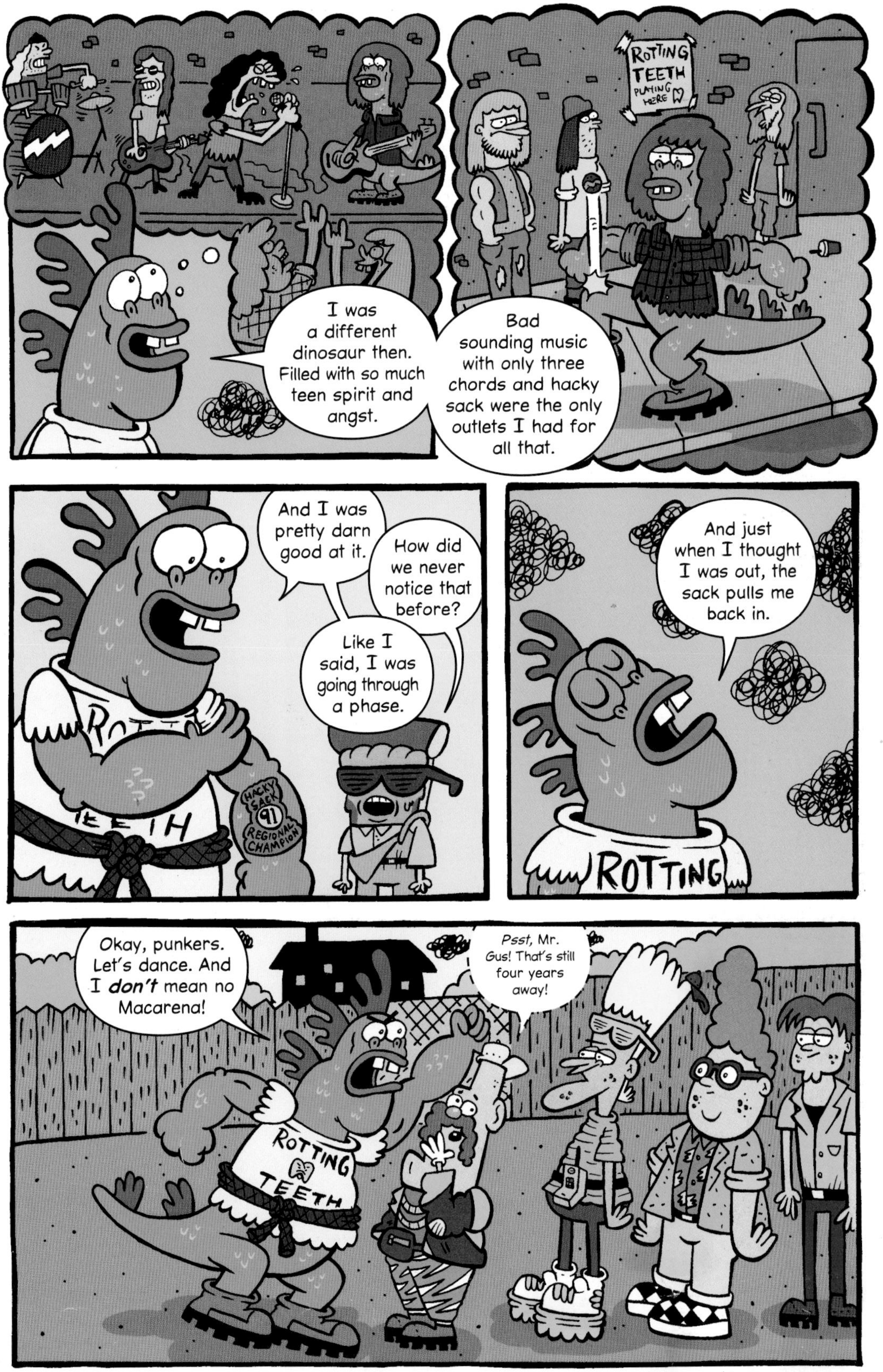
ROTTING TEETH PLAYING HERE
I was a different dinosaur then. Filled with so much teen spirit and angst.
Bad sounding music with only three chords and hacky sack were the only outlets I had for all that.
And I was pretty darn good at it.
How did we never notice that before?
Like I said, I was going through a phase.
HACKY SACK 91 REGIONAL CHAMPION
And just when I thought I was out, the sack pulls me back in.
ROTTING
Okay, punkers. Let's dance. And I ***don't*** mean no Macarena!
Psst, Mr. Gus! That's still four years away!
ROTTING TEETH

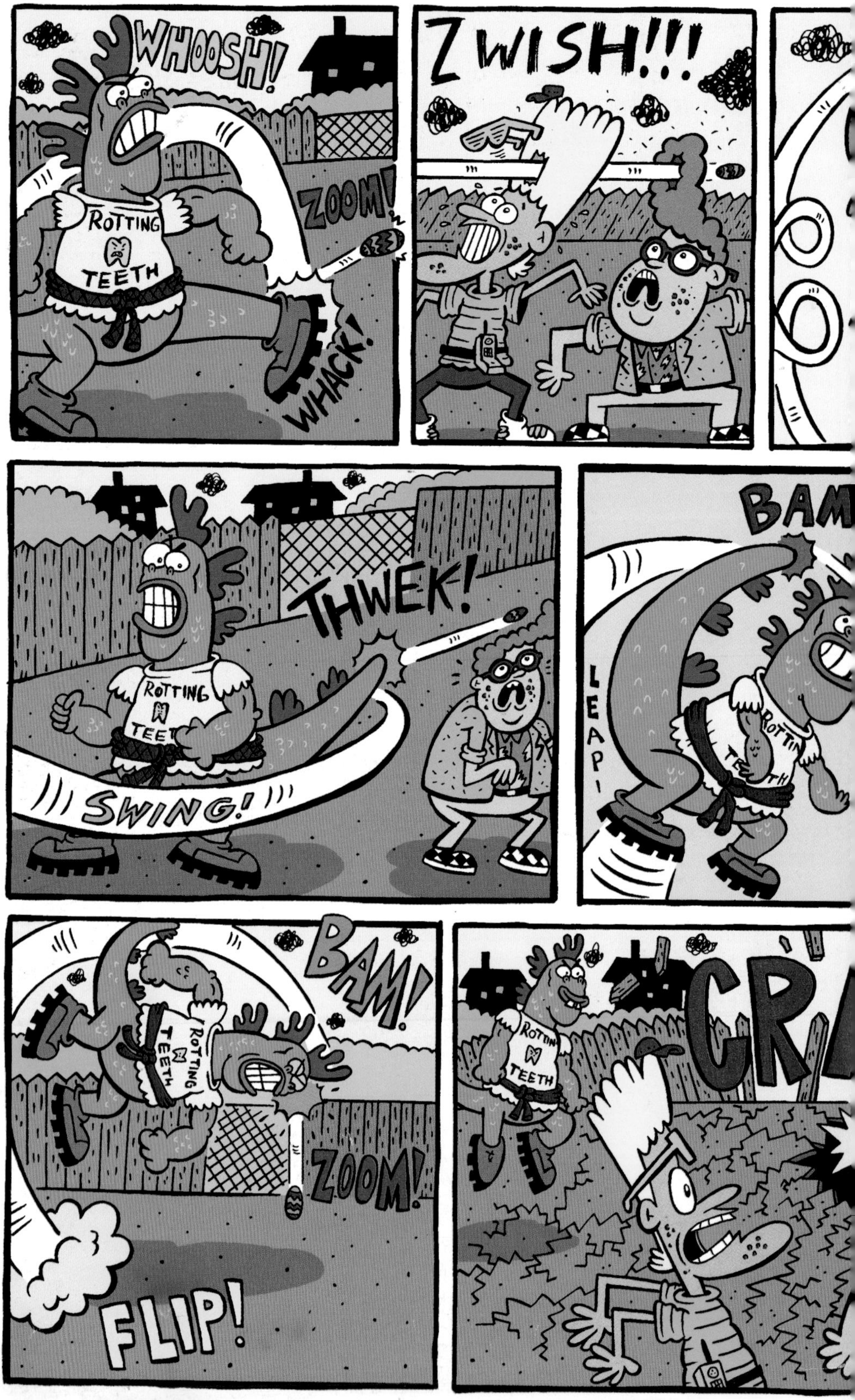
WHOOSH!
ROTTING TEETH
ZOOM!
WHACK!
ZWISH!!!
THWEK!
ROTTING
SWING!
LEAP!
BAM!
ROTTING TEETH
ZOOM!
FLIP!
TEETH

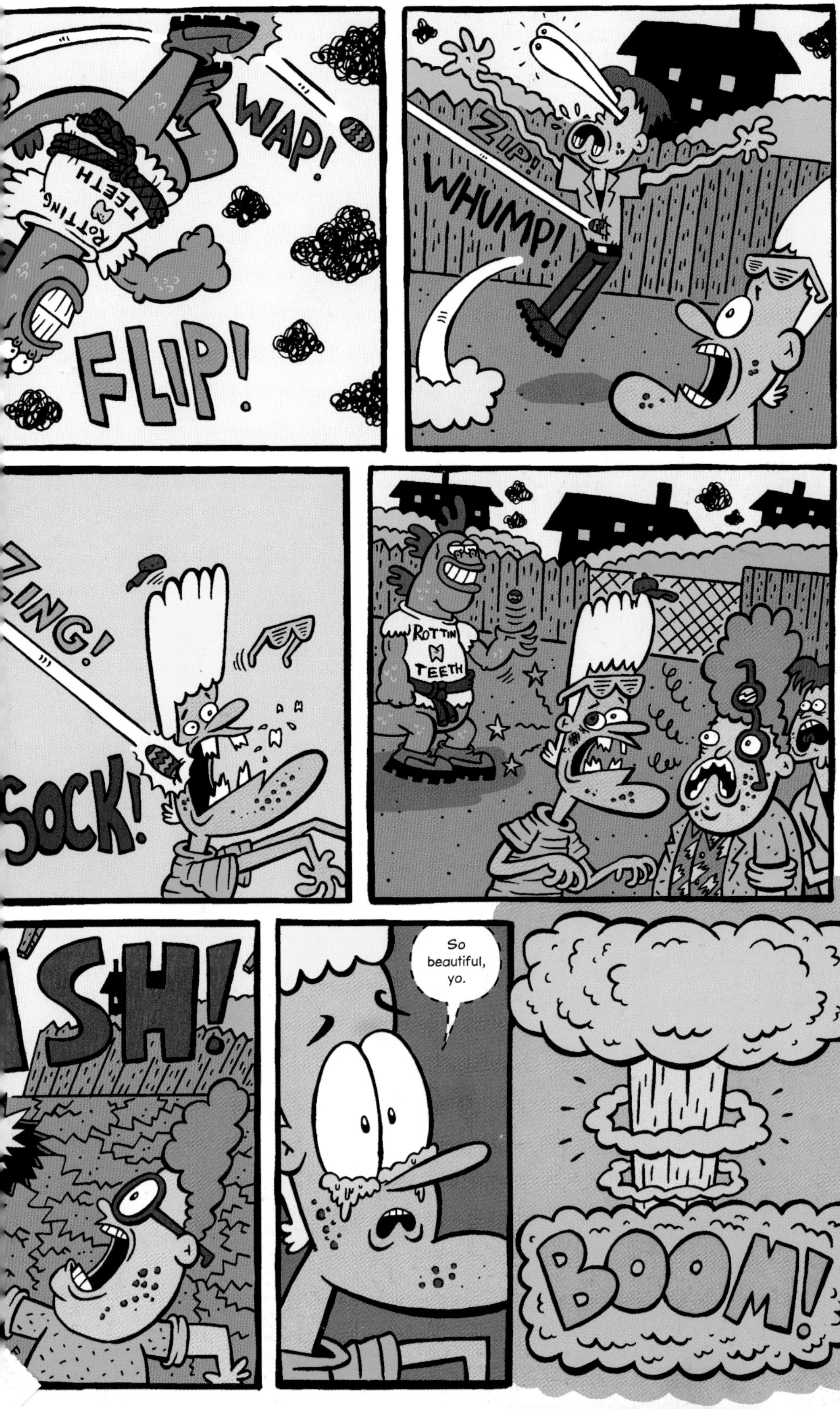
WAP!
ROTTING TEETH
FLIP!
ZIP!
WHUMP!
SOCK!
ROTTIN TEETH
So beautiful, yo.
BOOM!

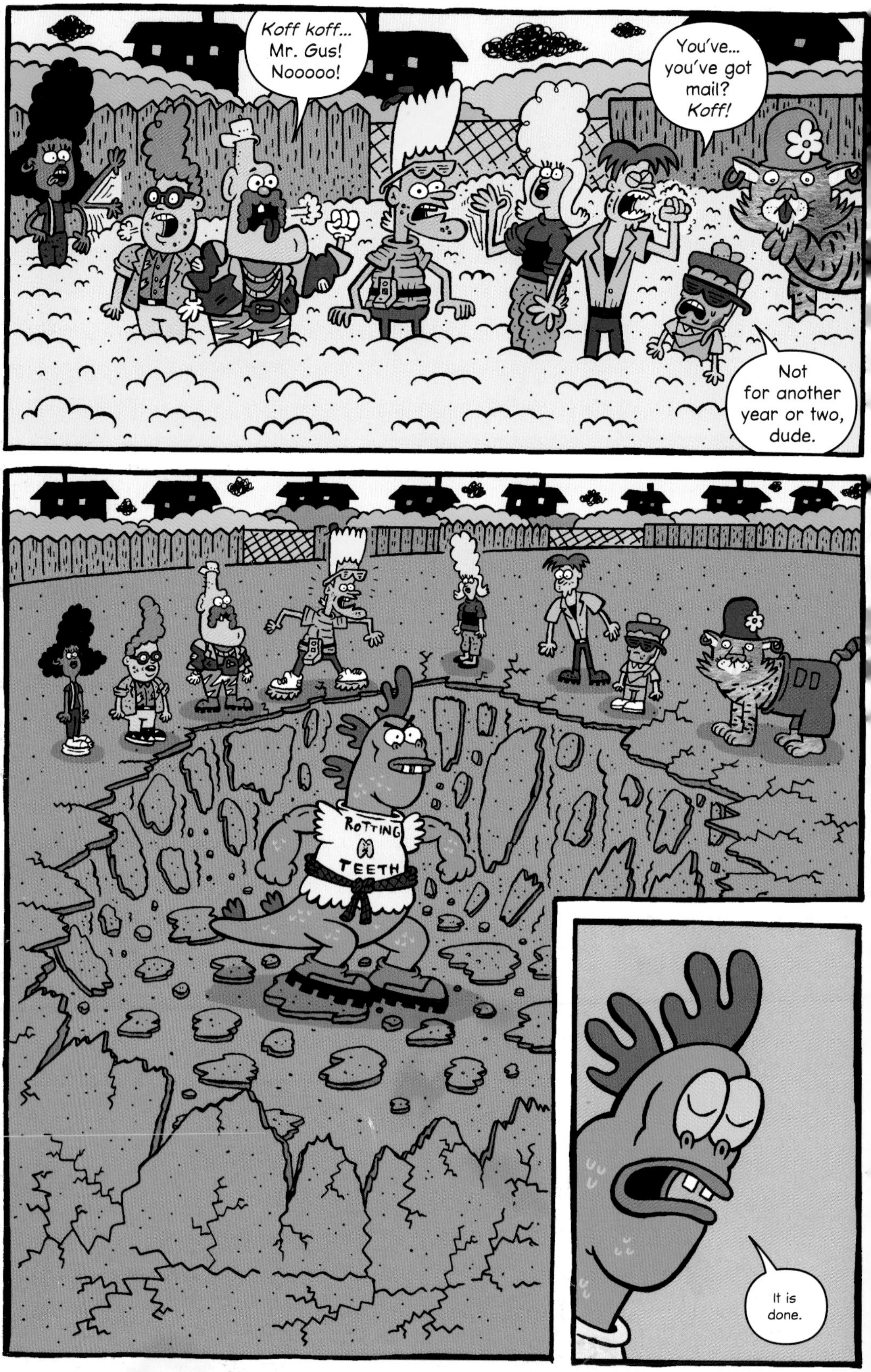
Koff koff... Mr. Gus! Nooooo!
You've... you've got mail? Koff!
Not for another year or two, dude.
ROTTING TEETH
It is done.

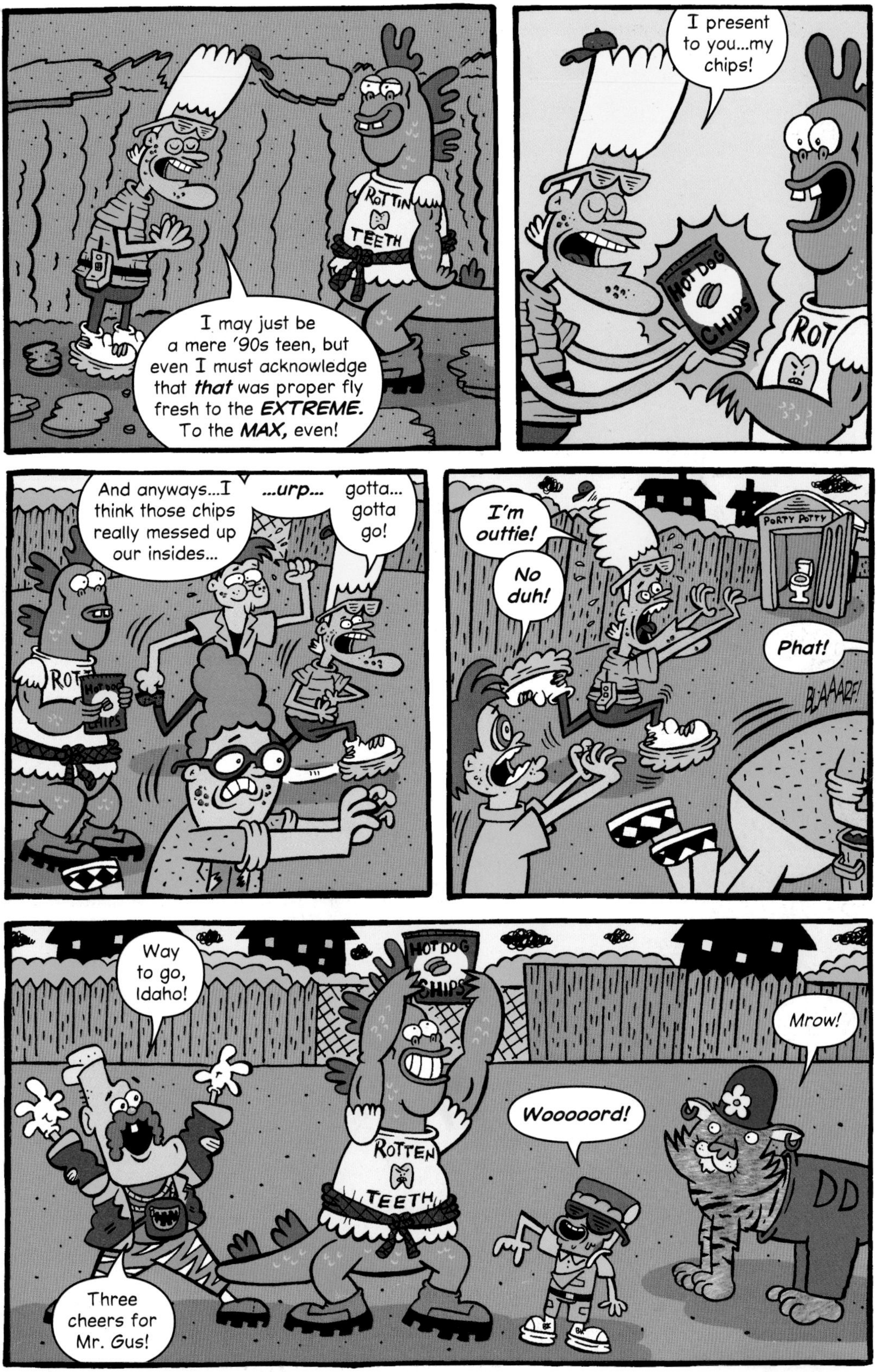
ROTTIN TEETH
I may just be a mere '90s teen, but even I must acknowledge that *that* was proper fly fresh to the ***EXTREME.*** To the ***MAX,*** even!
I present to you...my chips!
HOT DOG CHIPS
ROT
And anyways...I think those chips really messed up our insides...
...urp...
gotta... gotta go!
ROT
HOT DOG CHIPS
I'm outtie!
No duh!
PORTY POTTY
Phat!
BLAAARF!
Way to go, Idaho!
HOT DOG CHIPS
Mrow!
Wooooord!
ROTTEN TEETH
Three cheers for Mr. Gus!

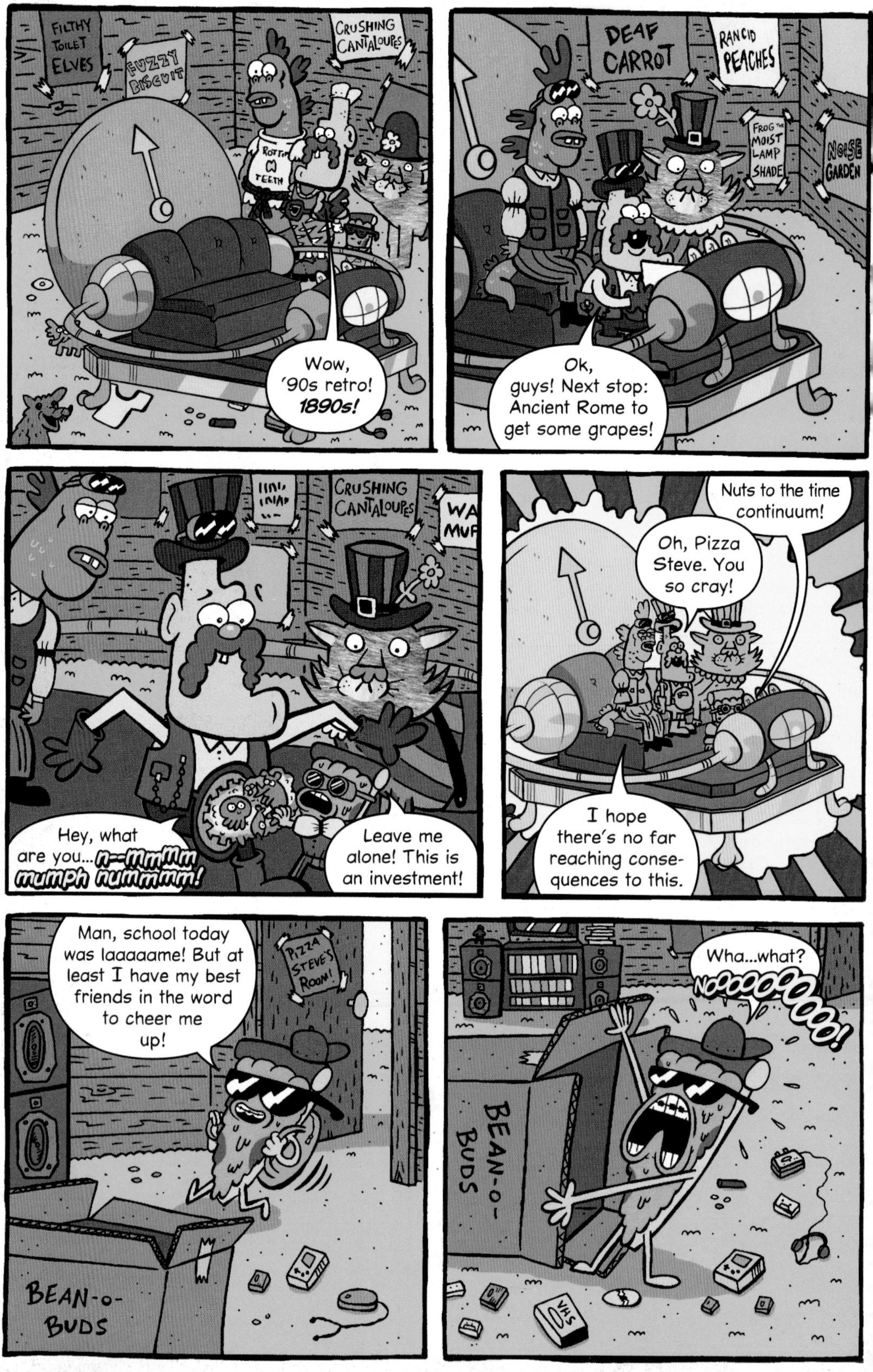
FILTHY TOILET ELVES
FUZZY BISCUIT
CRUSHING CANTALOUPES
ROTTIN TEETH
Wow, '90s retro! *1890s!*
DEAF CARROT
RANCID PEACHES
FROG THE MOIST LAMP SHADE
NOISE GARDEN
Ok, guys! Next stop: Ancient Rome to get some grapes!
CRUSHING CANTALOUPES
Hey, what are you... n--mmMm mumph nummmm!
Leave me alone! This is an investment!
Nuts to the time continuum!
Oh, Pizza Steve. You so cray!
I hope there's no far reaching consequences to this.
Man, school today was laaaaame! But at least I have my best friends in the word to cheer me up!
PIZZA STEVE'S ROOM!
BEAN-o-BUDS
Wha...what?
NOOOOOOOOOOO!
BEAN-o-BUDS
VHS

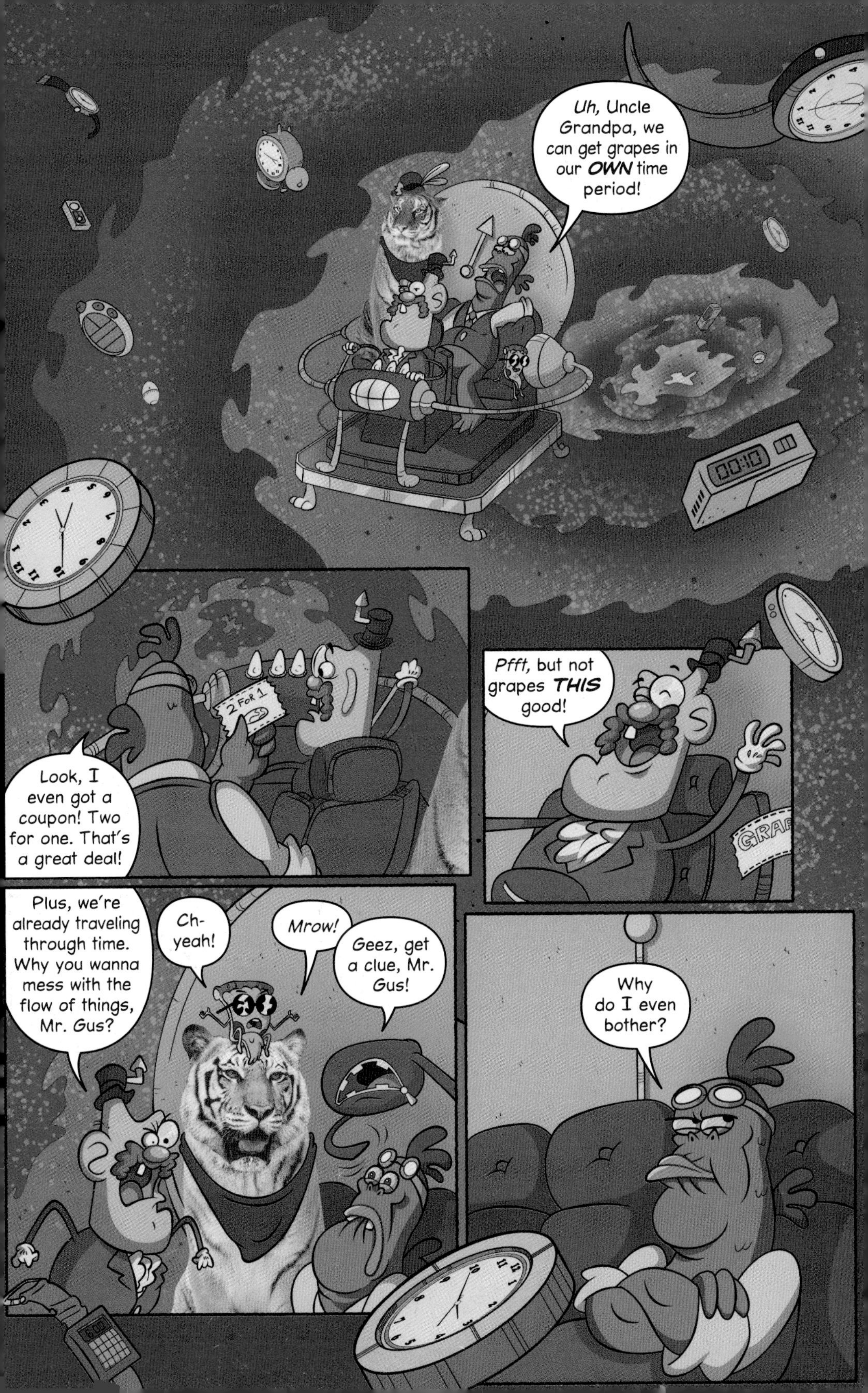
Uh, Uncle Grandpa, we can get grapes in our ***OWN*** time period!
00:10
2 FOR 1
Look, I even got a coupon! Two for one. That's a great deal!
Pfft, but not grapes ***THIS*** good!
GRAP
Plus, we're already traveling through time. Why you wanna mess with the flow of things, Mr. Gus?
Ch-yeah!
Mrow!
Geez, get a clue, Mr. Gus!
Why do I even bother?

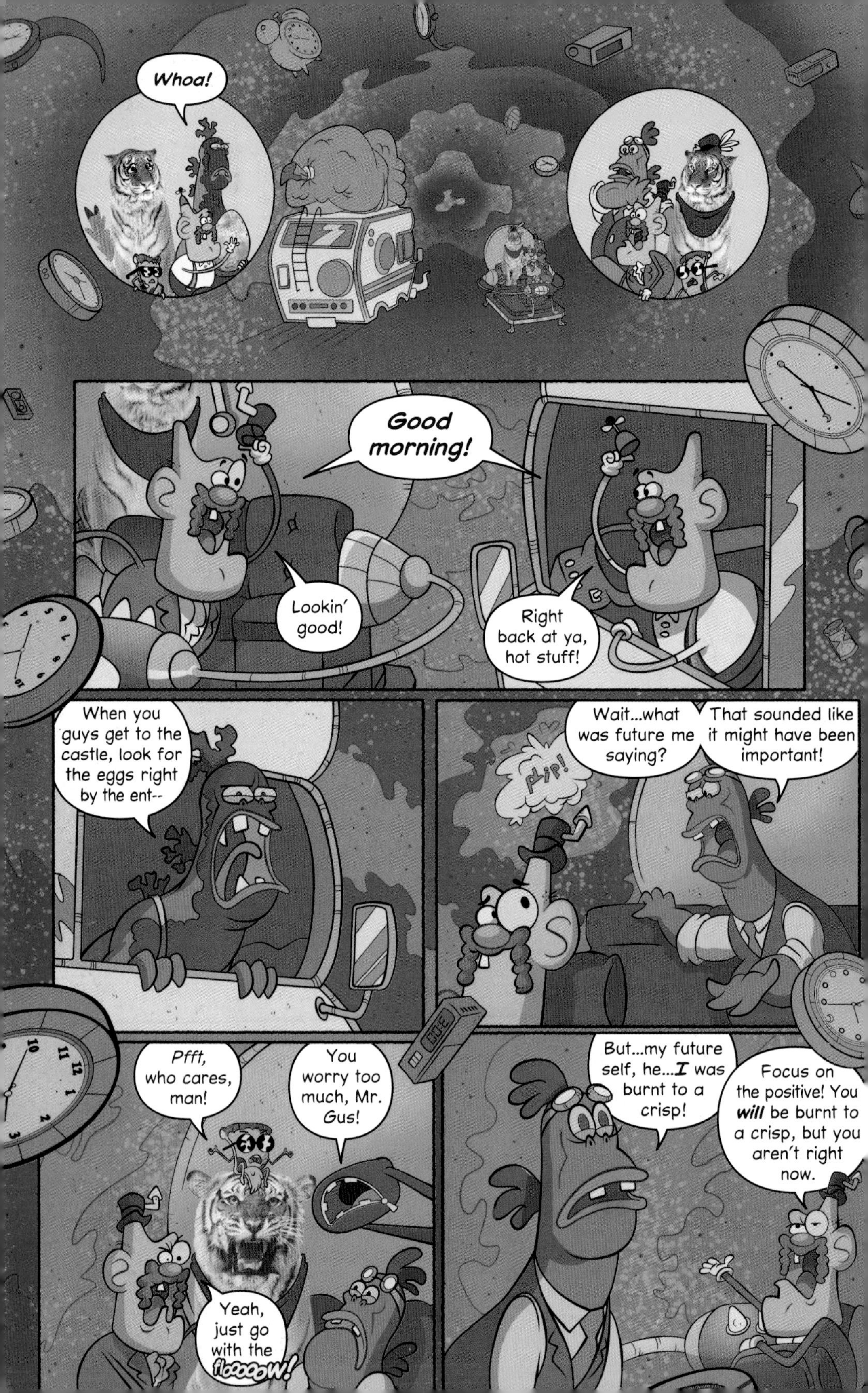
Whoa!
Good morning!
Lookin' good!
Right back at ya, hot stuff!
When you guys get to the castle, look for the eggs right by the ent--
pLip!
Wait...what was future me saying?
That sounded like it might have been important!
Pfft, who cares, man!
You worry too much, Mr. Gus!
Yeah, just go with the floooooW!
But...my future self, he...I was burnt to a crisp!
Focus on the positive! You will be burnt to a crisp, but you aren't right now.

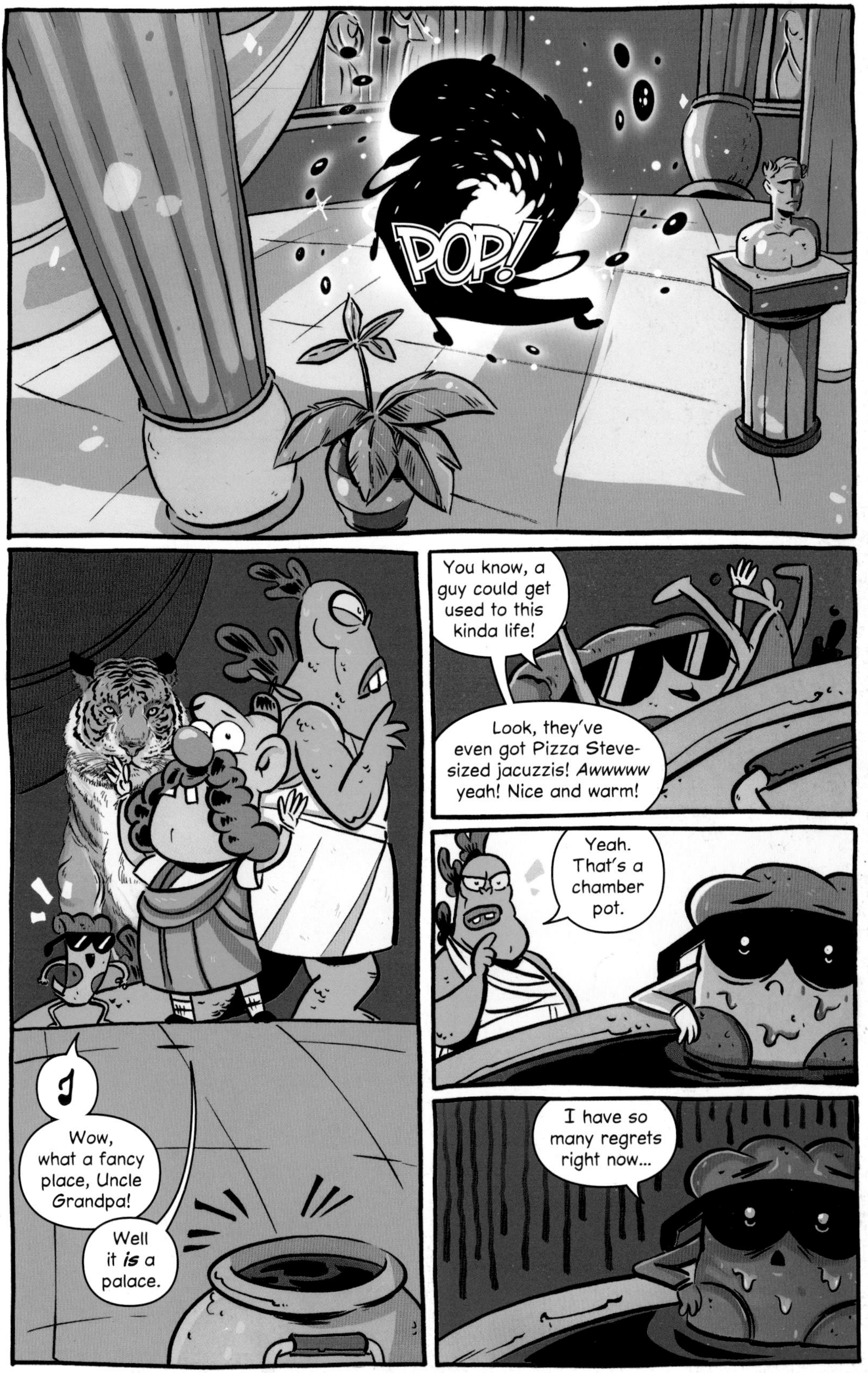
POP!
You know, a guy could get used to this kinda life!
Look, they've even got Pizza Steve-sized jacuzzis! *Awwwww* yeah! Nice and warm!
Yeah. That's a chamber pot.
Wow, what a fancy place, Uncle Grandpa!
Well it ***is*** a palace.
I have so many regrets right now...

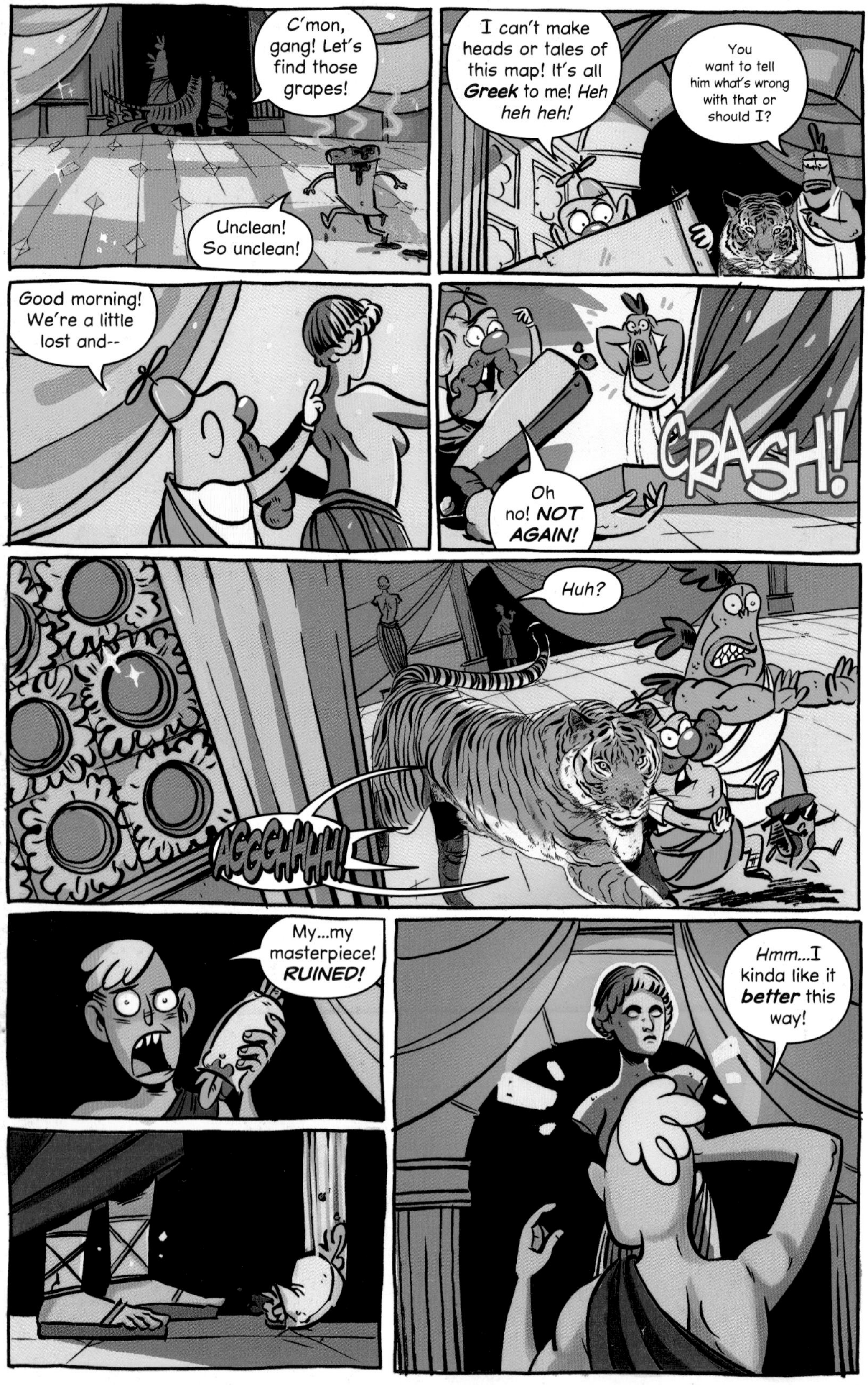
C'mon, gang! Let's find those grapes!
Unclean! So unclean!
I can't make heads or tales of this map! It's all **Greek** to me! *Heh heh heh!*
You want to tell him what's wrong with that or should I?
Good morning! We're a little lost and--
Oh no! **NOT AGAIN!**
CRASH!
Huh?
AGGGHHHH!
My...my masterpiece! **RUINED!**
*Hmm...*I kinda like it **better** this way!

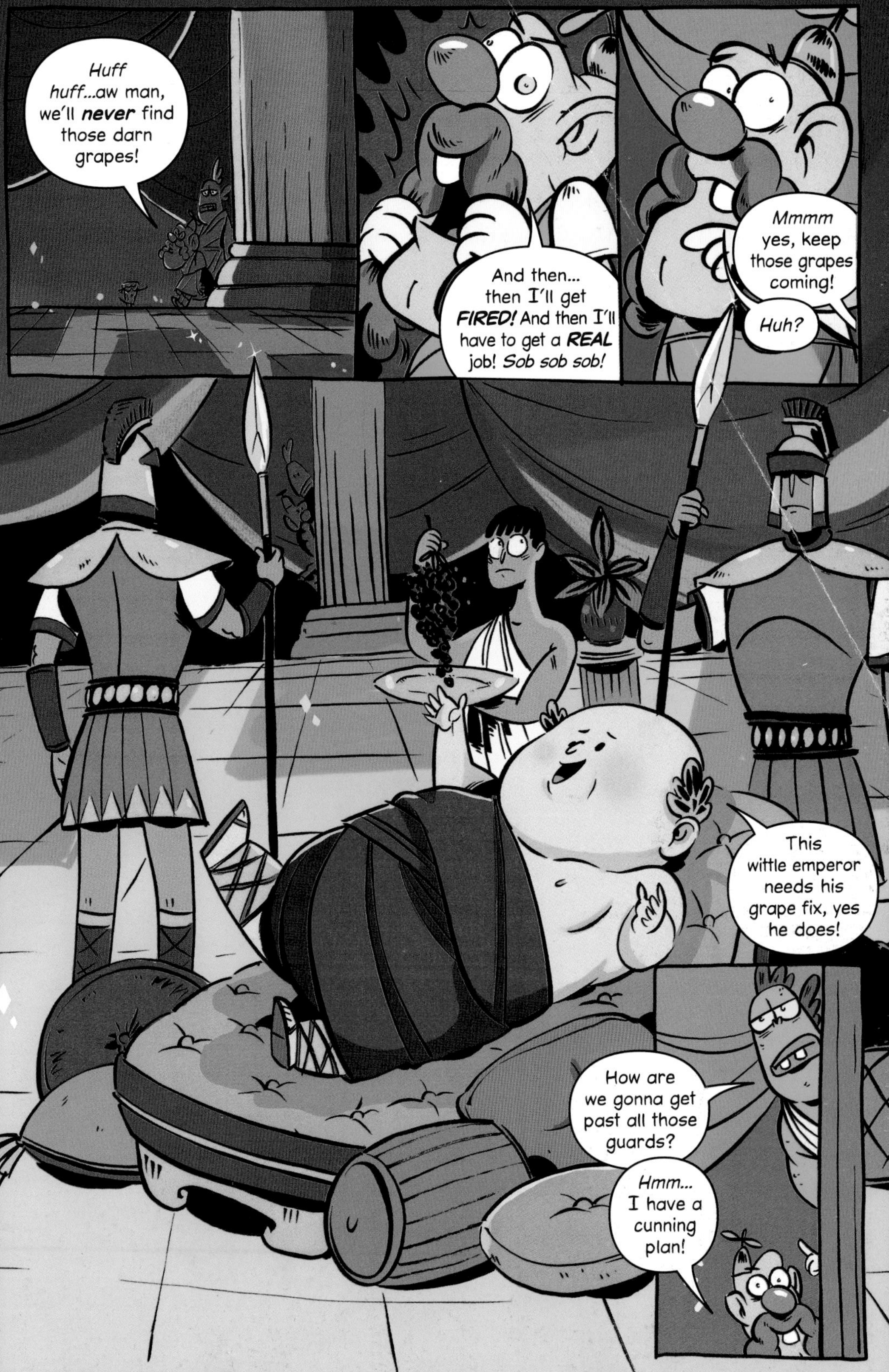
Huff huff...aw man, we'll **never** find those darn grapes!
And then... then I'll get **FIRED!** And then I'll have to get a **REAL** job! *Sob sob sob!*
Mmmm yes, keep those grapes coming!
Huh?
This wittle emperor needs his grape fix, yes he does!
How are we gonna get past all those guards?
Hmm... I have a cunning plan!

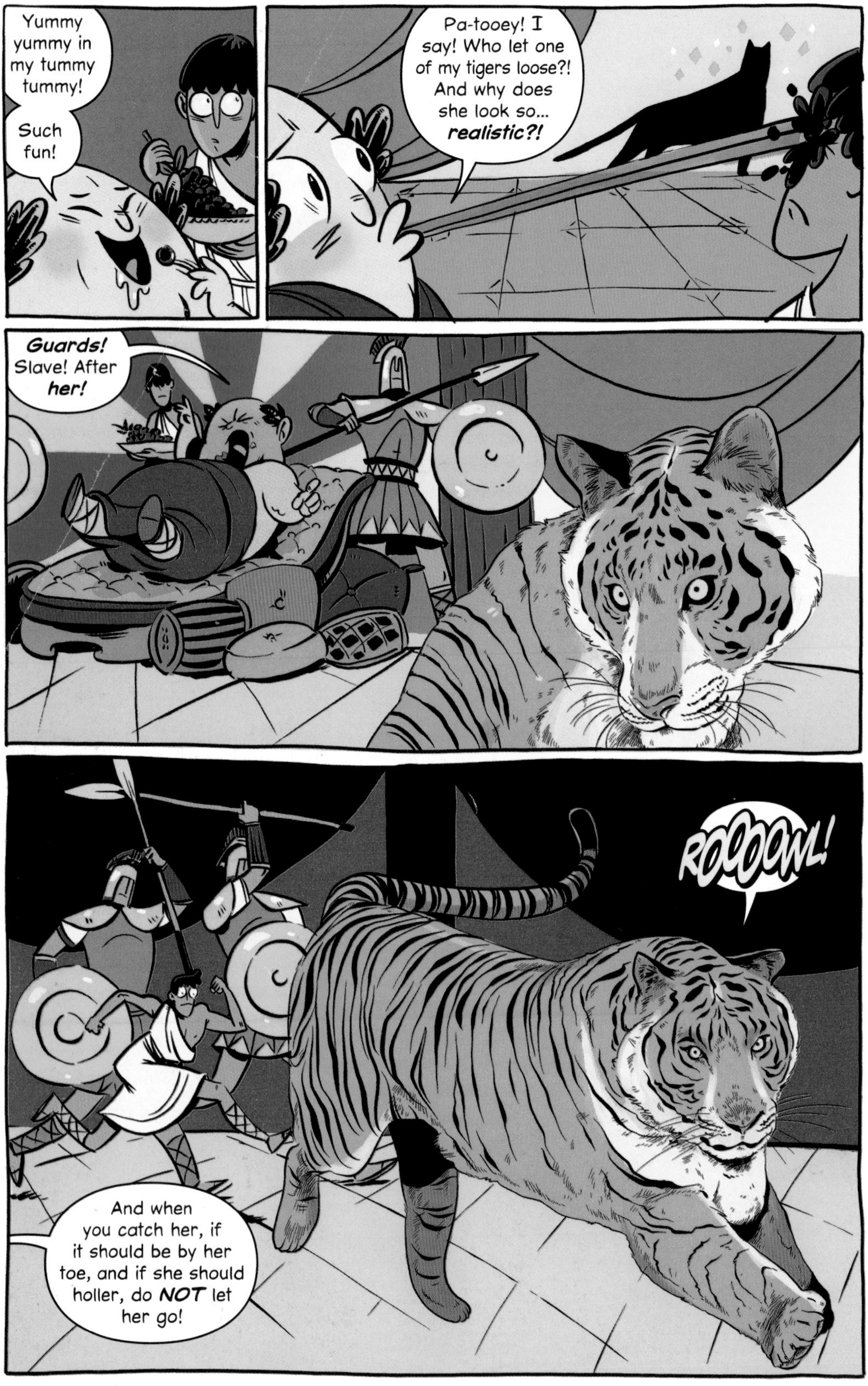
Yummy yummy in my tummy tummy!
Such fun!
Pa-tooey! I say! Who let one of my tigers loose?! And why does she look so... **realistic?!**
Guards! Slave! After **her!**
ROOOOWL!
And when you catch her, if it should be by her toe, and if she should holler, do **NOT** let her go!

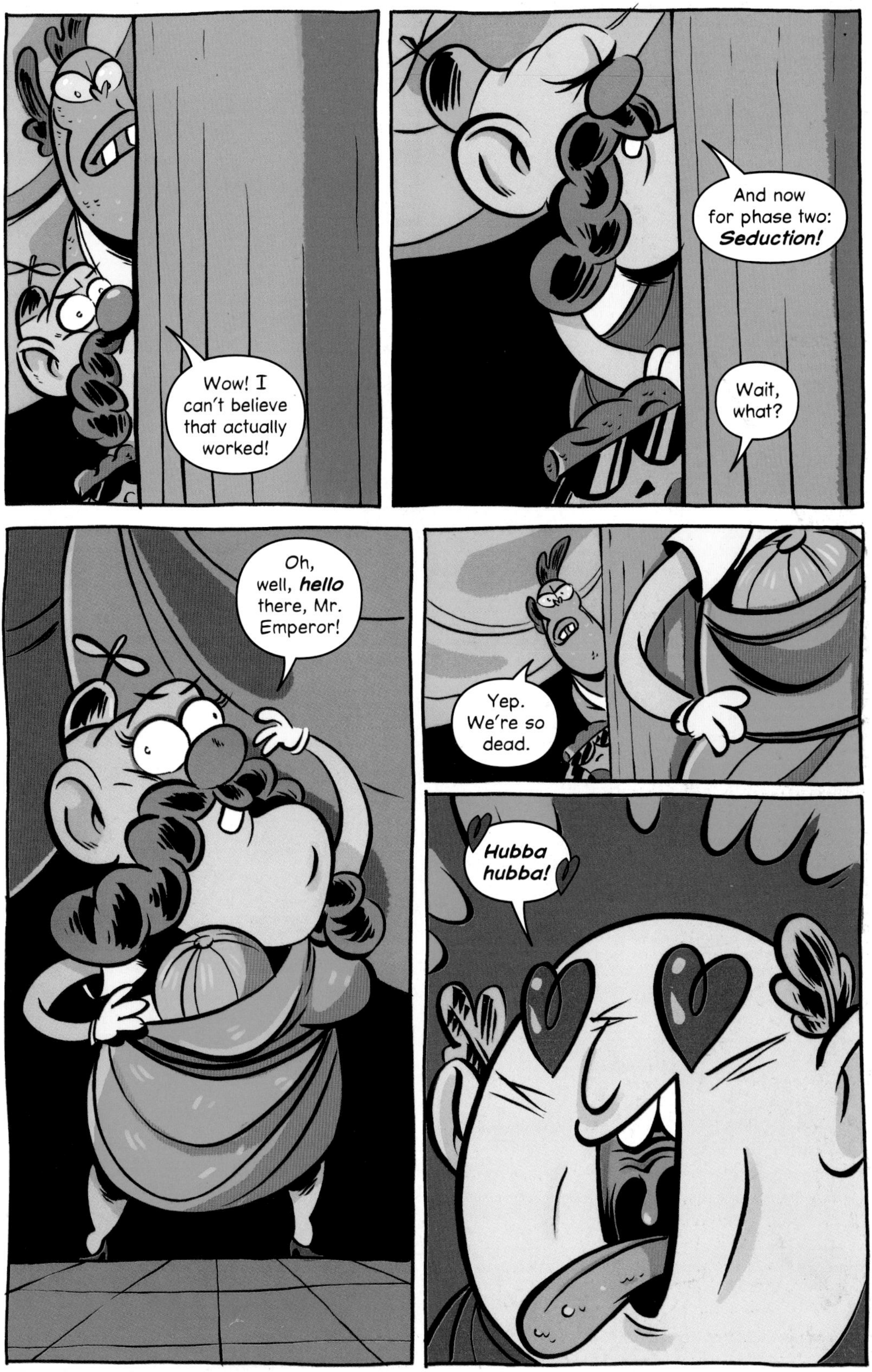
Wow! I can't believe that actually worked!
And now for phase two: ***Seduction!***
Wait, what?
Oh, well, ***hello*** there, Mr. Emperor!
Yep. We're so dead.
Hubba hubba!

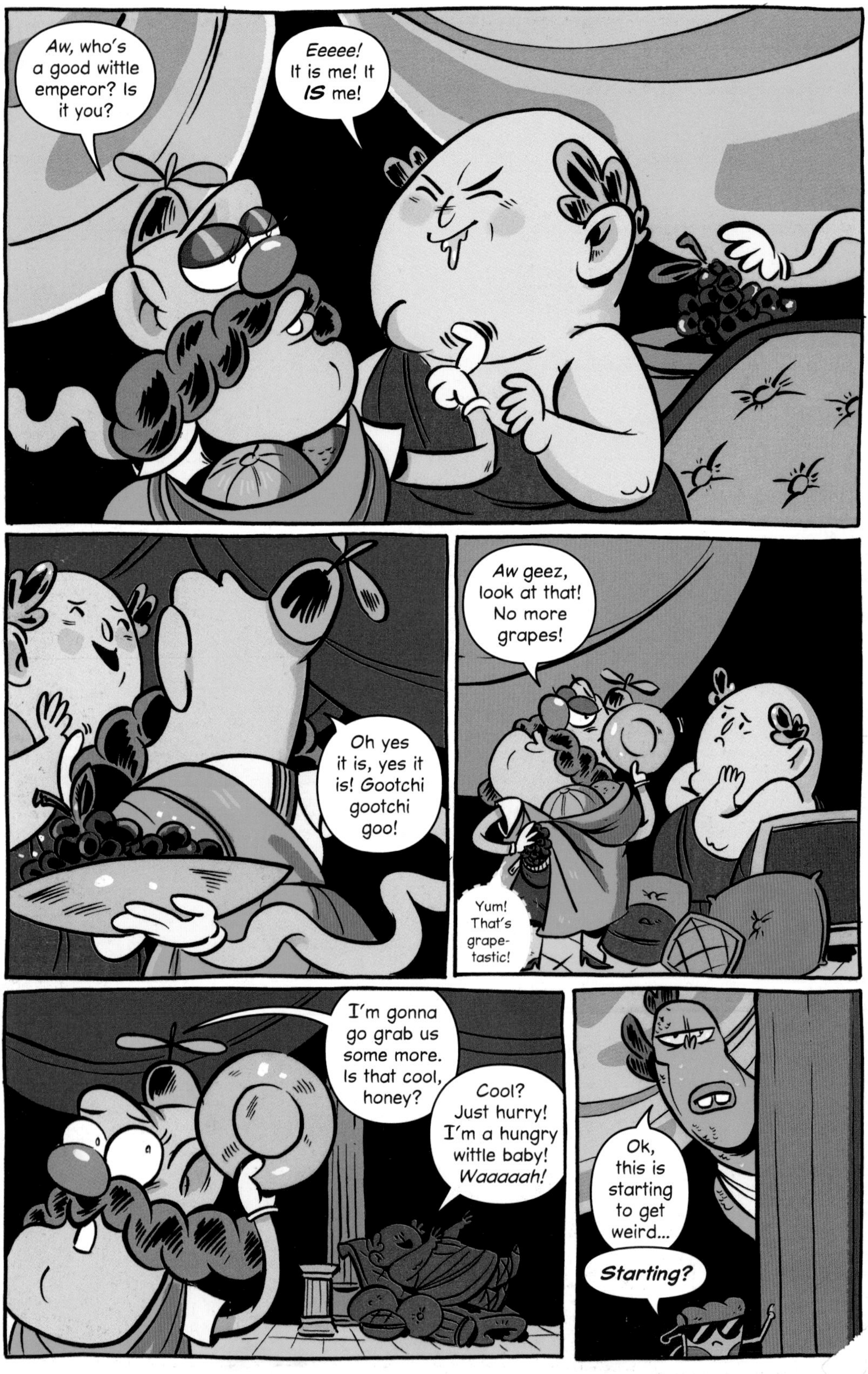
Aw, who's a good wittle emperor? Is it you?
Eeeee! It is me! It *IS* me!
Oh yes it is, yes it is! Gootchi gootchi goo!
Aw geez, look at that! No more grapes!
Yum! That's grape-tastic!
I'm gonna go grab us some more. Is that cool, honey?
Cool? Just hurry! I'm a hungry wittle baby! *Waaaaah!*
Ok, this is starting to get weird...
Starting?

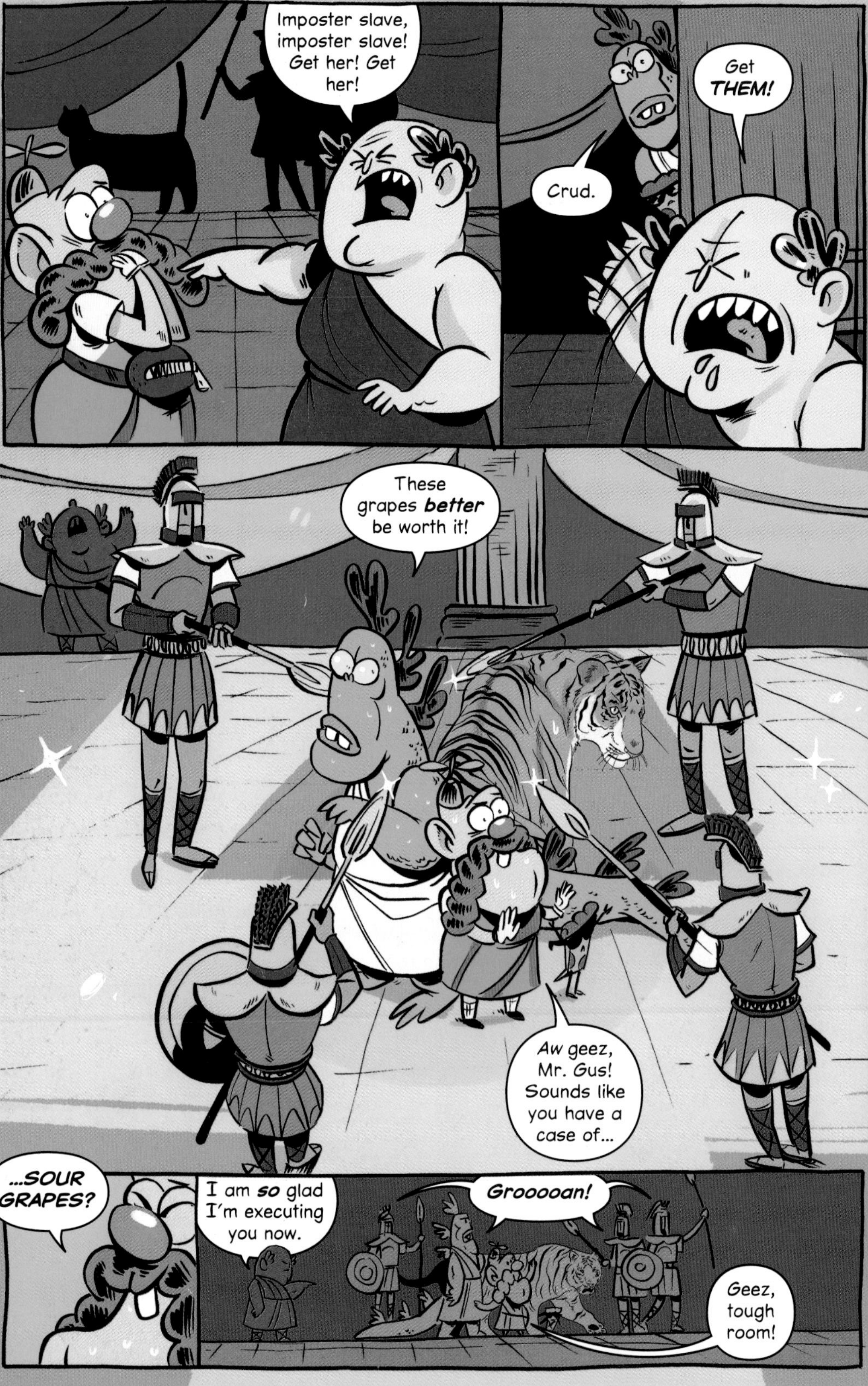
Imposter slave, imposter slave! Get her! Get her!
Get THEM!
Crud.
These grapes better be worth it!
Aw geez, Mr. Gus! Sounds like you have a case of...
...SOUR GRAPES?
I am so glad I'm executing you now.
Groooan!
Geez, tough room!

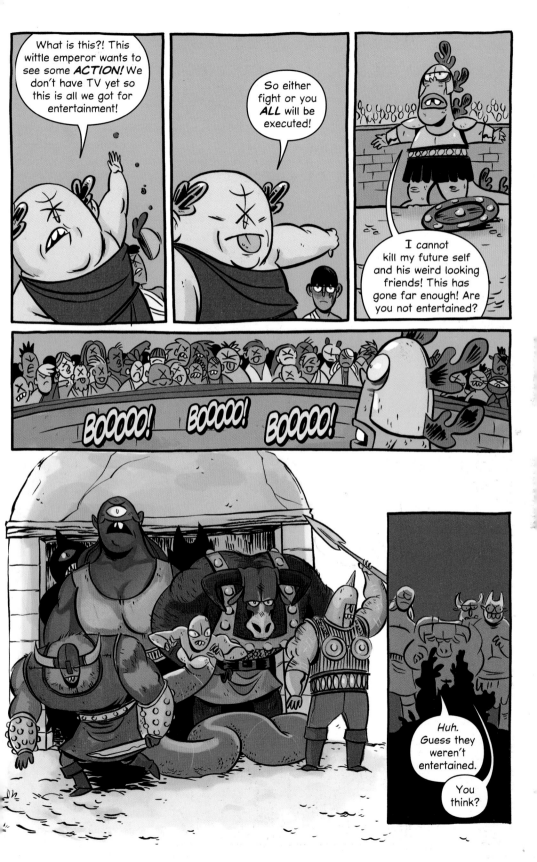

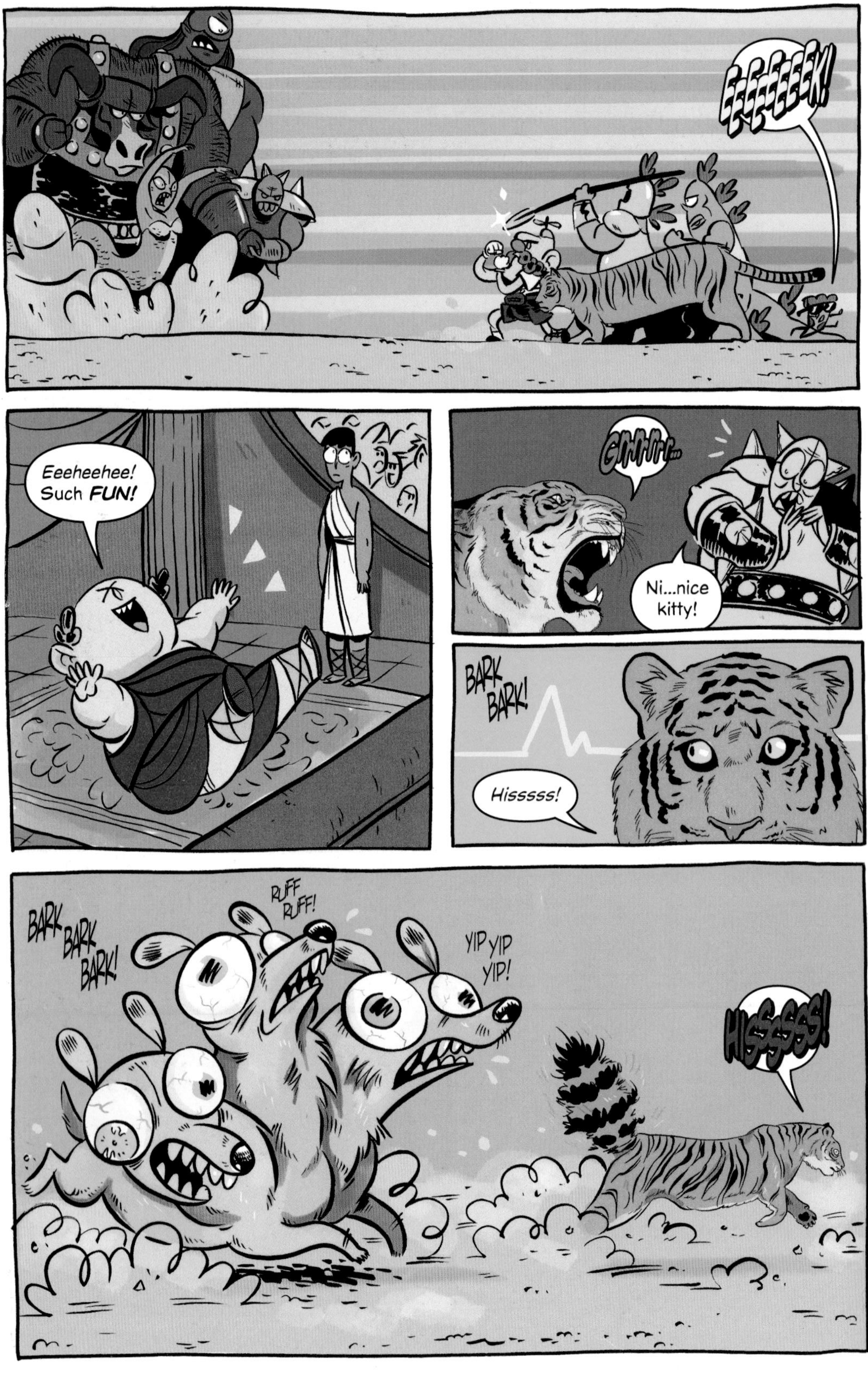
EEEEEEEEEK!
Eeeheehee! Such FUN!
Grrrrrr...
Ni...nice kitty!
BARK BARK!
Hissss!
BARK BARK BARK!
RUFF RUFF!
YIP YIP YIP!
HISSSSS!

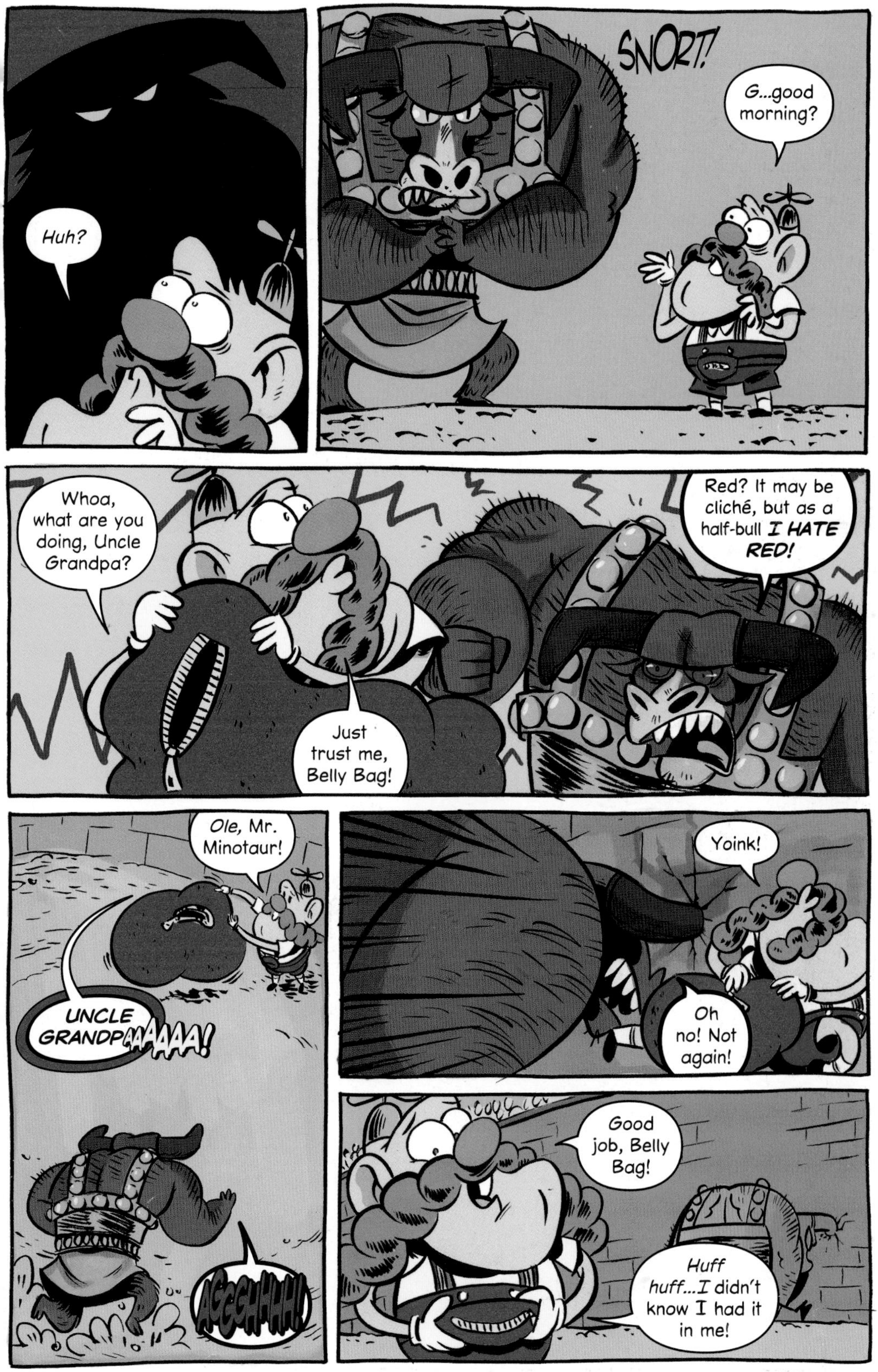
Huh?
SNORT!
G...good morning?
Whoa, what are you doing, Uncle Grandpa?
Red? It may be cliché, but as a half-bull I HATE RED!
Just trust me, Belly Bag!
Ole, Mr. Minotaur!
UNCLE GRANDPAAAAAA!
Yoink!
Oh no! Not again!
AGGGHHHH!
Good job, Belly Bag!
Huff huff...I didn't know I had it in me!

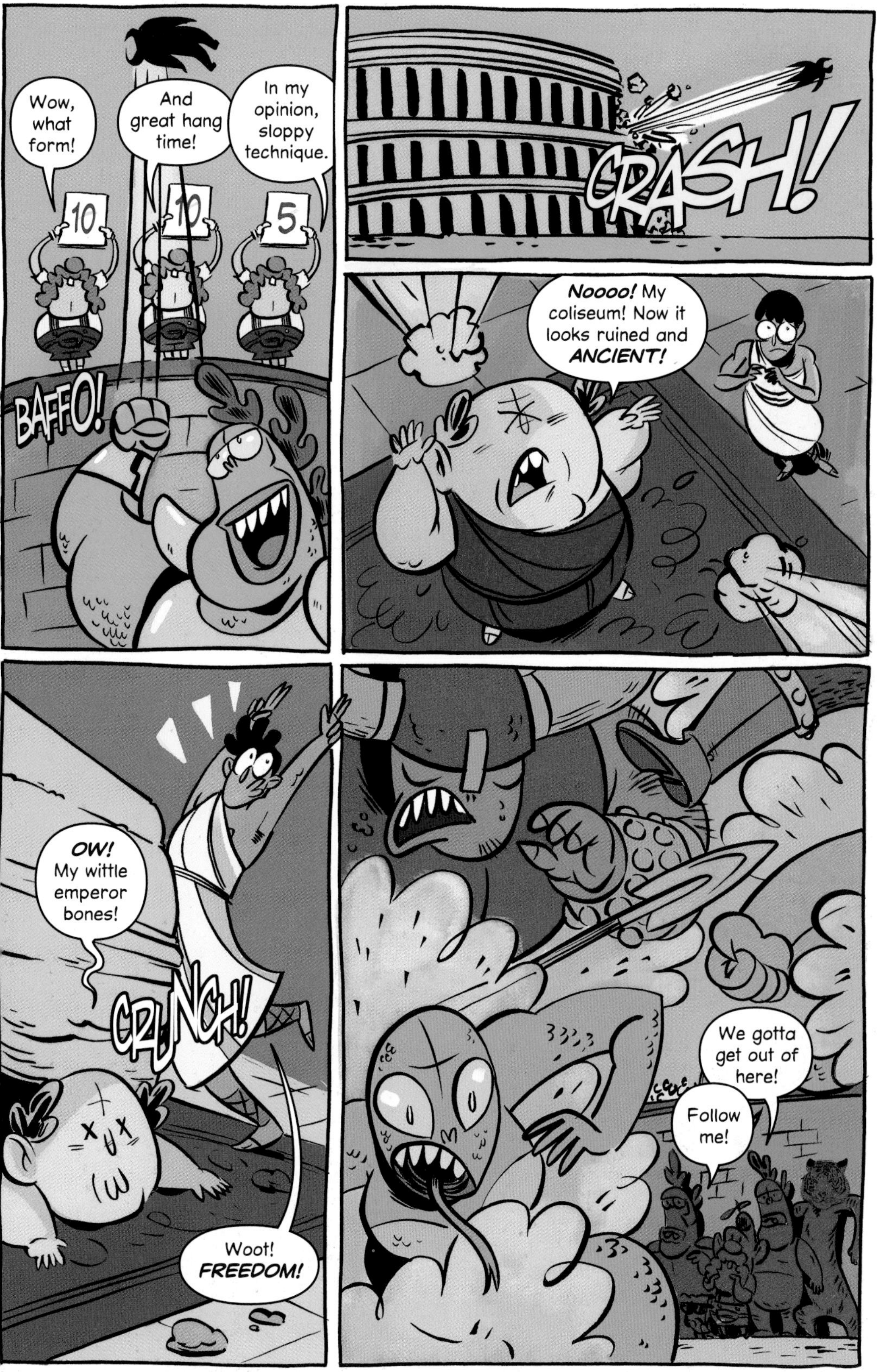
Wow, what form!
And great hang time!
In my opinion, sloppy technique.
10
10
5
BAFFO!
CRASH!
Noooo! My coliseum! Now it looks ruined and ANCIENT!
OW! My wittle emperor bones!
CRUNCH!
Woot! FREEDOM!
We gotta get out of here!
Follow me!

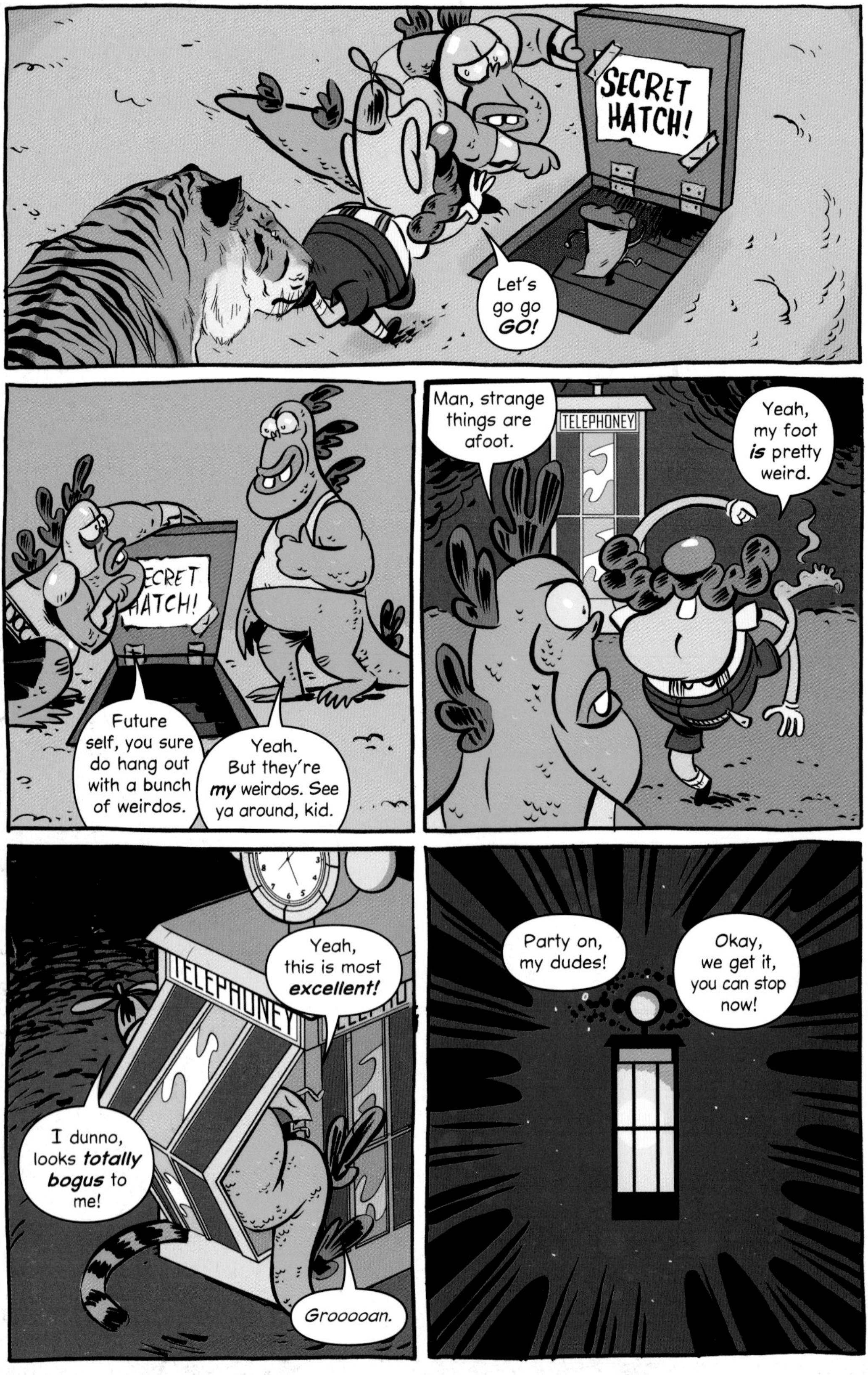
SECRET HATCH!
Let's go go GO!
SECRET HATCH!
Future self, you sure do hang out with a bunch of weirdos.
Yeah. But they're my weirdos. See ya around, kid.
Man, strange things are afoot.
TELEPHONEY
Yeah, my foot is pretty weird.
TELEPHONEY
Yeah, this is most excellent!
I dunno, looks totally bogus to me!
Groooooan.
Party on, my dudes!
Okay, we get it, you can stop now!

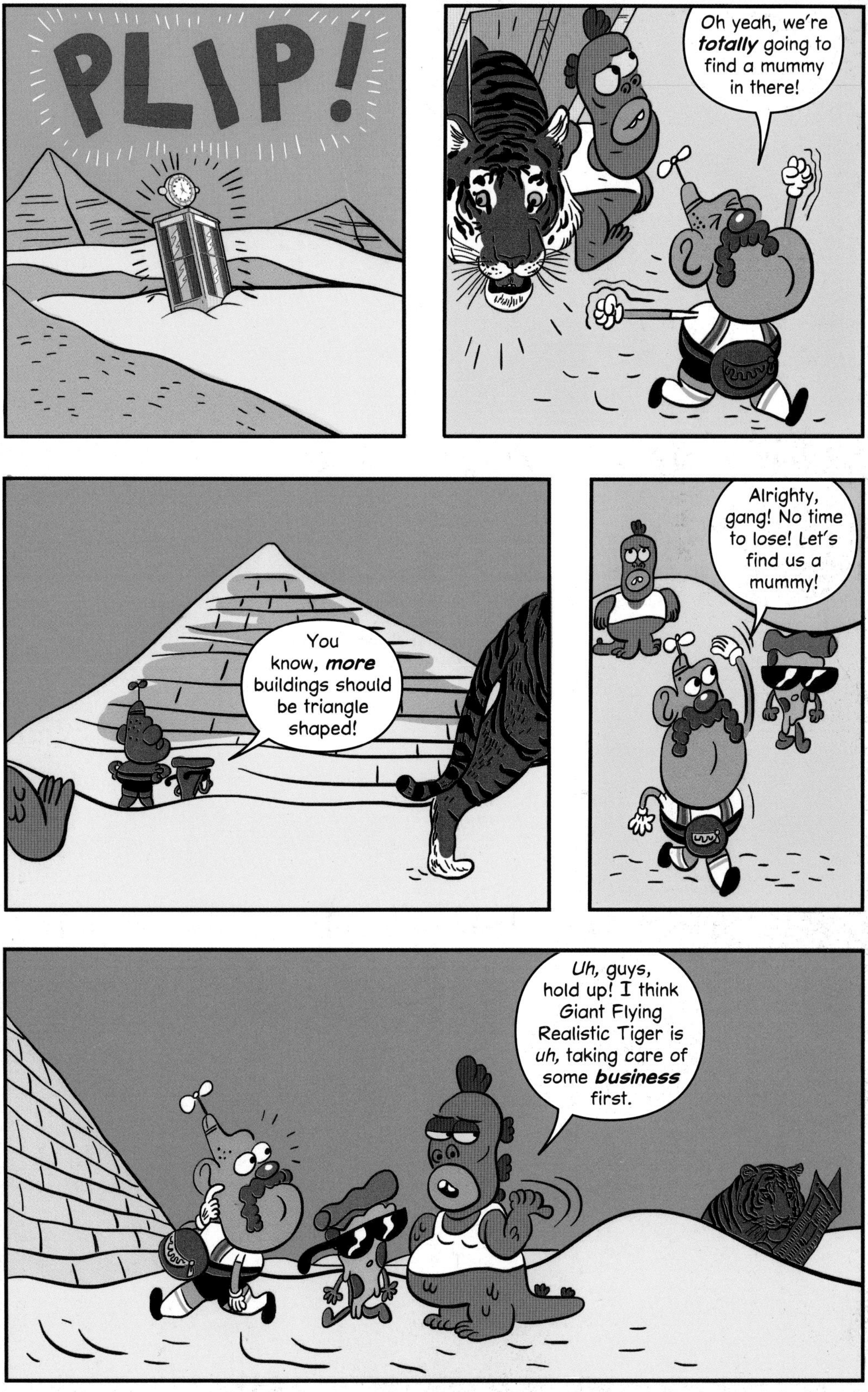
PLIP!
Oh yeah, we're *totally* going to find a mummy in there!
You know, ***more*** buildings should be triangle shaped!
Alrighty, gang! No time to lose! Let's find us a mummy!
Uh, guys, hold up! I think Giant Flying Realistic Tiger is *uh,* taking care of some ***business*** first.

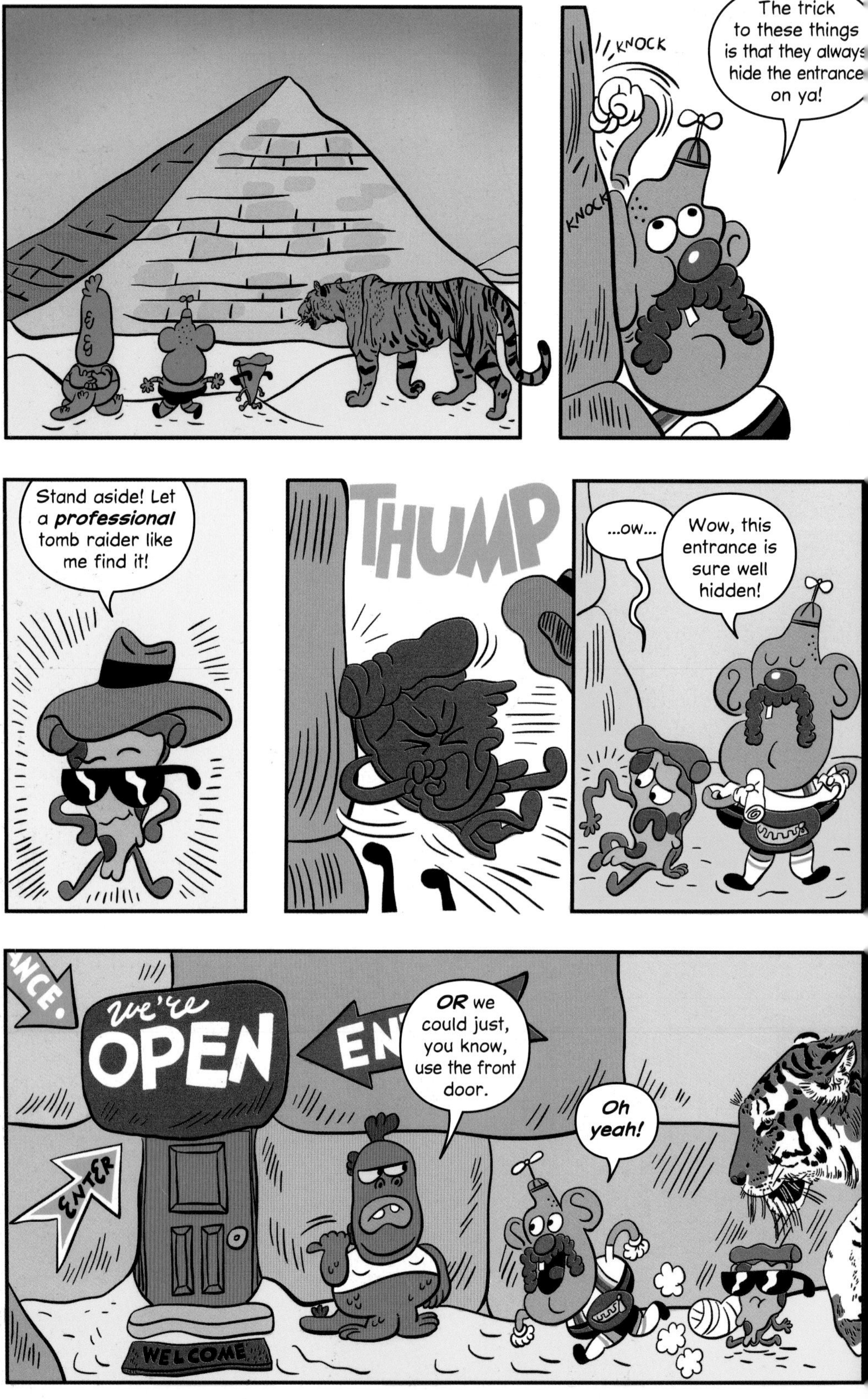
KNOCK
KNOCK
The trick to these things is that they always hide the entrance on ya!
Stand aside! Let a ***professional*** tomb raider like me find it!
THUMP
...ow...
Wow, this entrance is sure well hidden!
We're OPEN
ENTER
OR we could just, you know, use the front door.
Oh yeah!
WELCOME

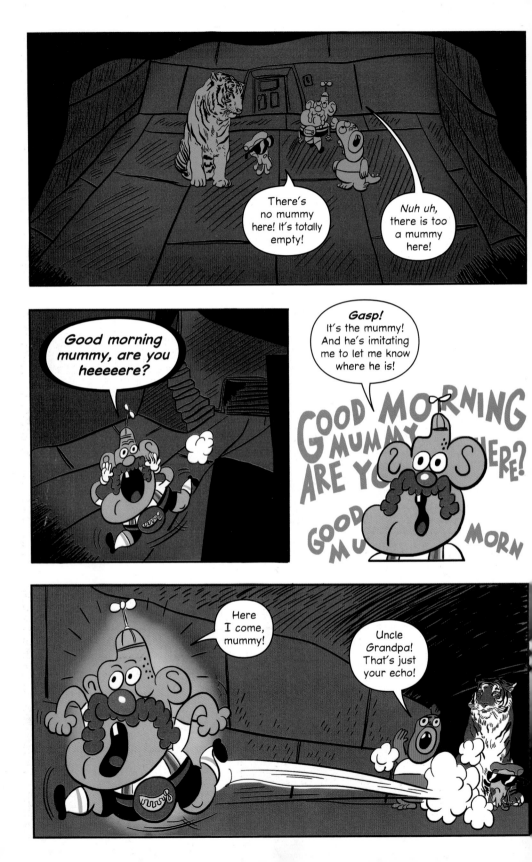

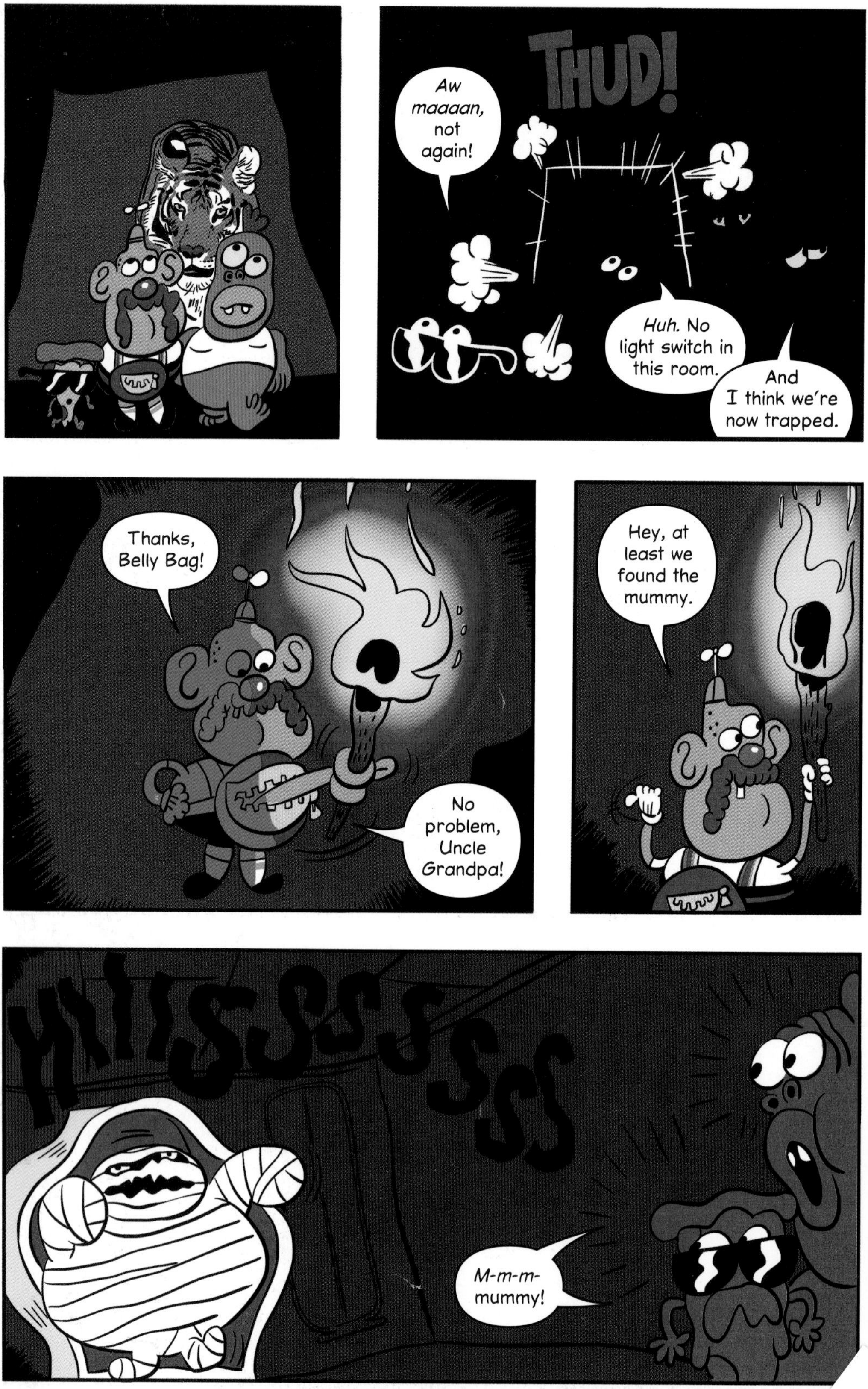
THUD!
Aw maaaan, not again!
Huh. No light switch in this room.
And I think we're now trapped.
Thanks, Belly Bag!
No problem, Uncle Grandpa!
Hey, at least we found the mummy.
HHISSSSSSS
M-m-m-mummy!

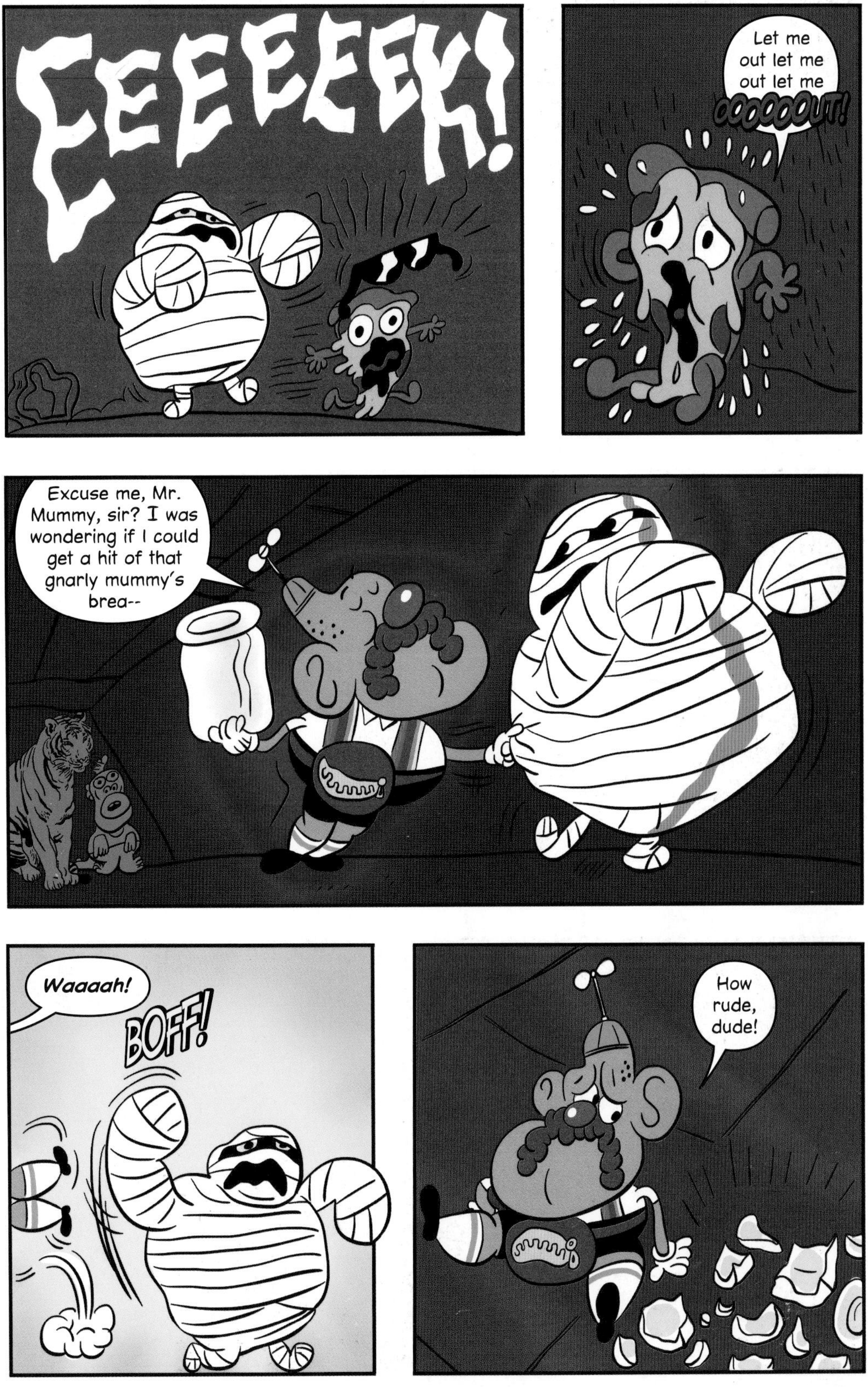
EEEEEEK!
Let me out let me out let me OOOOOOUT!
Excuse me, Mr. Mummy, sir? I was wondering if I could get a hit of that gnarly mummy's brea--
Waaaah!
BOFF!
How rude, dude!

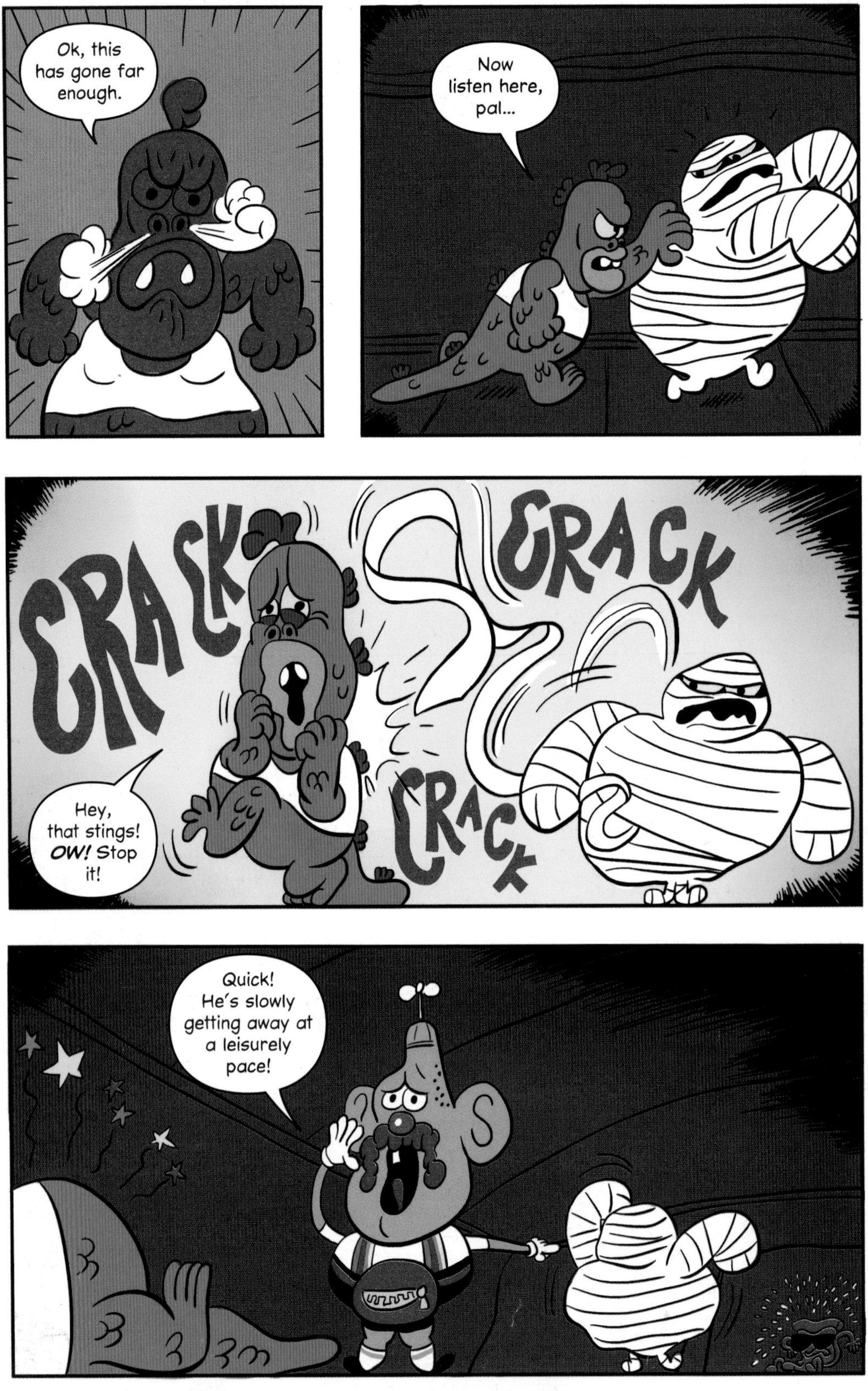
Ok, this has gone far enough.
Now listen here, pal...
CRACK
CRACK
CRACK
Hey, that stings! ***OW!*** Stop it!
Quick! He's slowly getting away at a leisurely pace!

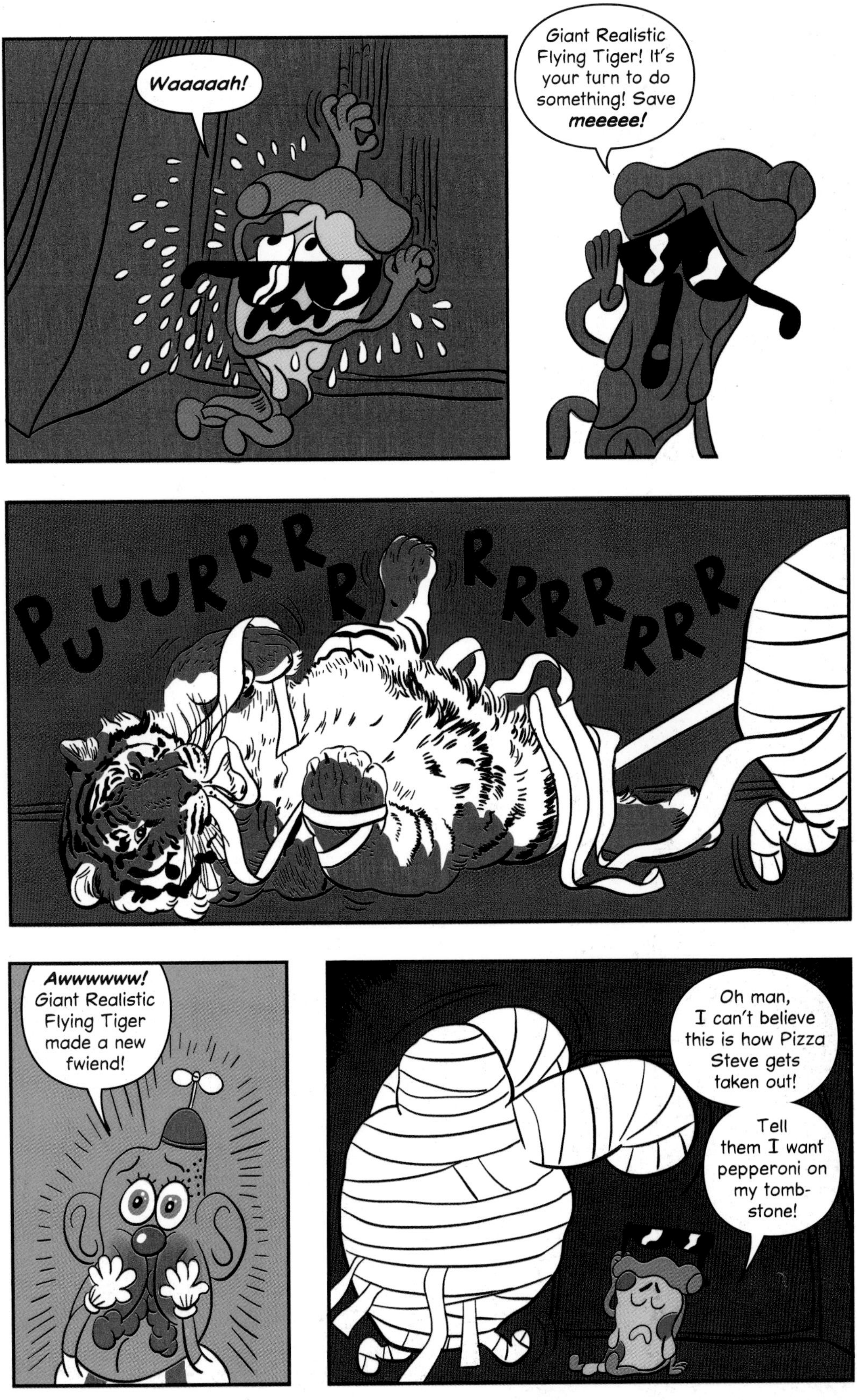
Waaaaah!
Giant Realistic Flying Tiger! It's your turn to do something! Save meeeee!
PUUURRRRRRRRRRR
Awwwwww! Giant Realistic Flying Tiger made a new fwiend!
Oh man, I can't believe this is how Pizza Steve gets taken out!
Tell them I want pepperoni on my tomb-stone!

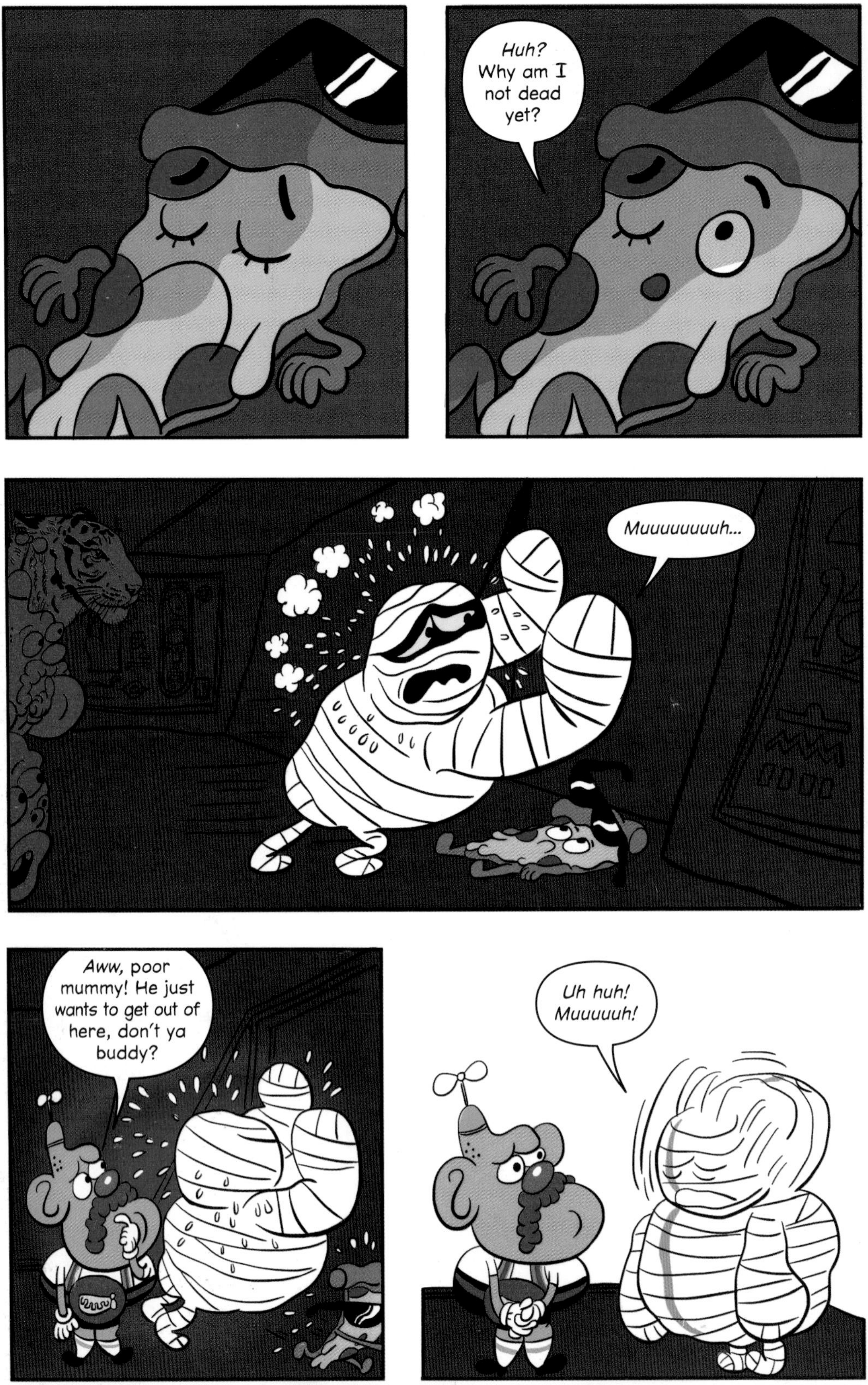

Huh? Why am I not dead yet?
Muuuuuuuuh...
Aww, poor mummy! He just wants to get out of here, don't ya buddy?
Uh huh! Muuuuuh!

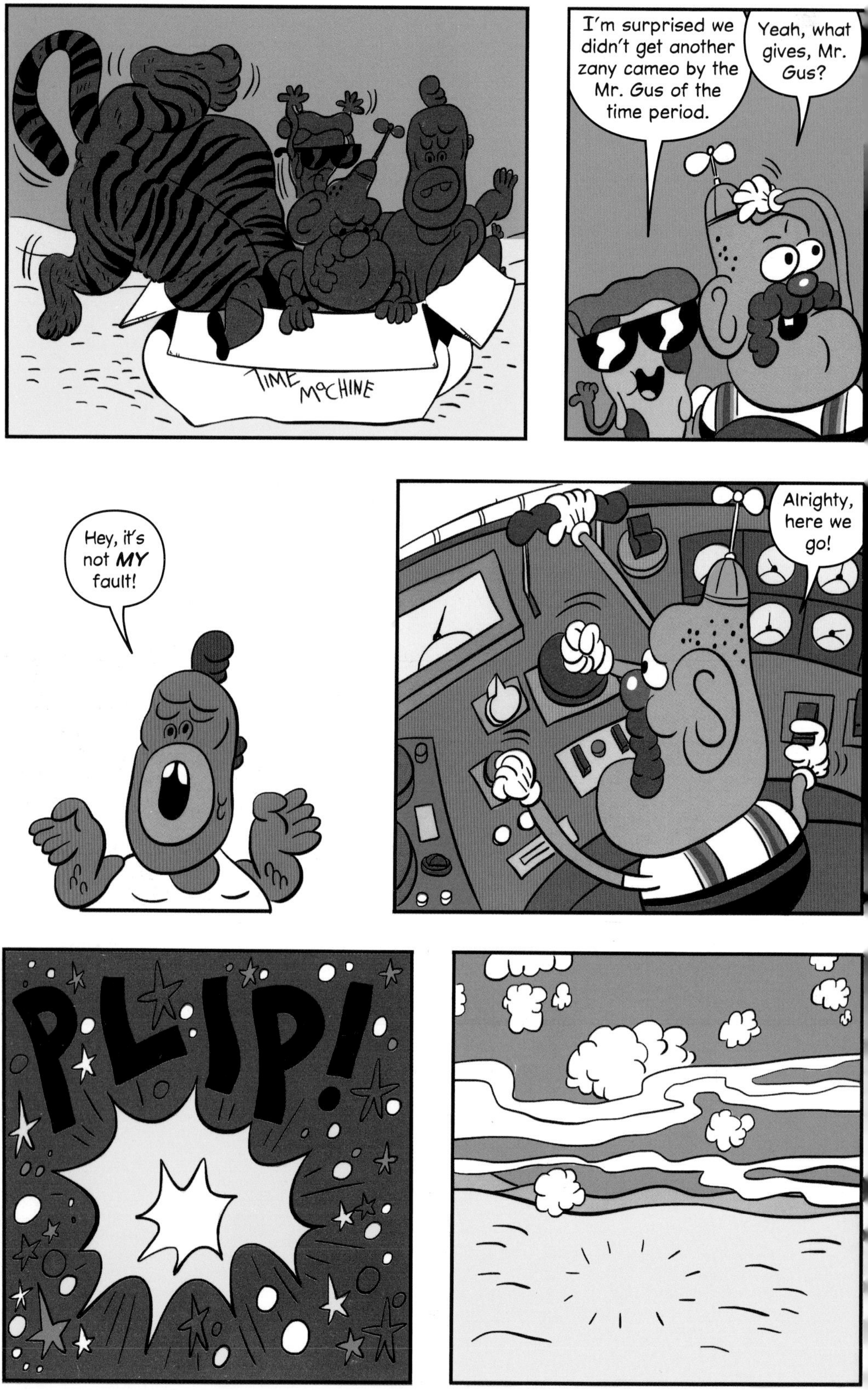
TIME MACHINE
I'm surprised we didn't get another zany cameo by the Mr. Gus of the time period.
Yeah, what gives, Mr. Gus?
Hey, it's not MY fault!
Alrighty, here we go!
PLIP!

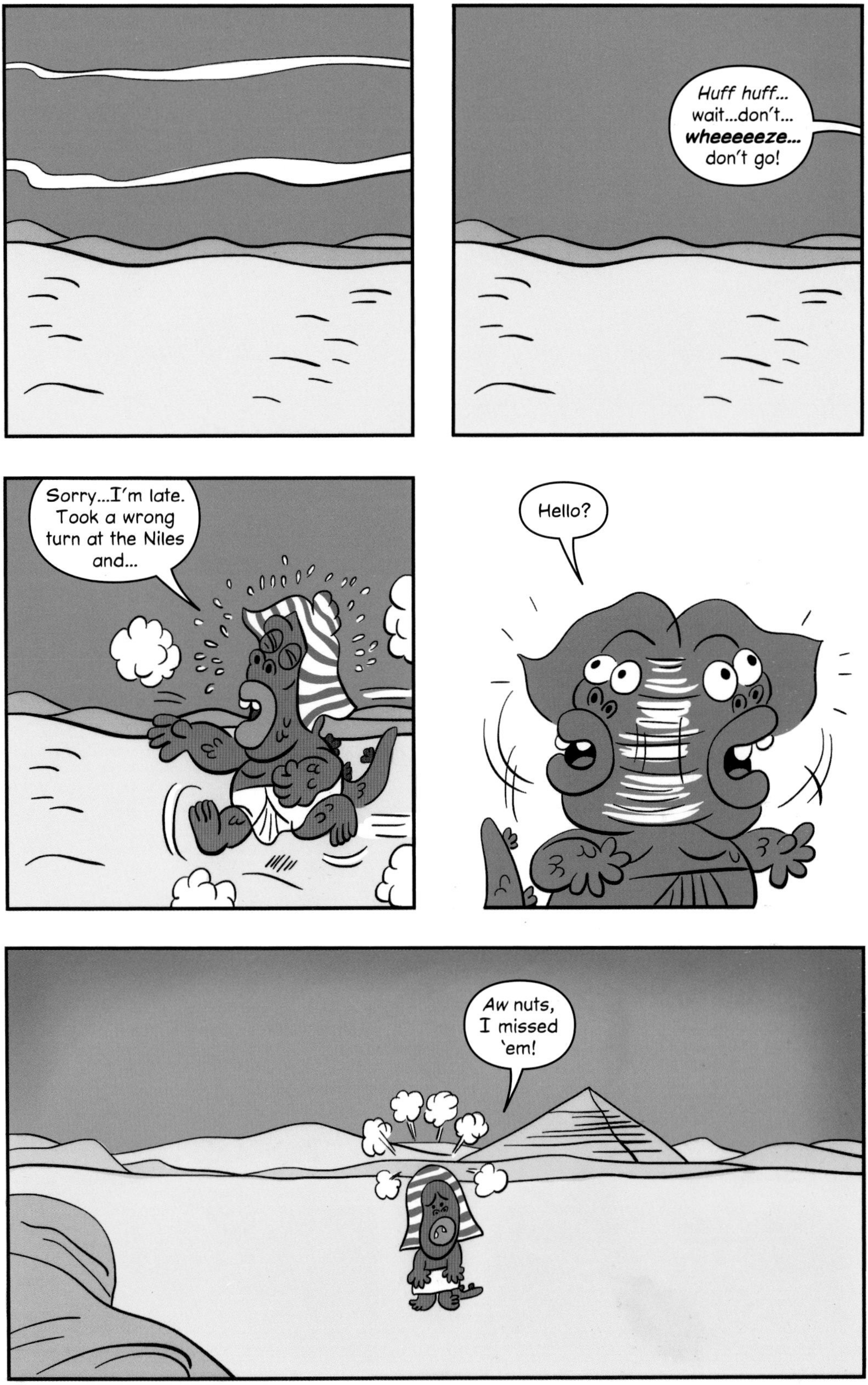

Huff huff... wait...don't... **wheeeeeze...** don't go!
Sorry...I'm late. Took a wrong turn at the Niles and...
Hello?
Aw nuts, I missed 'em!

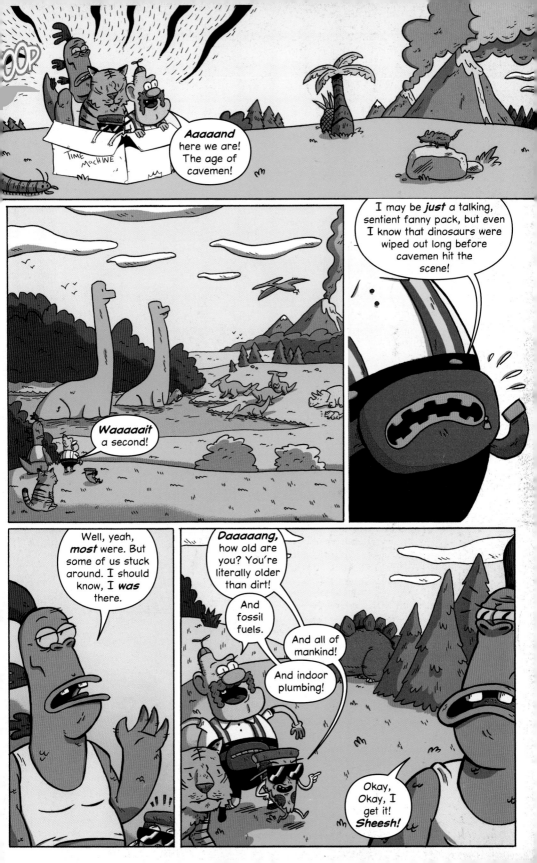

Older than the continents. Written word. Modern medicine. **Pizza bagels!**
Ugh.
Hey guys, LOOK!
It's our ancient ancestors!
Wait, pizza evolved from... rocks?
Makes sense when you consider how smart rocks are. *Heh heh.*
Hey! What did I ever do to you?

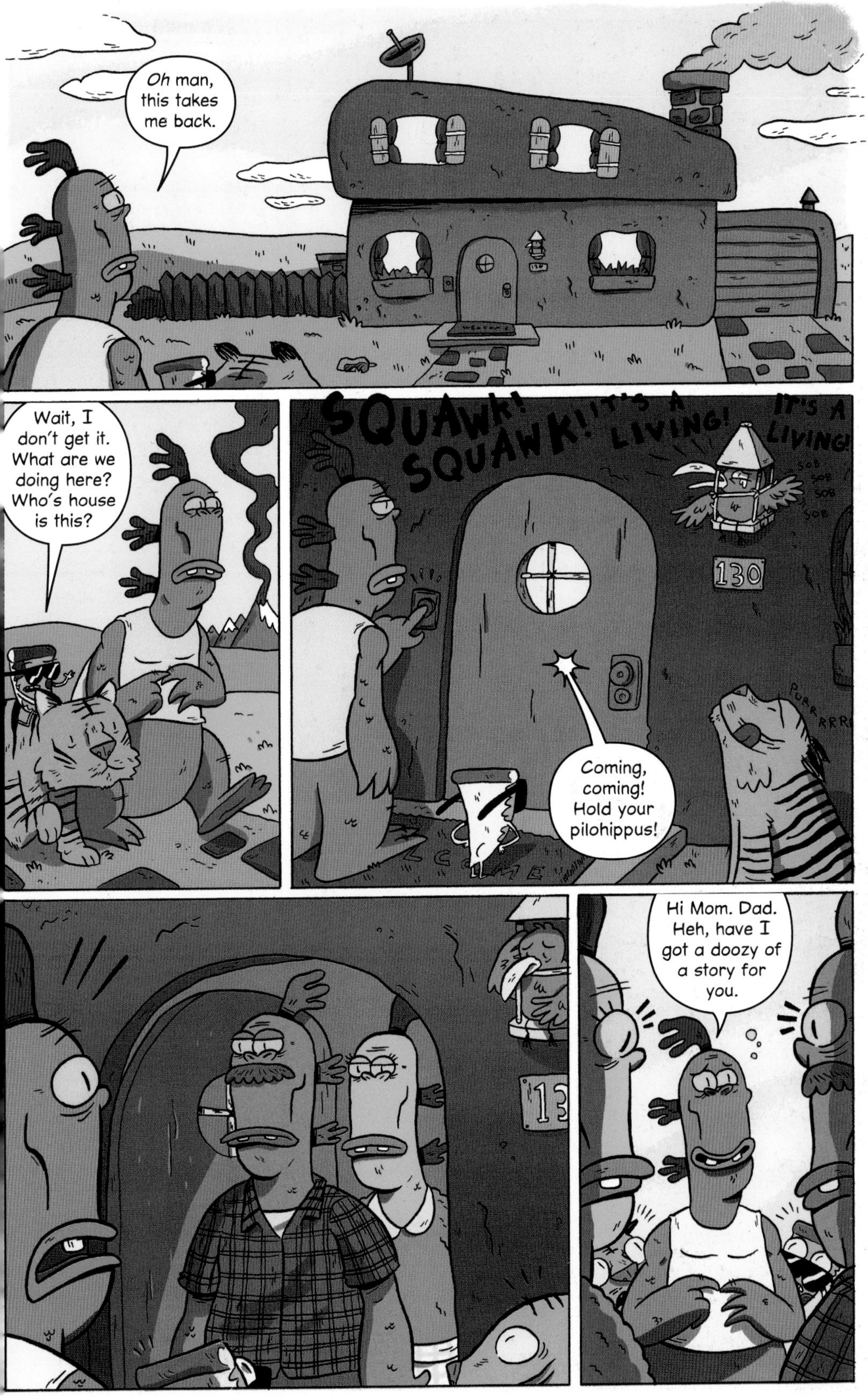
Oh man, this takes me back.
Wait, I don't get it. What are we doing here? Who's house is this?
SQUAWK! SQUAWK!
IT'S A LIVING!
IT'S A LIVING!
SOB SOB SOB SOB
130
Coming, coming! Hold your pilohippus!
PURRRRR
Hi Mom. Dad. Heh, have I got a doozy of a story for you.

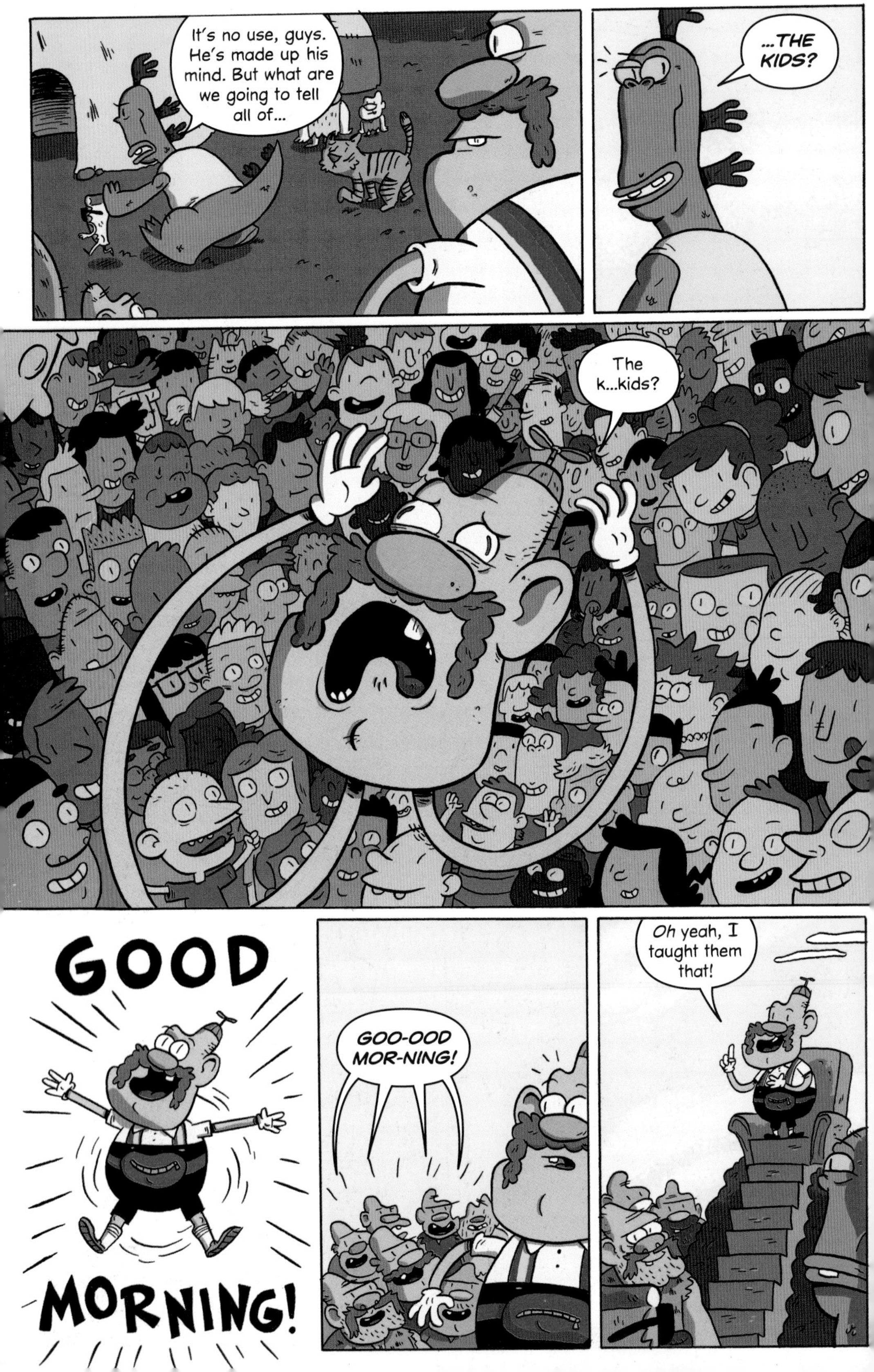
It's no use, guys. He's made up his mind. But what are we going to tell all of...
...THE KIDS?
The k...kids?
GOOD
MORNING!
GOO-OOD MOR-NING!
Oh yeah, I taught them that!

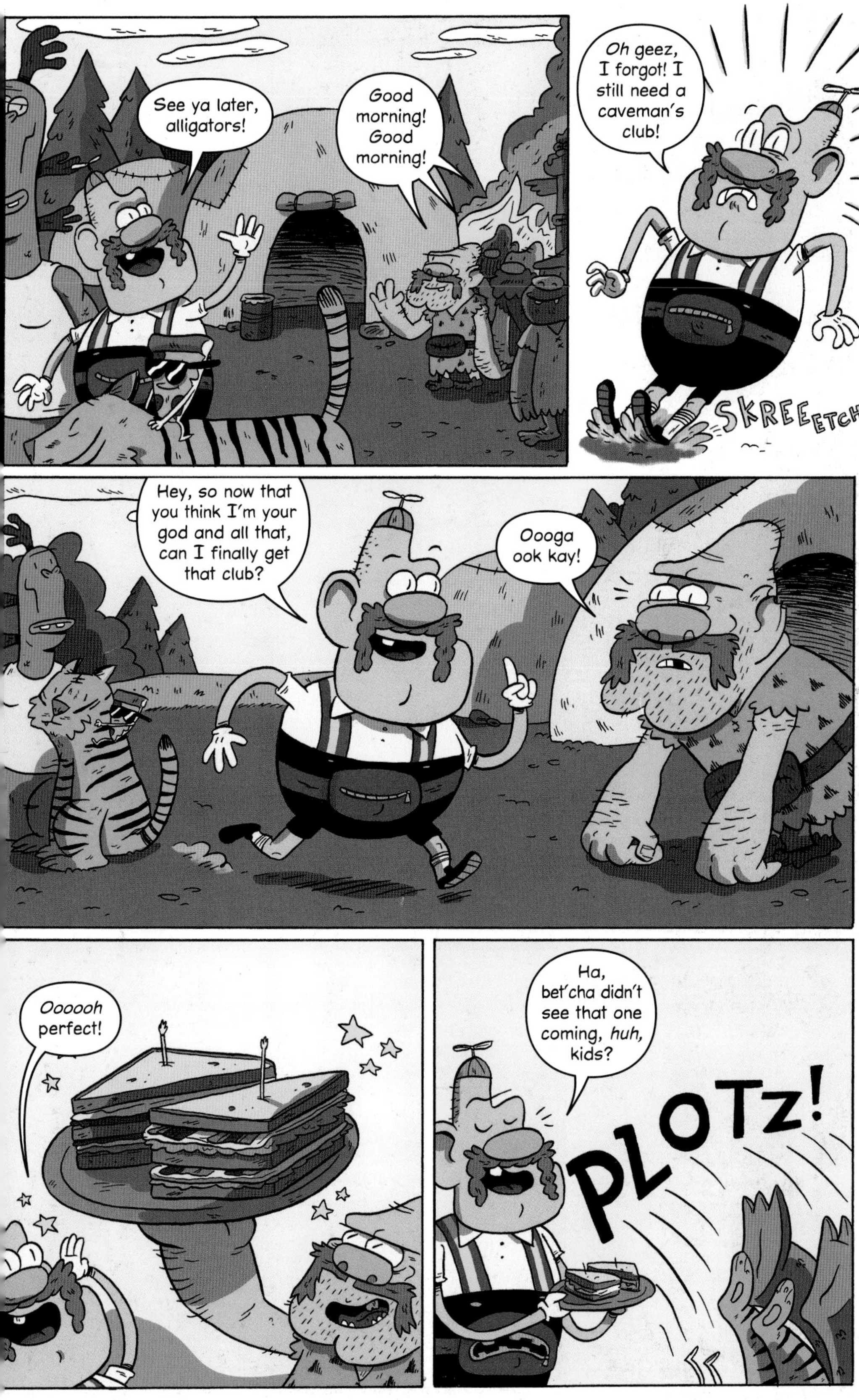

See ya later, alligators!
Good morning! Good morning!
Oh geez, I forgot! I still need a caveman's club!
SKREEETCH
Hey, so now that you think I'm your god and all that, can I finally get that club?
Oooga ook kay!
Oooooh perfect!
Ha, bet'cha didn't see that one coming, huh, kids?
PLOTZ!

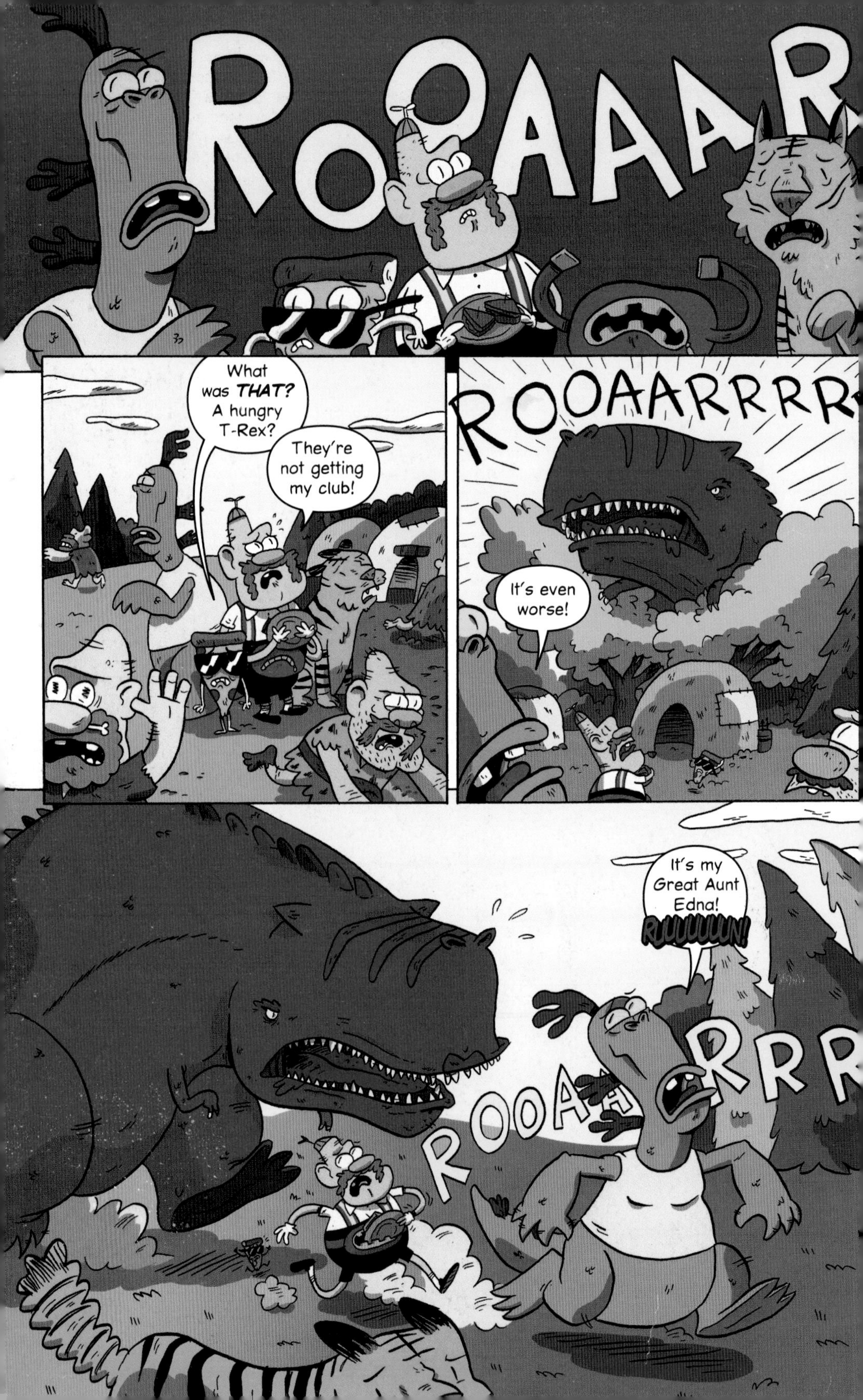
ROOAAAR
What was THAT? A hungry T-Rex?
They're not getting my club!
ROOAARRRR
It's even worse!
It's my Great Aunt Edna!
RUUUUUUN!
ROOAARRR

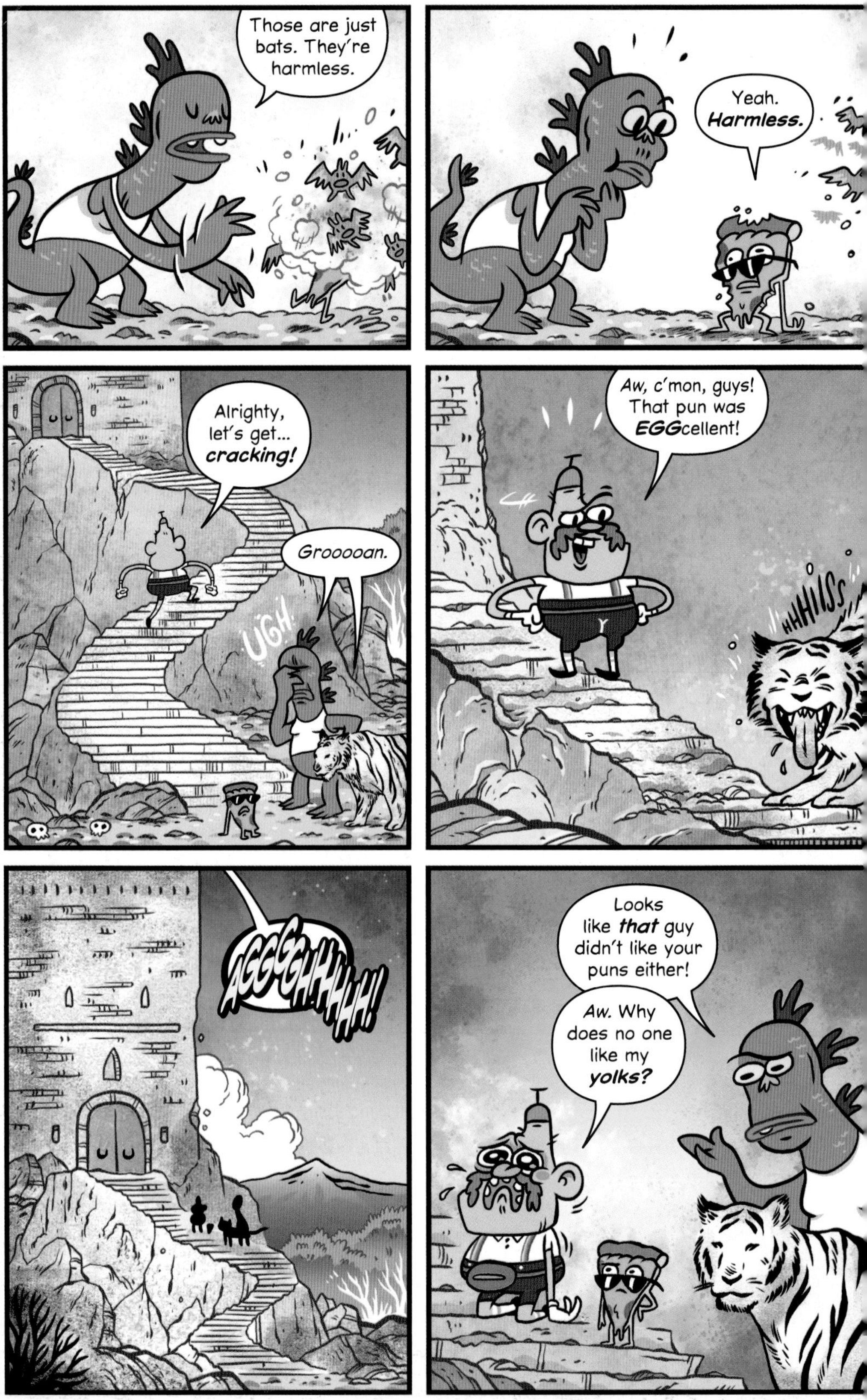
Those are just bats. They're harmless.
Yeah. **Harmless.**
Alrighty, let's get... ***cracking!***
Groooooan.
UGH
Aw, c'mon, guys! That pun was ***EGG***cellent!
HHHISS
AGGGGHHHHH!
Looks like ***that*** guy didn't like your puns either!
Aw. Why does no one like my ***yolks?***

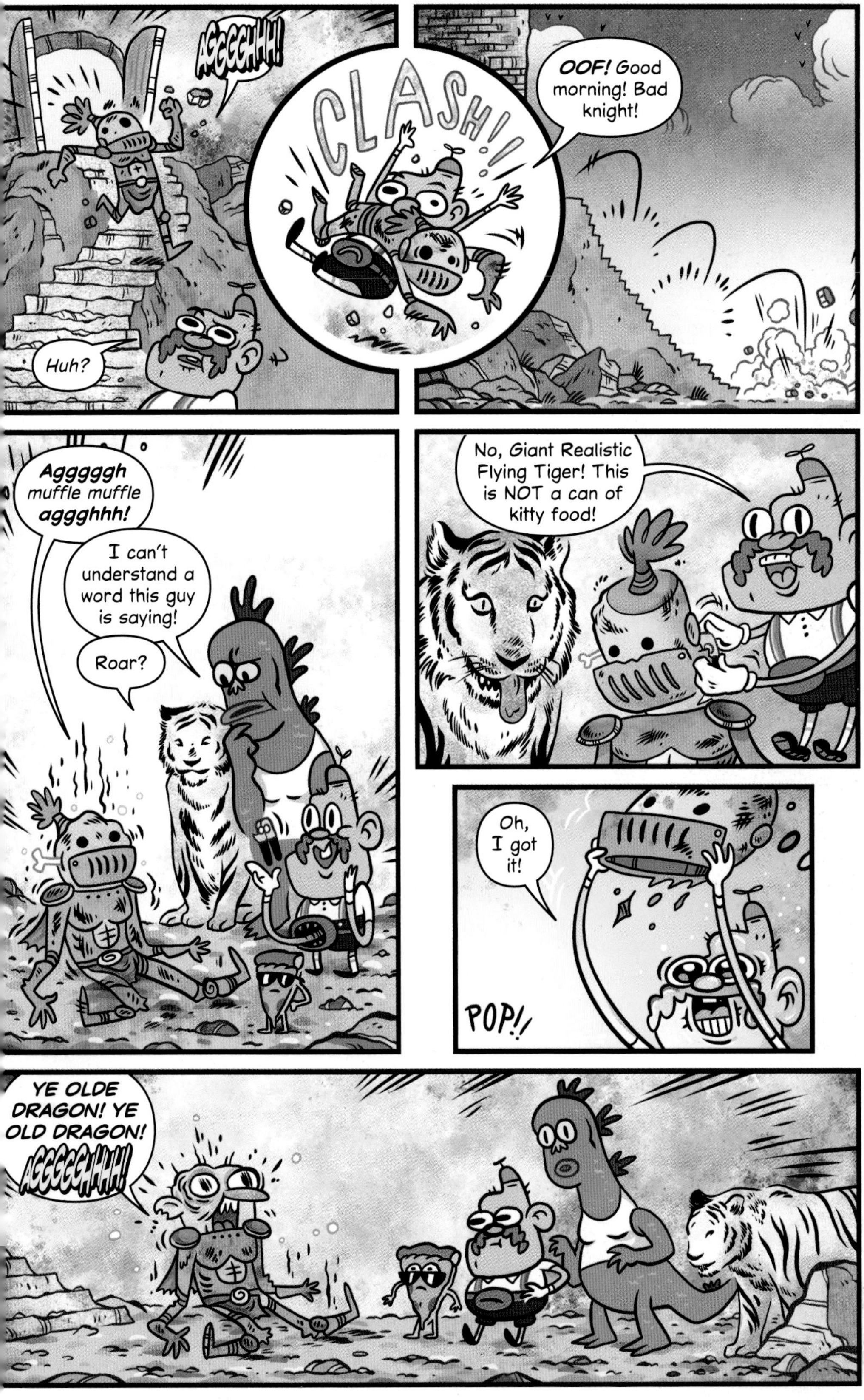
AGGGHHH!
Huh?
CLASH!!
OOF! Good morning! Bad knight!
Agggggh muffle muffle aggghhh!
I can't understand a word this guy is saying!
Roar?
No, Giant Realistic Flying Tiger! This is NOT a can of kitty food!
Oh, I got it!
POP!!
YE OLDE DRAGON! YE OLD DRAGON!
AGGGGHHH!

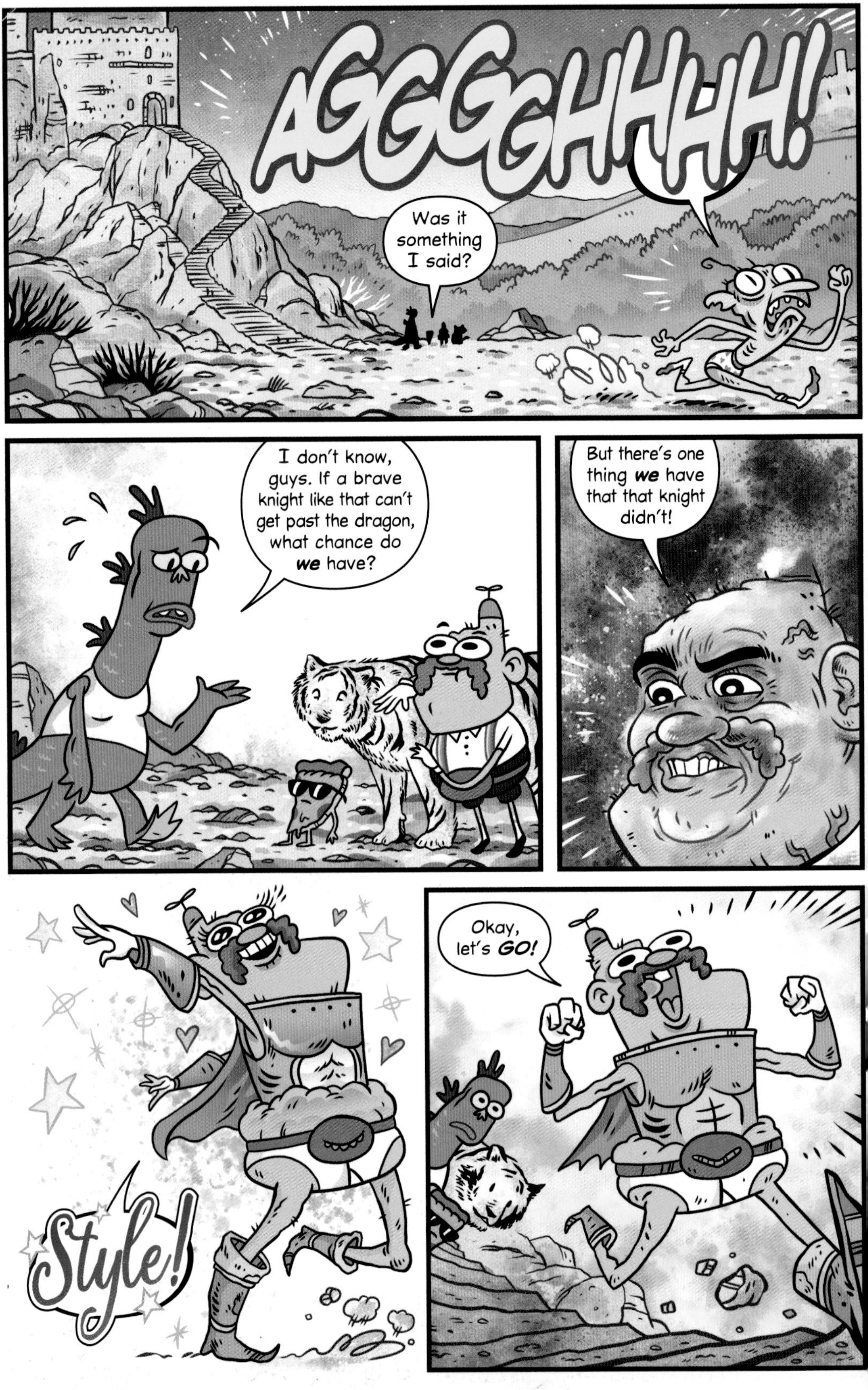
AGGGGHHHH!
Was it something I said?
I don't know, guys. If a brave knight like that can't get past the dragon, what chance do **we** have?
But there's one thing **we** have that that knight didn't!
Style!
Okay, let's **GO!**

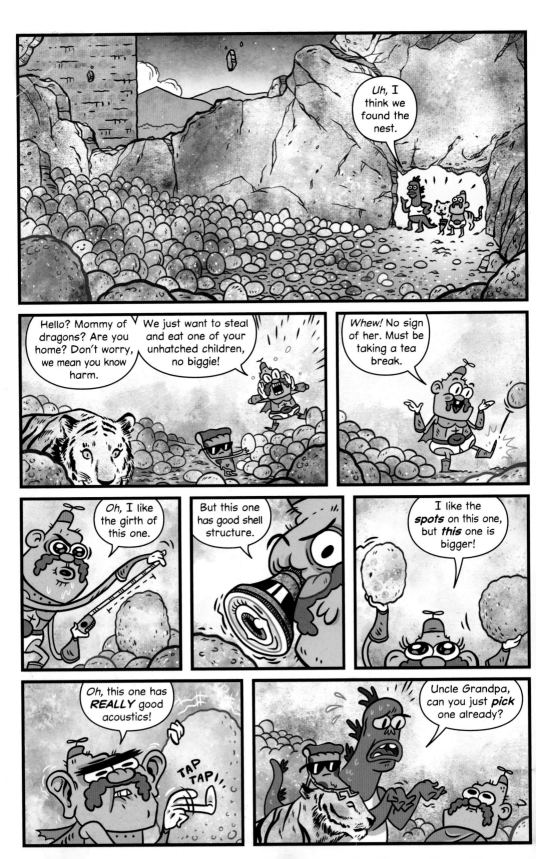

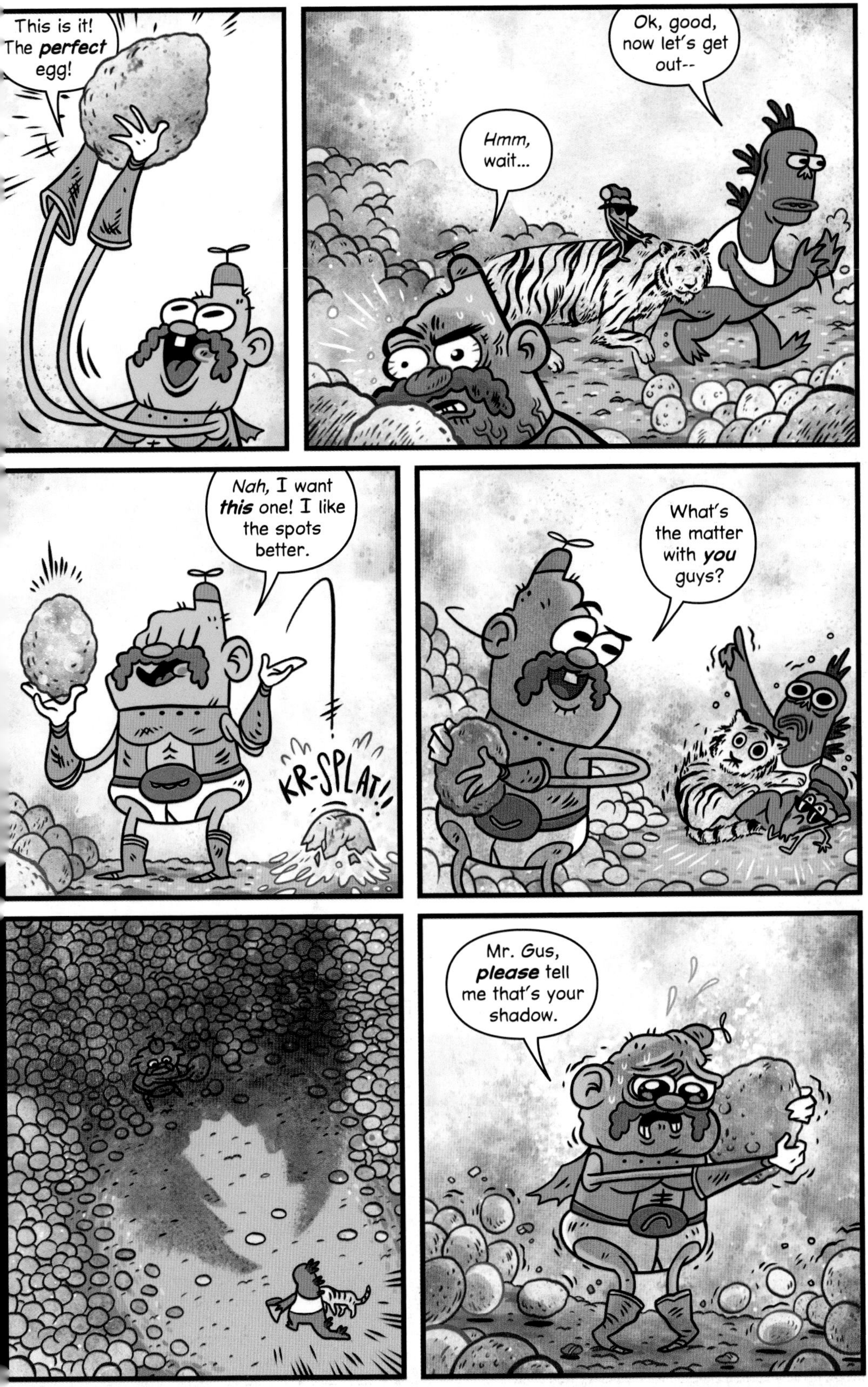
This is it! The *perfect* egg!
Ok, good, now let's get out--
Hmm, wait...
Nah, I want ***this*** one! I like the spots better.
KR-SPLAT!!
What's the matter with ***you*** guys?
Mr. Gus, ***please*** tell me that's your shadow.

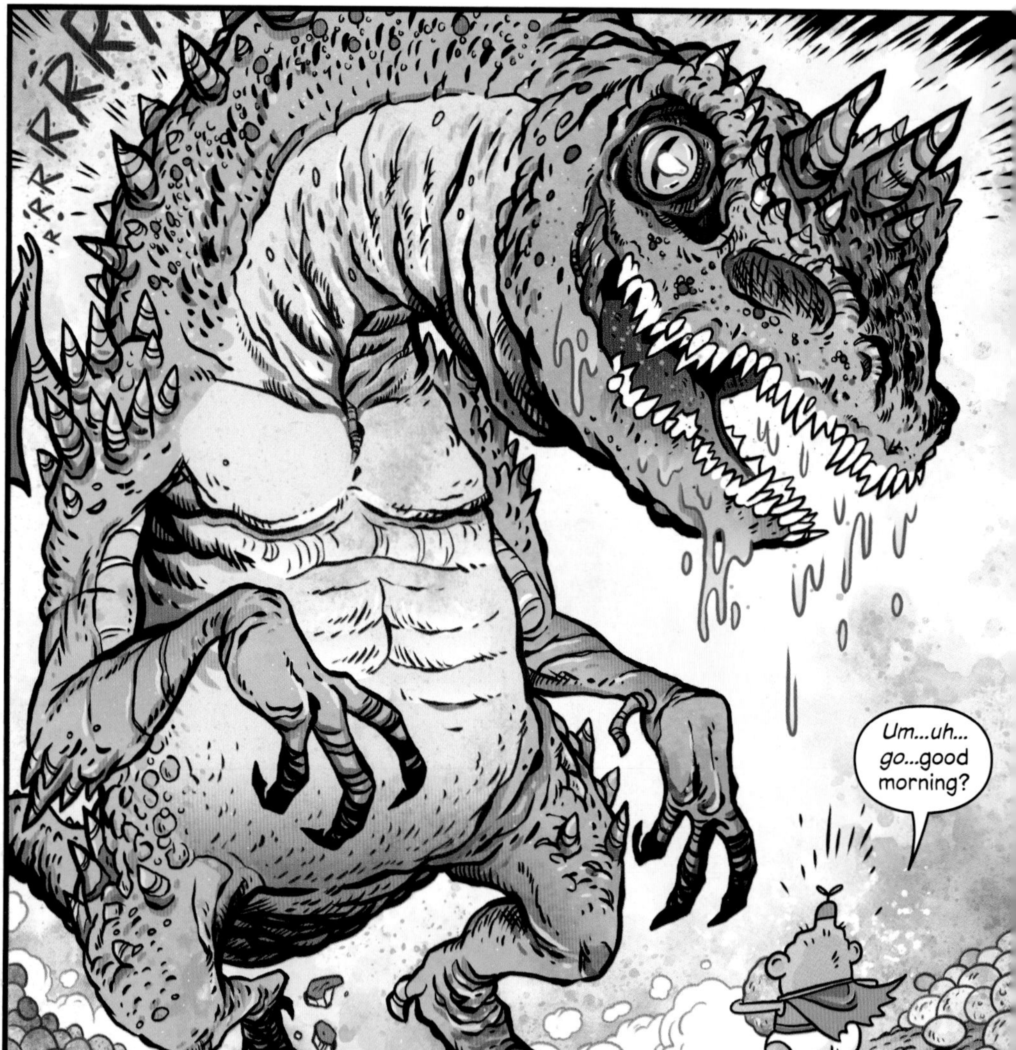
RRRRRR
Um...uh... go...good morning?

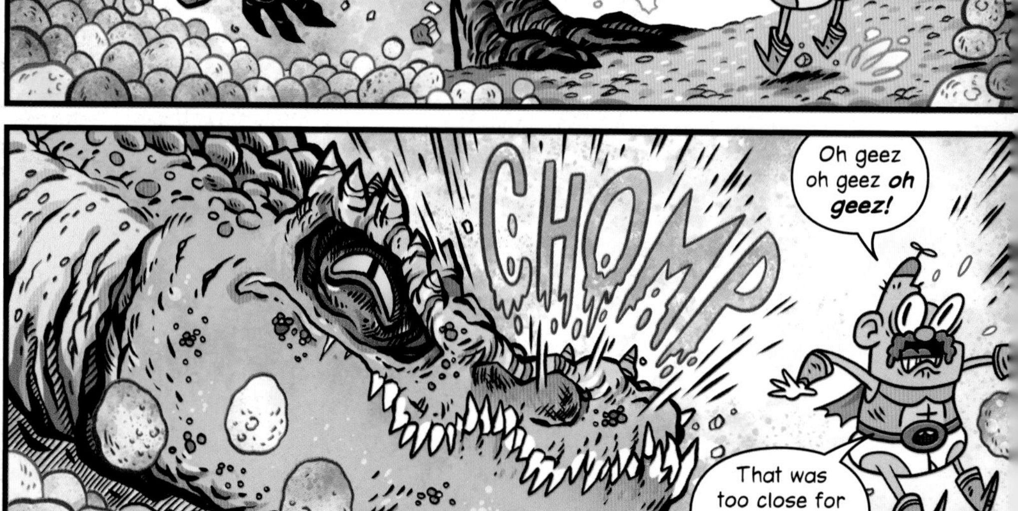
CHOMP
Oh geez oh geez oh geez!
That was too close for comfort, Uncle Grandpa!

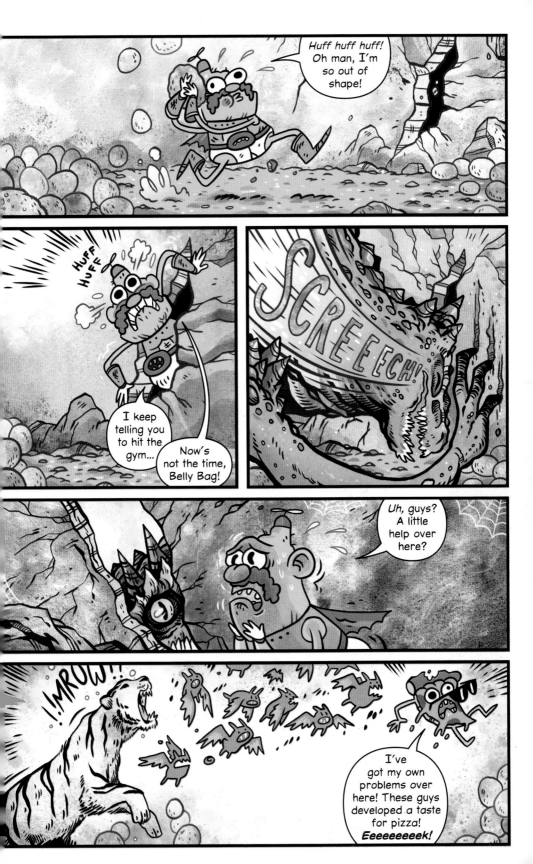

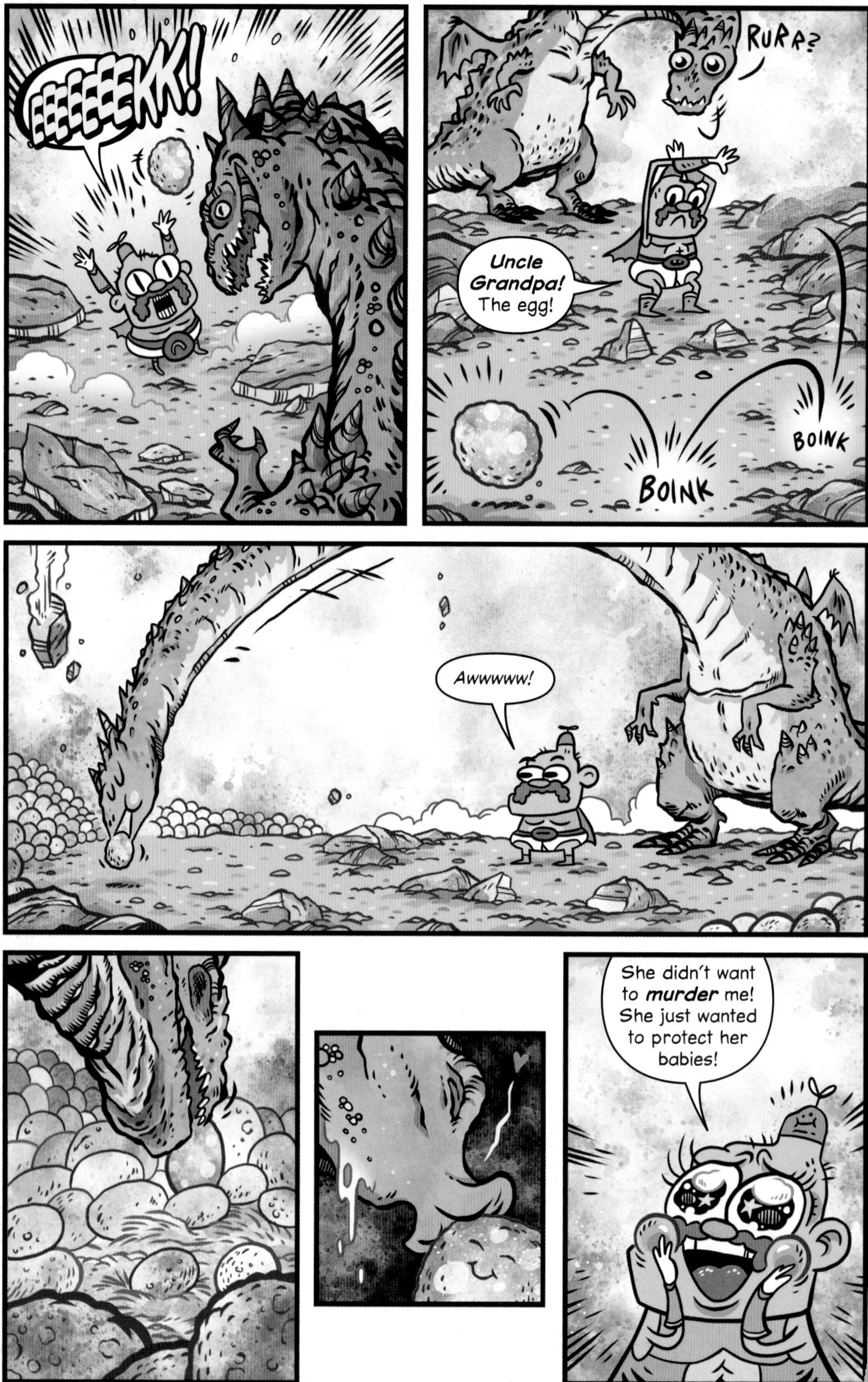
EEEEEEEEKK!
RURR?
Uncle Grandpa! The egg!
BOINK
BOINK
Awwwww!
She didn't want to *murder* me! She just wanted to protect her babies!

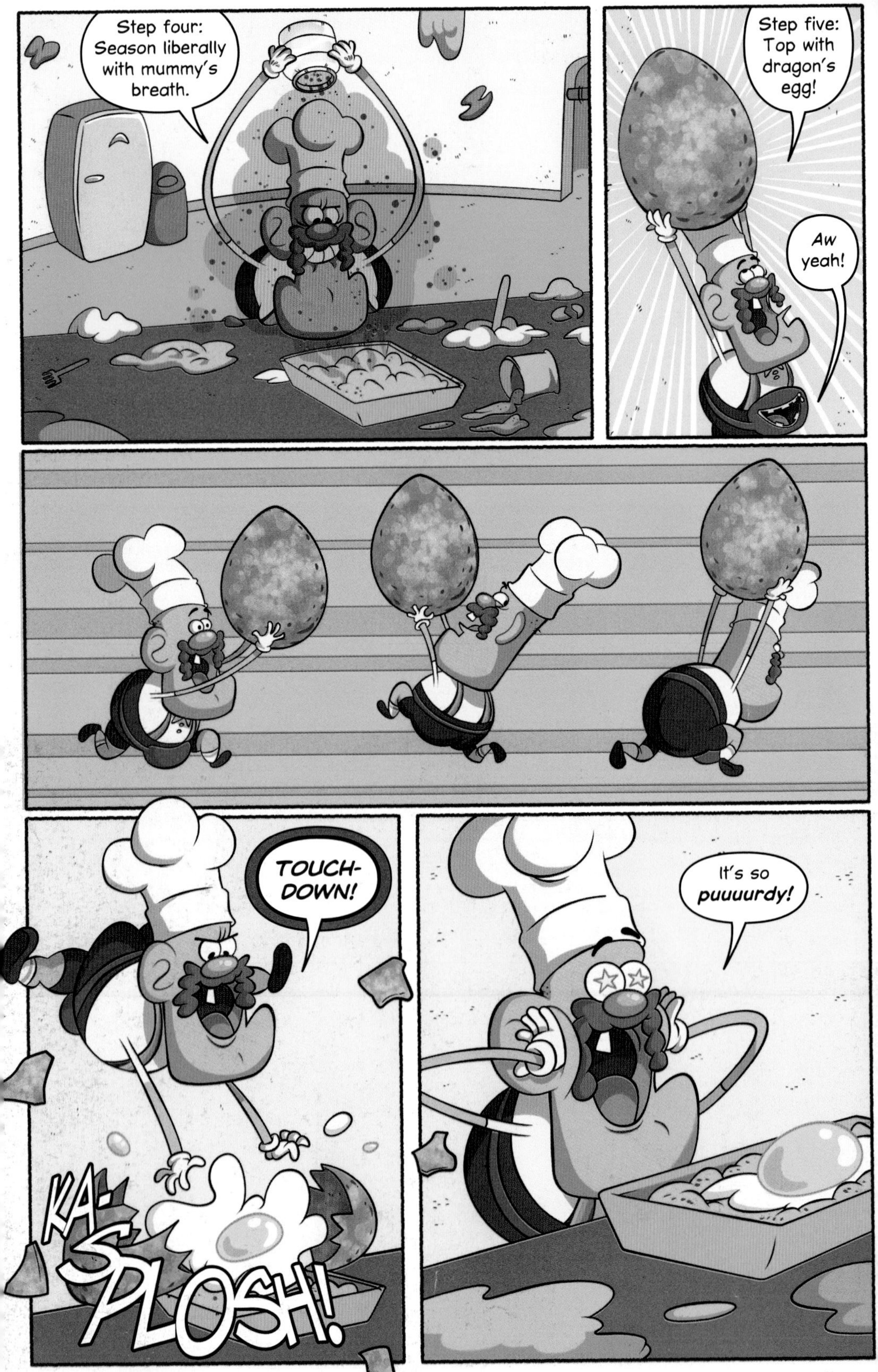
Step four: Season liberally with mummy's breath.
Step five: Top with dragon's egg!
Aw yeah!
TOUCH-DOWN!
KA-SPLOSH!
It's so puuuurdy!

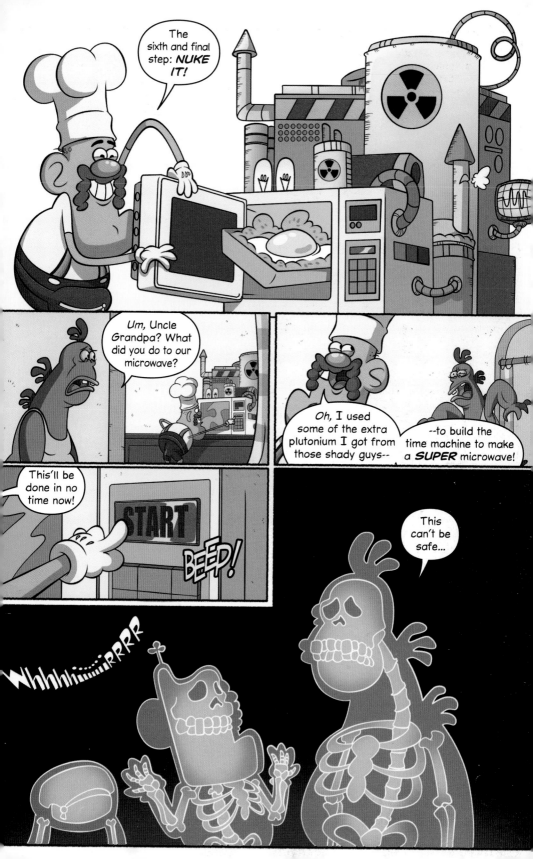

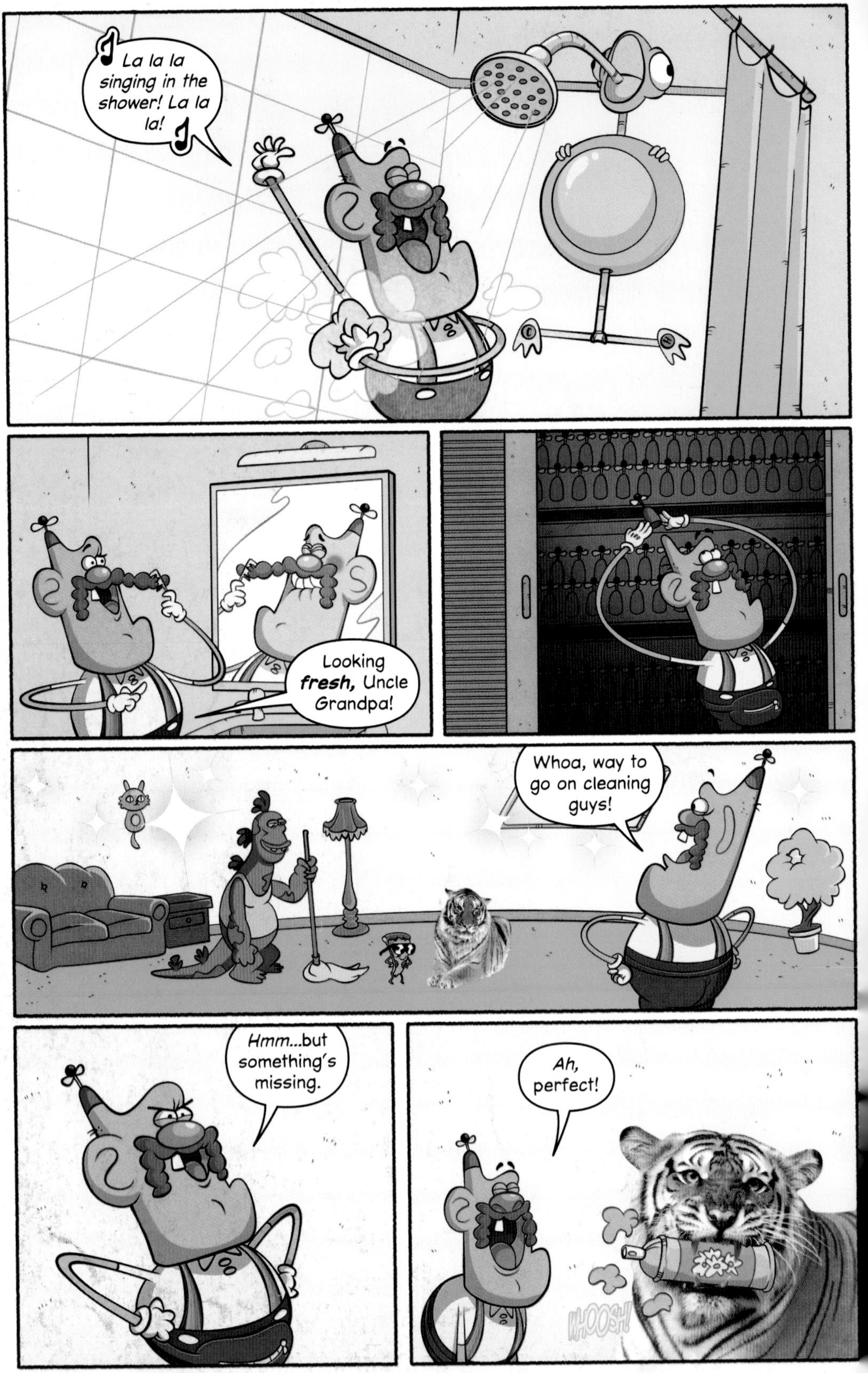
La la la singing in the shower! La la la!
Looking *fresh,* Uncle Grandpa!
Whoa, way to go on cleaning guys!
Hmm...but something's missing.
Ah, perfect!
WHOOSH!

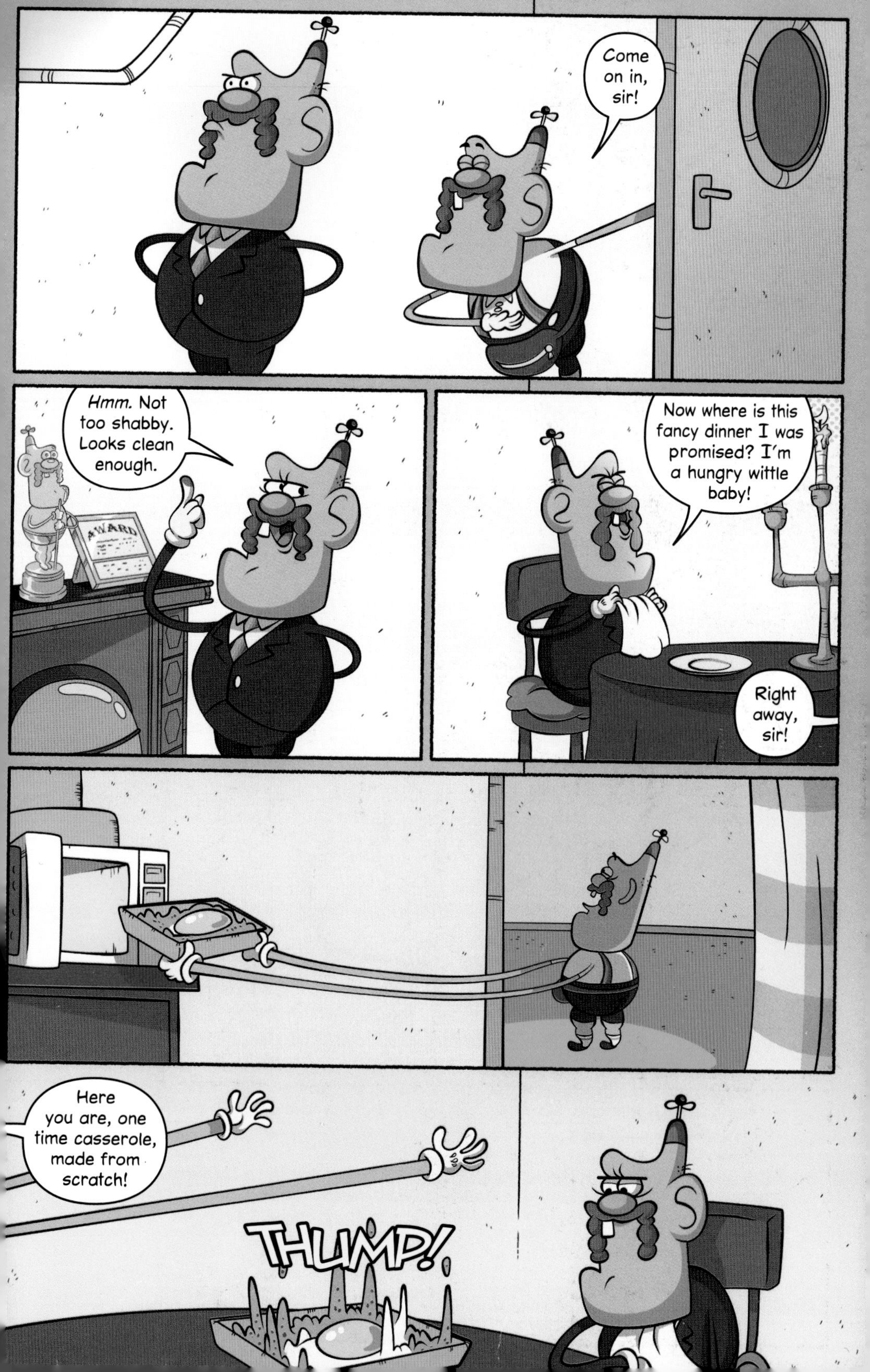

Come on in, sir!
Hmm. Not too shabby. Looks clean enough.
AWARD
Now where is this fancy dinner I was promised? I'm a hungry wittle baby!
Right away, sir!
Here you are, one time casserole, made from scratch!
THUMP!

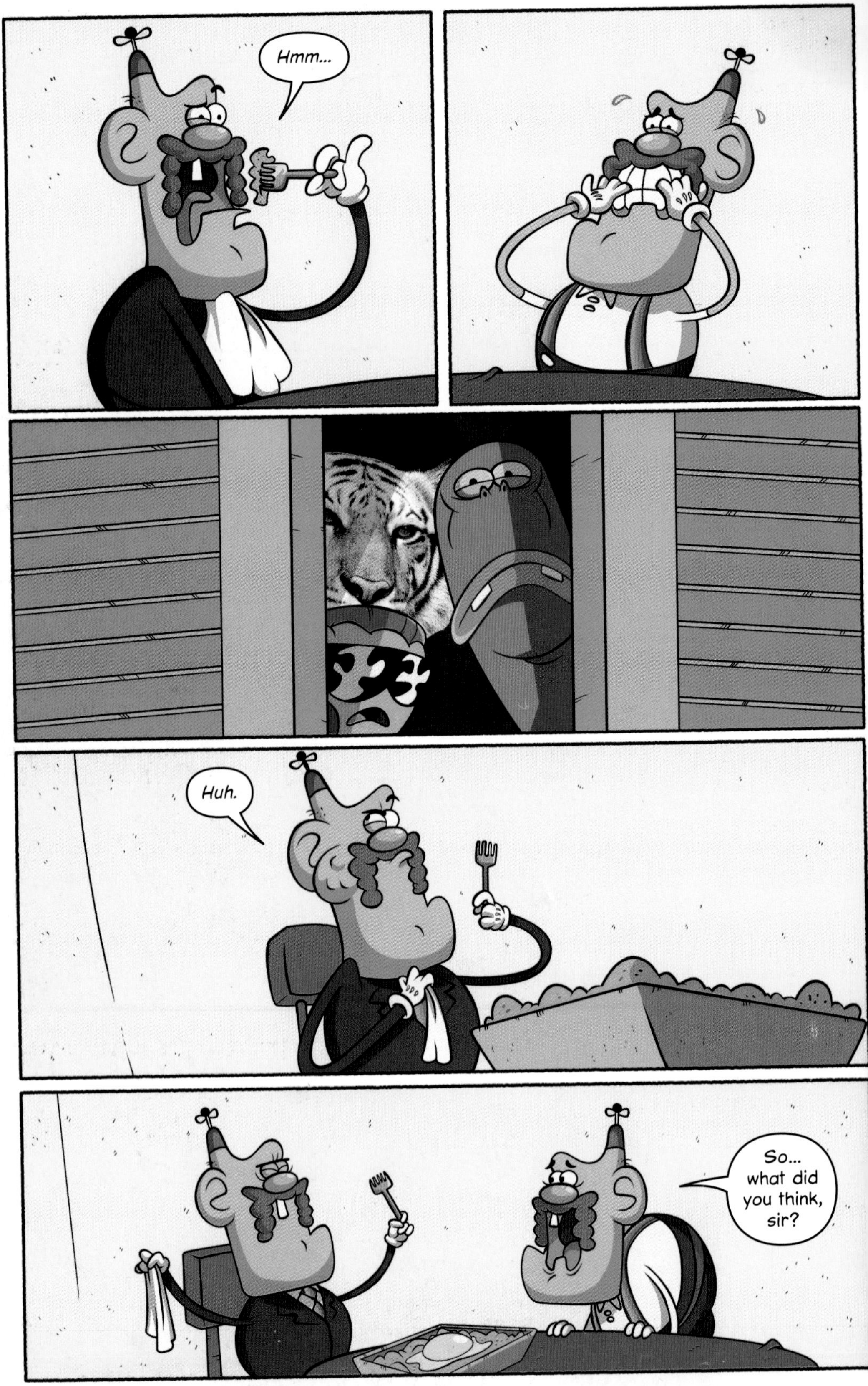

Hmm...
Huh.
So... what did you think, sir?

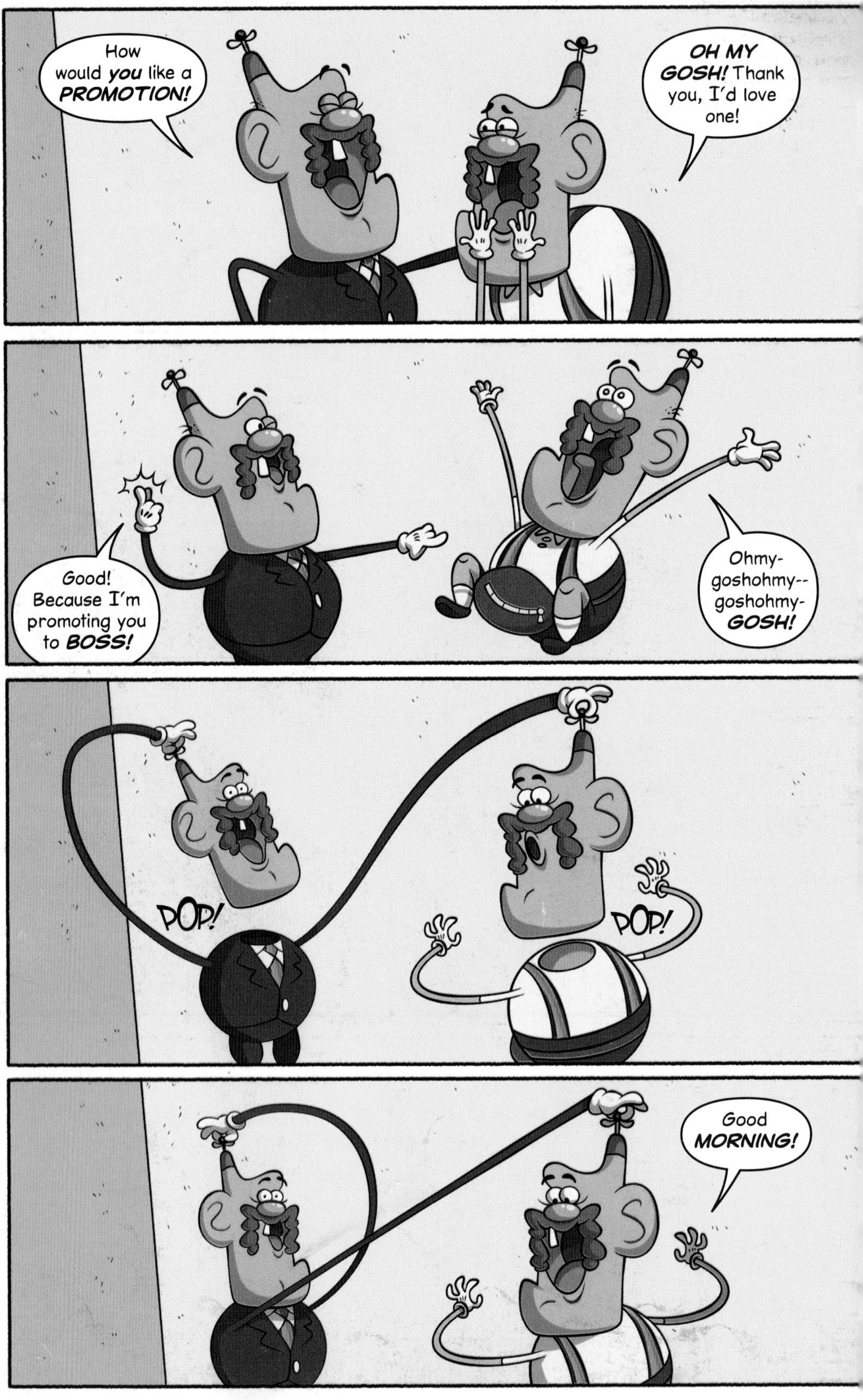
How would you like a PROMOTION!
OH MY GOSH! Thank you, I'd love one!
Good! Because I'm promoting you to BOSS!
Ohmy-goshohmy--goshohmy-GOSH!
POP!
POP!
Good MORNING!